PENGUIN METRO READS
THE BOY WITH A BROKEN HEART

Durjoy Datta was born in New Delhi, and completed a degree in engineering and business management before embarking on a writing career. His first book—*Of Course I Love You . . .*—was published when he was twenty-one years old and was an instant bestseller. His successive novels—*Now That You're Rich . . .*; *She Broke Up, I Didn't! . . .*; *Oh Yes, I'm Single! . . .*; *You Were My Crush . . .*; *If It's Not Forever . . .*; *Till the Last Breath . . .*; *Someone Like You*; *Hold My Hand*; *When Only Love Remains*; *World's Best Boyfriend*; *Our Impossible Love*; *The Girl of My Dreams*; and *The Boy Who Loved*—have also found prominence on various bestseller lists, making him one of the highest-selling authors in India.

Durjoy also has to his credit nine television shows and has written over a thousand episodes for television.

Durjoy lives in Mumbai. For more updates, you can follow him on Facebook (www.facebook.com/durjoydatta1) or Twitter (@durjoydatta) or mail him at durjoydatta@gmail.com.

the
boy
with a
broken
heart

DURJOY DATTA

Penguin
metro reads

An imprint of Penguin Random House

PENGUIN METRO READS

USA | Canada | UK | Ireland | Australia
New Zealand | India | South Africa | China

Penguin Metro Reads is part of the Penguin Random House group of companies
whose addresses can be found at global.penguinrandomhouse.com

Published by Penguin Random House India Pvt. Ltd
7th Floor, Infinity Tower C, DLF Cyber City,
Gurgaon 122 002, Haryana, India

Penguin
Random House
India

First published in Penguin Metro Reads by Penguin Random House India 2017

Copyright © Durjoy Datta 2017

All rights reserved

10 9 8 7 6 5 4 3 2 1

This is a work of fiction. Names, characters, places and incidents are either the
product of the author's imagination or are used fictitiously, and any resemblance
to any actual person, living or dead, events or locales is entirely coincidental.

ISBN 9780143426585

Typeset in Bembo STD by Manipal Digital Systems, Manipal
Printed at Thomson Press India Ltd, New Delhi

This book is sold subject to the condition that it shall not, by way of trade
or otherwise, be lent, resold, hired out, or otherwise circulated without the
publisher's prior consent in any form of binding or cover other than that in
which it is published and without a similar condition including this condition
being imposed on the subsequent purchaser.

www.penguin.co.in

the boy with a broken heart

20 July 2002

What should I start with? 'Hi' or 'Dear Diary'? 'Hi' is too casual, and 'dear' sounds a little archaic. Maybe if I go deeper into the question, I will find my answer. Who's it I'm writing for? For an older me who wouldn't even have the time to read this? For a sister who would pull my leg endlessly if she finds out about this? For the best friend I don't have? Or for the boyfriend that I have vowed never to make?

OK, let me forget about finding a reason, and get straight into it.

Tomorrow a new chapter starts in my life and I intend to make it count. Tomorrow's the day everything will change; it's like one of those moments in movies where the girl is walking on the street and she's confused and lost, her eyes teary and her steps unsteady, but then slowly a sense of confidence seeps through her, slowly filling her up, submerging her in hope and possible joy, and she's smiling, and then she's running, sprinting away from her past, leaving behind all that she has been through, charging at her future, laughing like crazy. Eighteen years is a long time to spend with eyes looking at the ground like a good girl, steps slow, words soft and barely audible, and a constant, polite smile. Now it's all going to change. It has to. Doesn't it?

Is it rude not to introduce myself?

Here goes.

Hi! I'm Advaita Vaid, daughter of Om Prakash Vaid and Nilima Vaid, the younger sister of Divya Vaid. I am from

Dehradun and I live with Mumma, Papa, Di, Dadaji (Grandpa), Buaji (Papa's sister), Fufaji (Buaji's husband), Manish Chachu (father's younger brother) and my two cousins, Karan Bhaiya and Anshuman Bhaiya, in a house as old as time, in a room which I share with three others, and there's not one part of this sentence that I am not dying to change.

21 July 2002

'You can do anything you want once you're in college,' Mumma had always said to me while I was in school.

Anything.

I took her up on this and asked her if her words still stand, and if I could seriously do *anything* now that it was my first day of college. She stared at me and I think she was wondering if I would put her through the same sleepless nights and the same humiliation that Divya Di had put her through before dropping out of college in her second year.

'Don't steal from anyone,' she said.

That was unfair. The last time either Divya Di or I— famed shoplifters of pens, chocolates and newspapers, and later, even filching hard cash—had been caught stealing was three years ago when we stole three hundred rupees from the *shagun* envelopes at our second cousin's wedding. We were then banned from attending the other functions, but I have heard the paneer wasn't anything to write home about and the ice cream had finished an hour before the *phera*s. In my defence, I'm a much better thief than Di (the debacle was all her fault), although she can jump, run, kick and punch her way better than me. That was the last time Di and I ever stole at a wedding. Mumma would not let us out of her sight. But neither Mumma nor Papa has ever scolded us for finding things with us that we didn't own. 'Everyone steals,' says Papa, who has always been at the receiving end of thievery. So the two of us are just trying to balance the scales little by little.

Mumma was arguing with an aunty from the neighbourhood when I got back home from my largely disappointing first day in college which chiefly comprised of filling up one form after another, being polite to seniors, and watching boys and girls trying to fall in love at first sight.

'The stitches have come apart,' the aunty groused loudly.

'It was perfect when I gave it to you. You must have gained weight, bhabhiji,' said Mumma. 'But fine, I will stitch it again, it'll cost forty rupees.'

Before the aunty could protest, Mumma said, with a strategic touch on the aunty's arms and a kind look in her eyes, 'You're my friend, what kind of person would I be if I don't give you a special rate.'

This doesn't always work. Di tells me that she has seen Mumma being spat on, pushed around, her sewing machine smashed, and on one occasion slapped around by a few aunties on the allegation—which is probably true—that she steals cloth. And even if she didn't steal, there's no denying that it's Mumma's cunning and tenacity that have paid for Di's and my schooling.

Mumma has two part-time tailors, Iqbal and Altaf, working for her. Mumma often says she owes her entire business to these two men, but they are never allowed inside our house on Dadaji's and Buaji's instructions. They drink out of earthen tumblers which we have to break after their use.

'At least Altaf Chachu can come inside, he always gets Natkhat and Kismis toffees for me!' I often protested when I was little. I saw them so often that I grew up believing that Altaf was my cousin chachu. I didn't care much about Iqbal who never came bearing toffees.

'Your buaji and dadaji don't like them because they are Muslims,' Mumma often used to say

'Buaji and Dadaji like no one! Not even us!' I would reply.

It was later that I realized that their hatred towards Altaf and Iqbal stemmed from not only the fact that they were Muslims, but also that they belonged to lower-caste Hindu families which had converted to Islam two generations ago, exhausted by the indignity they had suffered at the hands of upper-caste Hindus.

As for Dadaji's hatred towards us, it had to do with the fact that Papa, the eldest son in the family, had chosen to marry Mumma, a lower-caste woman. Papa had betrayed Dadaji, a proud, jingoist Brahmin who had spent his youth defending the exalted position of Brahmins, their pure blood and the need for untouchability in Mohyal meetings across the state. Mumma and us had put him in quite an awkward position.

Our relatives, which is another word for bloodsucking monsters, have never failed to point that out to Divya Di and me even when we were too young to understand any of this.

'Look at you sisters, you get your complexion from your father,' they used to say. 'You are lucky to not get anything from your ma. Look at your father, white like milk, and your mother . . . *chii chii*.'

'But Papa is a *langda*! He can't even walk!' Divya Di and I would chime.

Papa, the son of a tall, authoritative and respected homeopath, Dr Vaid, was a cripple. Sometimes he would use a stick, but most times Papa would just hobble around with a bright smile on his face, hoping it would deflect the attention from his crooked leg. As if he owed it to the world to be cheerful at least.

When we said this, the relatives would be shocked, and soon accusations would fly left and right, and fingers would be pointed at Mumma for having taught us to disrespect Papa by calling him langda.

'Where else would they learn such a thing from! No matter where these people get married, they will always be guttural. It's useless to teach them civility.' They would gasp and start chanting, Buaji being the loudest of them all, 'Ram, Ram, Ram!'

Papa would later give us chocolate. It was he who had taught us to call him langda if anyone berated Mumma; he would also say it wasn't Mumma who was lucky but him.

23 July 2002

What is it about siblings that there's never a day they don't want to strangle each other? In the past few months there has rarely been a time that the transistor in our room has not been switched on. We even sleep with that damned thing on, lest she misses hearing the '*Dola Re*' song from *Devdas* for the billionth time. Though there's little doubt that Shah Rukh Khan is a living god, there has to come a time when you have heard the song so many times that you would rather hear your nails scratch against the blackboard. But Divya Di has only made it worse by borrowing a mini stereo which plays the song repeatedly from its tinny and defective speakers.

'Where did you get this from?' I asked.

'A friend,' said Divya Di, and gave no further explanations. We have learnt over time that it's useless to ask her for any explanation because she's more adept at lies than Shah Rukh is at breaking hearts and dying in his films.

'How was college?' Mumma asked, pouring hot *kadhi* into my bowl.

'You didn't make pakoras? What's kadhi without pakoras?' I grumbled.

'You sister is trying to lose weight,' she answered.

'I have to be fifty-five kg before the end of this month,' said Divya Di, who already looks malnourished—gorgeous but malnourished. There are times Mumma and I can't keep our eyes off her when she combs her long, black hair, pulls them into a tight pony, and wears the snug salwar kameezes

7

Mumma stitches for her. Growing up, her high jawline, the smooth, glistening skin, and her sharp, piercing eyes, always seemed like an oddity when she drove a cycle around the neighbourhood. She should have been at the back of an air-conditioned Honda City. Every few days, Mumma burns little red chillies, or slaps the ground with a slipper to save her from the evil eye. When I was younger, all I wanted was to look like my big sister but I am short by Divya Di's enviable and baffling five-foot-ten by an embarrassing eight inches. She is taller than the seventeen-year-old twins Karan and Anshuman Bhaiya, both of whom still hope to grow taller than her to save their masculine pride. They would be crushed if Dadaji's towering height isn't passed on to them, and only to Di. Divya Di continued, 'There are auditions for a Punjabi music video next month. There's a lot of money in it.'

'Many girls are auditioning,' said Mumma, scraping the leftover kadhi on to her plate. 'Girls are even ready to wear shorts for it. Keep your hopes low, *beta*.'

'Ma, it's not *that* kind of a video. We have been instructed to wear only salwar kameez,' said Divya Di.

These days Divya Di has been practising the steps to '*Dola Re*' all afternoon in the room, which meant Mumma and I had to divide her cleaning responsibilities amongst ourselves.

'She dances like a dream, doesn't she?' Mumma said as we watched her in rapt attention. She swirled and bent and swayed like she was possessed, and when she crashed heartbroken to the floor as the song ended, she had put to shame Aishwarya Rai and Madhuri Dixit and anyone else who'd tried dancing to that song.

'Goddess,' I whispered to Mumma, because it was true. And then told Divya Di, 'Enough of dancing. Now make Mumma and me some tea. We have been working so hard.'

'How was it?' she asked, panting and sweating and beautiful.

'OK-ish, it could have been much better,' I teased her.

'Nonsense, it was beautiful!' said Mumma, and got up to make her patent overboiled, too-sweet-for-anyone tea.

Except for Papa, none of us can make good tea. Buaji never fails to remind us about this every evening when Dadaji and she are back from the clinic and we make them tea. We make it bad purposefully to exact our little revenge—death by a thousand cups of bad tea. Dadaji would complain about it to Buaji, and not us, as if our sight and our words would make him impure. Not once has he called us by name, and has chosen to call us '*vo ladkiyan*'.

'Do you think Buaji will let me do the video if I'm selected?' asked Divya Di later at night.

Last year, she was chosen from hundreds of girls to star in a music video which she firmly believed would be her ticket out of this town, towards a better life for all of us. Two days before the shoot, Buaji had found out that Divya Di had lied and she would have to wear a short skirt for the video, and thus be forever labelled a raging whore. Despite the five thousand rupees that she was being paid, Buaji had grabbed Divya Di by her hair and locked her in the storeroom for three days.

'BUAJI! Take the money! Let me do the video! I PROMISE I WON'T WEAR SHORTS,' Divya Di had screamed till she lost her voice.

But Buaji had just glared at Mumma and Papa, and said, 'That's what your daughter's *izzat* is worth? Five thousand rupees? Take that from me and slap your daughter! Had you slapped her earlier she wouldn't have—'

'Di, we don't have to bring that up again,' Papa had said.

'People never forget. You think they will ever stop talking about how your Chamarni daughter opened her legs for that boy and—' Buaji's voice trailed off as if she couldn't bring herself to say anything more.

I think Buaji's problem was only partly with what Divya Di would have to wear or what she had done in the past to besmirch the honour of our family. What she feared most was that we would have a future, we would have money and hope, and that was unacceptable to her.

If I were to rate how much we are loathed by members of the Vaid household, Buaji would be right at the top, followed closely by Dadaji and then by Fufaji and his sons, Karan Bhaiya and Anshuman Bhaiya, who have been taught and conditioned to be effective in their hatred; they are followed by the last of the lot, Manish Chachu, who's too self-absorbed to care.

If Papa's elder brother, Anil Tauji, were alive, things might have been different, but why cry over spilt milk? We had learnt early in life that if you're a mixed-caste family with a crippled father, and two girls with stained reputations, you would only have each other for support and love.

I've learnt over a period of time that Buaji reserves a secret stash of hatred and nastiness for Divya Di, who had turned out to be the complete opposite of the abomination of a child that Buaji had predicted would come out of the unholy, lusty marriage between Papa and Mumma. Divya Di was a beautiful child, and that grated on Buaji. She was the polar opposite of Buaji who's cracked, burnt and ugly, a pain to look at. Maybe looking at Divya Di reminded her of how lizard-like and horrible she looked. Mumma has strictly asked us not to comment on Buaji's looks, has even scolded and slapped us on numerous occasions, but we only do that because she's exactly like that on the inside. Cracked like barren earth. Shrivelled up. Flaky. Disgusting.

I've heard that Buaji had 'accidentally' dropped Divya Di twice when she was just about twenty days old in the hope that the pretty child that had come out of the womb of my dark, untouchable mother would break her skull and die.

27 July 2002

This family of ours has one and only one dream—to have a house of our own, to run away from where we live now—and everything converges towards that dream. Every suit and salwar Mumma sells, every railway and bus ticket Papa books as an agent, every dance class Divya Di teaches, it's with the hope that one day we will be able to move out of our one room in Dadaji's ancestral house and have at least a one-bedroom house. Wouldn't that be an upgrade from the single room we have been living in?

Till now there's been scant progress on that dream, but hope is what takes us from one day to another. On some Sundays all four of us take a bus to the outskirts, towards Haridwar, to inspect the buildings under construction, have futile conversations with property dealers where we talk about square feet and carpet area and monthly instalments, and then walk around apartments where other people lived, and imagine what would it be like to live in one of them.

'At least it's not a fool's dream,' Mumma said, holding up today's paper. The Dalit Maha Sabha had organized a Dalit women's rally in Andhra Pradesh asking for land redistribution so that they would also have land of their own

'Nothing is going to happen,' said Mumma before using the newspaper to pack my lunch.

Despite her surname now being Vaid, Mumma feels a kinship towards all lower castes. Despite our hatred for all things Brahminical, Di and I have revelled in the privilege

11

of our surnames. Neither Di nor I were made to feel inferior in school because everyone knew us as the Vaid sisters, granddaughters of a respected, old Mohyal Brahmin. But we were never made to forget it once we were home. We were constantly reminded that we were impostors, with unclean blood, and *lucky* to be living in a Brahmin household. The definition of 'lucky' being dubious at best. All three of us would rather live in a caste-less, religion-less household than be lucky.

There should be a research on the long-standing side-effects of your brothers constantly calling you Churi or Chamar, and asking you to clean the septic tank and then laugh.

'That's what your destiny is, to clean our shit, roll around at our feet, Chamarni!' they would say.

'Our destiny is also to carry your dead bodies. Isn't that exciting? I am wondering what we would do with your dead, defenceless bodies,' Divya Di would say.

'Leave it to the dogs? Nah, too easy,' I would answer. 'Parade them naked? Oh. Wait. Leave them with the pigs. Play football with your beheaded heads? Hockey with your balls? Endless possibilities. Wouldn't that be wonderful?'

They would run away, crying.

For three hours after another unsatisfactory day in college, at a cyber café near my old school, I typed out CVs for diploma holders and college graduates who needed them for jobs in Delhi, Mumbai, Kolkata and Bengaluru. Cities with bigger roads, shorter clothes, taller buildings and longer nights. The eagerness in their eyes as I handed over the printed CVs made me want to type one out for myself as well.

'Where did you learn to format like that?' asked a boy when I took some novel keyboard shortcuts. 'School. I was the computer lab monitor,' I answered, and added gruffly, 'You can go if you're done.'

Divya Di would have been proud. She's always been wary of seeing boys around me.

'Of course I worry about you being around boys. You're so beautiful and stupid!' Divya Di has always told me.

'I'm not, you are. I'm the ugly duckling and you're like . . . the swan,' I would often say.

'I will slap you if you say that once more. Every model in Delhi looks like me, and there are millions. But you, look at your eyes, as if they were plucked out of a stuffed toy, all black and deep and sparkly, and your cute little face that feels like the morning itself. And see, see, just look at your lips, so bubblegummy. It's like you're still a child. Look at how you go pink in your cheeks when someone tells you that.'

'I'm so short and you're like—'

'And you hobble around like a little duck, quack, quack. It's so adorable. They should put you in an assembly line and make thousands of you. Stress levels will plummet, I am telling you. Love at first sight everywhere. Like this.' She would snap her fingers.

'Please, Di—'

'Mumma *kasam*, I would be you in a heartbeat,' Divya Di would say. Mumma kasam was sacred. It wasn't as if we believed that the cosmos would conspire to rob Mumma of her life if her stupid kids lied, but it was a pact between us. To not lie under Mumma's oath. And every time she would say that, I would immediately feel beautiful.

But it's not as if I have given her many chances to worry about boys being around me.

Both she and I have been quite unlucky with making friends with either gender. We were always the poorest in class, and even for little children, it's hard to keep up with friendships when you don't have a single rupee to spare.

Especially when the parents of other children tell them not to mix with the Vaid girls. Dirty uniforms, empty lunchboxes, no presents, birthday parties, and return gifts, and barely passing marks—nothing was in our favour. It was worse because despite our limited intelligence, we were in a school beyond our means.

It kept getting tougher as we grew older. Di and I were known to steal things, And Mumma was dismissed as the slimy vamp, and Papa the wicked cripple.

Our fate was finally sealed when Di was branded a *bad girl* after her affair with Vibhor Gupta. From then on we were bad influences.

Coming back to the typing. For three hours of easy work, 120 rupees is a lot. If I get three hours of typing work every day, I would be earning 3600 rupees a month, and that would change a lot of things around the house. But it would also require every young person in Dehradun to wake up to a dream of wanting to leave this sleepy town.

But today was a good day overall. Divya Di got paid for the month she had spent teaching a family dance to '*Dola Re*'; so the Vaid kids were rich today! We all pooled in and bought a second-hand cooler after taking permission from Buaji. Some luxury that.

29 July 2002

Fufaji has fallen ill. Unfortunately, Dadaji says it's nothing more than a stomach infection, and it will pass. We wanted it to be much worse.

Divya Di opted for cancer. 'You can't pick cancer,' I argued about Divya Di's choice. 'It will be a long, expensive path to death. And you know how Dadaji is, this is about his beloved *damad*, and what wouldn't he do for him.'

We discussed other morbid ways Fufaji could die swiftly and economically till Mumma asked us to stop.

'As if you don't want the same,' said Divya Di.

'I don't,' said Mumma, checking dress materials for holes and defects. Then she added softly, 'And can you please not say such things so loudly?'

If you think of it—Divya Di and I have talked about this at length—Fufaji dying a horrible or non-horrible death would be of no use to us. But Buaji's death would throw the entire power equation of the Vaid house into a tizzy. Dadaji runs this house like a feudal lord, brandishing his walking stick like a sword at dissidents. Despite his advanced age, he's built like an ox, at six-foot-three towering over all of us, and his bony arms still retained the power and swiftness from his youth. It's said when he was younger, he could have crushed a skull with his bare hands. And if rumours are to be believed, a few men have lost a part of their hearing after a good slap from Dadaji.

But most of his dirty work is carried out by Buaji, who took over as his deputy/crony/compounder at the clinic after

Anil Tauji passed away. That was an entirely unnecessary death. I have been told that Anil Tauji loved Papa and all of us. He was a kind, brilliant man who was supposed to take over work from Dadaji when the right time came.

'He was the light of Dadaji's eyes, and I was the scourge,' Papa often said. 'He was tall and really handsome, while I reminded your dadaji of his failure. He couldn't keep me around him. I was embarrassing.'

The failure Papa was talking about was the dent in the pride Dadaji took in his homeopathy when Papa was struck down with polio. Dadaji hadn't got any of his children vaccinated, and advocated against it, for he believed that homeopathy medicines had made vaccines superfluous. While Anil Tauji, Buaji and Manish Chachu grew up to be healthy adults, Papa was crippled—a constant, living reminder of Dadaji's failure, which was there for everyone to witness. Naturally, Papa had gotten us vaccinated, but then he had gotten thrashed by Dadaji in front of the entire neighbourhood. That was the last nail in their relationship. It was the day that Mumma and Papa had decided they wouldn't spend their lives in this house, and started to work towards it. It was Anil Tauji who had helped Papa realize that.

'We had finally broken free of this toxic joint family. We had our own house, just the four of us. It was a good time,' Papa had told me.

'Were we happy?'

'Very happy, Advaita. You should have seen your didi and mumma! Ah, such smiles!' Papa had said tearfully. 'Your Anil Tauji had managed everything. He paid us for everything without telling your dadaji or dadiji. The rent, the deposit, the furniture, everything. Your Tauji knew that staying in that house with your dadaji wasn't good for you and your sister. But your dadaji knew there was no way I could have that kind of money.'

'Did Dadaji ask you where you got the money from?'

'He assumed that I had been filching from the house for years, having fallen to your mother's insatiable greed. There was a lot of talk around the town. People wondered why I had shifted away from the family. Most of them piled the blame on your Mumma. But your Tauji made Dadaji not take any steps against us.'

'But then Tauji fell sick?'

'He was diagnosed with a terminal illness a month after we had moved out of the house. Then Buaji came back from Delhi.'

I am told that Buaji had descended like a hawk on the house when Anil Tauji was told he won't survive his long-standing illness. She then laid claim to the house, the clinic, anything of value, and poisoned Dadaji's ears against Mumma and Papa, whom she already loathed. Even after all those years, she hadn't forgiven them. Her grudge had become sharper, more insidious. She squatted in the house like a cunning scavenger. Your Fufaji came with her, lugging a few suitcases too many, and never left.'

'But why did we move back? We could have stayed away.'

Papa had sighed. 'It wasn't by choice. We were made to after your Tauji passed away, beta.'

'How could they do that!' I had asked angrily.

Papa had held my hand, the way you would while telling someone a horrible story. 'When Anil Tauji passed away, Dadaji turned his grief into wrath. We bore the brunt of it. Dadaji held a lot more power than he does today in our community. People listened to him. Everyone in Dehradun knew someone who had been treated by Dadaji. Your dadaji never had the money, but he was listened to, respected, and feared.'

'Dadaji threatened you?'

'Your dadaji got us thrown out of the house we had rented, stripped us of our belongings, accused us of theft, and made sure we didn't find a place to stay. He had been ready to see us starve to death. Three days we waited outside the gate till finally your dadiji strode into the courtyard and threatened to light herself if your dadaji didn't let us inside.'

I was four at the time but I have faint memories of the little row house we had shifted to. But it could also be that I am constructing these memories from what I have heard. But Divya Di remembers clearly the house, the little garden, the old neem tree, and the tulsi planted by Mumma.

Papa told me Dadiji kept Dadaji from harassing us when we first moved in. But things changed swiftly when she passed away. After Dadiji died, Buaji wanted to throw us out, but she soon she realized that having three girls around in the house meant not having to pay for a maid. We are also treated as such.

We weren't allowed to use the bathroom—we still aren't—so Papa had to make one outside by the garden. We still use that. There's no running water or power there. We also have a separate kitchen. It's in a shed on the roof. This is because Buaji doesn't want her food to be mixed with Mumma's, though farcically, Mumma's the one who cooks for everyone.

'She can't see us happy,' Mumma had once said after a particularly rough day. While the septic tanks of all the houses were getting cleaned by the jamadars sent by the municipal corporation, Buaji had joked in front of the entire colony, 'We don't need one, we have a jamadarni right in our home.'

Mumma had protested strongly and when the shouting match between the two had reached a feverish pitch, Dadaji had intervened. He chased the jamadars out of the house, and asked Mumma to clean it.

'*TU NAHI KAREGI TO KAUN KAREGA!* (Who will do it if not you?)' Dadaji had shouted.

Mumma had spent six straight hours carrying buckets of faeces from our house tank to the municipal truck. The whole lane watched with dupattas and handkerchiefs covering their noses, while little children vomited, not being able to bear the stench. Mumma had fainted twice, and both times Dadaji had swung his stick at Papa's foot to stop him from going to Mumma's help. Such stupid, stupid love.

And when she was done and shivering in her bed with high fever, Dadaji had said, 'WHY DIDN'T YOU DIE! MY SON WOULD HAVE BEEN ALIVE HAD YOU PEOPLE NOT STOLEN FROM US. WE COULD HAVE GIVEN HIM BETTER TREATMENT! YOU STOLE FROM MY DYING SON! THIS IS WHAT YOU DESERVE!!'

That was grossly untrue, but it didn't matter. Not only did Buaji and Dadaji believe it, so did everyone else who knew us. That's why no one really raises an eyebrow when they treat us badly in this house.

It's easier to say this in hindsight, but Mumma and Papa think they should have rode it out when Dadaji had not let them inside the house. They think they should have pulled Divya Di out of school for a couple of years and scraped through. Over the years, the more Dadaji's reputation had grown as a fiercely protective father of an unfortunate daughter, and as a legendary doctor for the have-nots, and also as the tragic man whose eldest son had died in his arms, people saw Papa in the worst of lights. Over the years, he has been called 'ungrateful', a 'thief', an 'abomination', and if it had been anyone else, he or she would have crumbled.

The cooler has been shifted to Buaji's room for the day to make Fufaji feel better.

It's so hot without it. How quickly did I get used to that? I'm telling you, the Vaids are born for luxury.

4 August 2002

Karan Bhaiya and Anshuman Bhaiya, the seventeen-year-old twins and the apples of Dadaji's eyes, are conditioned to hate us, think of us as inferior, belittle us and break our spirits—and they really have been taught well. But unlike Mumma and me, Divya Di still sees some good in them, and believes they will turn around some day, fall to their knees and apologize. She has grown up with them. When they were twelve and had started to truly own their role of vile and crafty bastards who revelled in our misery, Divya Di used to defend them and try to paint a picture of their past niceness.

'They never let me carry my bags when they were younger.' 'Despite Buaji telling them not to, they would share their paneer with me. Even you, but you don't remember.' 'They used to polish your shoes, remember?'

Even now, Divya Di's only disappointed in them, not angry like the rest of us. So today, Divya Di had taken to a pleading tone with them, hoping they would see sense. They didn't. Despite Di's and my fervent protests, Karan Bhaiya and Anshuman Bhaiya had decided to fix things themselves. And that after Divya Di had already fixed it the best she could; they thought it was their brotherly duty to do so, because from the moment Divya Di and I had turned thirteen, the honour of the Vaids rested purely on how we behaved and conducted outside the house.

They had missed a previous opportunity to prove themselves to be worthy men, men who could bravely pick up cudgels and rods and hockey sticks, and defend the women of their family if the need arose. Three years ago, they couldn't do anything when it was rumoured that Divya Di had lost her virginity to a boy named Vibhor Gupta. When she was grilled and slapped about at home on whether the rumours were true, she had been mum. She bore the beatings for a month without a frown; even Karan Bhaiya and Anshuman Bhaiya, years younger than her, had hit her with authority. Barely fourteen then, they had planned for days to accost the guy and beat him up, only to realize that someone else had already done it for them. Vibhor Gupta had been beaten within an inch of his life, his house ransacked, and his scooter burnt. His college classroom had been set on fire, and his admission (and Di's) had been cancelled. The person who had done it was Meghnad Sharma, an influential boy of politically connected powerful parents from Saharanpur who had been hopelessly in love with Divya Di since her school days. He had quite a reputation for getting into fights and scuffles on a daily basis; he had even paid a couple of visits to the police station, but his uncles were in charge there.

But when I first saw him, he didn't come across as a bad guy. It had started harmlessly enough.

He would wait outside our school patiently for it to end and then watch us till the time we boarded the bus. A few months later he started driving alongside the bus, stealing shy glances at us, smiling softly. Divya Di and I stopped sitting by the window to save ourselves from the embarrassment. Other girls called his stalking cute, and wanted to switch places with her.

Once Divya Di started going to college, he was there too, leaning on his car with his friends, watching Di every day. When he finally mustered up the courage, Divya Di turned him down.(At that time, she was in love with a college mate, but no one knew this except me. I had stumbled across the powerful love letters they had written to each other.) The rejection changed something in Meghnad, who started camping out in front of our house, his eyes cold, his body stiff. Warnings by Mumma and Papa helped only for a brief while, as it turned out that Dadaji knew Meghnad's father. So his transgressions were labelled as 'things boys do'. Divya Di started to take longer routes to college to avoid him, and when he caught on to that, she stopped going to college altogether. The more Di pulled away from him the more invasive and aggressive he got.

He would then be found near our house at all times of the day, waiting for Di to step out, and try to talk to her. Sometimes he would grab her dupatta or her hand. It was only when Di threatened to shout and cry would he let go. Then the calls started. Once a day, and then twice a day, and after that till Buaji pulled the cord out of the phone.

Twice he had banged the door in the middle of the night and then ran away when Dadaji walked out, brandishing his stick. Of course, Buaji and Fufaji had pointed their fingers at Divya Di.

'You must have encouraged him,' they had said.

And then, out of the blue, the rumour spread like wildfire that Divya Vaid and Vibhor Gupta had had sex in the library after college hours. In a small town like ours, people live for rumours like this, and soon a bunch of people substantiated them, saying they had always suspected there was something going on between the two. The rumour never sat well with me because I knew that Vibhor Gupta had ended the relationship with Di—leaving her a crying mess for weeks—and left her for another girl months before the whispers started.

So why didn't Divya Di own up to the truth?

I had gotten my answer in the weeks that passed. Meghnad's trips to our house trickled to a stop. The last time he had camped outside our house, he and his friends had broken alcohol bottles, screamed profanities for an hour in the middle of the night, and spray-painted the word '*RANDI*' on the boundary wall. It took Divya Di and me the better part of a day to smudge it into a large black blot.

Divya Di told me one day, 'Boys like Meghnad? They won't accept a girl who has been with another man. It's against their masculinity.' In fact, it was Di who had concocted and spread the rumour. She had said, 'Look at it this way. Vibhor has left town and gone to Delhi, and I don't have to deal with Meghnad any more.'

Karan and Anshuman Bhaiya had let go of the opportunity then, but they weren't going to let it go now.

'Madhuban Hotel, that's where the *madarchod* is staying!' said Karan Bhaiya, twirling the bat in his hand.

He's the one with stupid bravado, while Anshuman Bhaiya, a wimp, is the more cunning of the two.

'We will beat the shit out of him,' said Karan Bhaiya.

They sped off on Dadaji's scooter before we could make them see sense. We got on our cycles and followed. They shot out of sight pretty quickly.

Earlier that evening, during the auditions, the Punjabi singer had decided to join Divya Di's dance and put his hands in places he shouldn't have. Expectedly, Divya Di punched his nose hard enough to break it, and threatened to call the cops. They threw her out of the hotel. The Vaid brothers weren't satisfied with this narrative. Is a brother a brother if he doesn't meddle in his sister's affairs?

We found the Vaid brothers, paragons of brotherhood, avengers of their sister's pride, sitting with bloodied noses on the pavement outside the hotel. The singer had left, leaving behind his troupe to deal with my brothers.

Karan Bhaiya was all bloodied while Anshuman Bhaiya didn't have a scratch. They were brothers, but they couldn't be more different from each other. Karan Bhaiya seeks out fracas and dives headlong into them; he's not the one into plans, his only plan is his fist. Anshuman Bhaiya, on the other hand, is cowardly and cunning. Only last week, he had freaked out like a child when Divya Di had filled up his school bag with frogs. He had taken revenge by spitting into our food.

'Let him come to the city the next time,' said Karan Bhaiya. 'We will see how he leaves.'

It was already late, so Di and I rode back home, chained our cycles to the electric pole, and were clambering over the fence when the lights came on in the house. The news of the fracas in the hotel, and our brothers' heroic stand had reached the elders too.

Out came Dadaji, swinging his cane, blaring, 'WHERE DID THE TWO OF YOU GO?'

Dadaji strode towards us and raised his stick and stopped just short of Di, who had scrunched herself into a ball.

Divya Di stammered softly, 'It . . . it wasn't my fault . . . that singer . . .'

Buaji said, 'I had asked her not to go.'

Fufaji asked Papa to keep us under her thumb. '*Bechkar izzat khaa jaengi ye dono.* (They will sell our honour.) Money is not everything, Prakash.'

Buaji added sternly, 'Two girls, and both are like this. *Badiwali* was always like this, characterless, but now even *chhoti* is getting out of hand, visiting cyber cafés and what–not!'

We know that Dadaji, even with his reputation of a respected homeopath, is capable of dangerous violence. Even today, everyone cites what he had done to those three poor boys who had broken into his clinic more than two decades ago. Dadaji had scouted out three teenagers who had burgled his clinic and brought down his stick on them. It was a miracle they survived the cracked skulls, broken ribs and smashed jaws. Onlookers will still tell you that he would have killed them that day had people not intervened. The boys were poor Dalits, and Dadaji too respected to be touched, so the matter was buried under the carpet. Over the years, Dadaji has given plenty of examples of how savage he could get with his stick. Every few months, the stick has to be replaced, for that's how long it lasts.

Dadaji stood there, looked at us and Mumma and Papa alternatively, shook his head derisively, and turned and strode inside.

Later at night, Dadaji made Karan Bhaiya and Anshuman Bhaiya remove the fuse of the line to our room, plunging us into darkness and heat. The door to the terrace was locked.

Mumma burst out laughing at their childishness.

All four of us sweated like pigs in our room.

7 August 2002

I consider myself an optimist, and optimists like me aren't stupid or out of touch with reality; what they do have is a thicker skin, a higher threshold of pain, and an eye on the bigger picture. Despite repeated disappointments, I had allowed my college the benefit of the doubt. My big plan was to inveigle my way into college festival councils, make myself indispensable to the treasury or the sponsorship department and do what this country is great at——a scam. Unfortunately, the college professors decided that first-year students were too young to be a part of the more important departments and should be relegated to infrastructural and organizational roles that I had no interest in. Why else would I want to be in this shitty excuse of a college? You can pretty much get a degree without going to college. A degree that's worth nothing. Vaids, anyway, have always been indescribably bad in studies. It's a marvel that Divya Di and I have finished school. Karan Bhaiya and Anshuman Bhaiya have had to change schools twice because of failing in the eighth and ninth classes. And yet, Buaji and Fufaji foster a strange dream to put these blockheads in an engineering college. So every extra rupee in the house goes into the fund for these two jackasses whom Buaji is obsessed with seeing as engineers.

Now back to my college.

I had to wait for other opportunities, and girl did I stumble on one.

My class, full of unambitious slackers, were letting their library cards go waste, and that's where I found my little opportunity.

I collected nineteen library cards from different students, and stacked together at home the newest editions of the text and reference books recommended by the professors. Within a week, while the students were too busy ingratiating themselves with social hierarchies to care about books, I had cyclostyled copies of all the books I had chosen.

I waited for exam time, when panic would reach a critical mass; all students were now looking for the books that were neatly stacked in the Vaid house. Classic hoarding. The photostat bhaiya and I turned in a neat profit of 4500 rupees.

But this time the four of us weren't buying anything. The money is hidden in a shoebox in our Godrej almirah.

Papa got us aloo *tikki* to celebrate, but he had to wait outside the house till Buaji, Fufaji and the wastrels were out of the way. We lit agarbattis before we ate to keep the smell from wafting towards anyone's noses.

'Look at them! The electricity bill is going through the roof; they don't pay their share and then eat tikkis every day! The gall of that woman,' Buaji would shout otherwise.

It was good money, but temporary money, and nothing that would get us out of this house. But you got to celebrate your little victories.

Something else happened today and I'm not sure what to make of it.

There was this boy in the library today.

Hands dug in his pockets, he walked around, head bent, scouring the spines of books, pausing longer at the bigger ones as if imagining what they must be about, his soft lips moving slowly, relishing the names on his tongue, smiling softly as if remembering something, and then moving on. Twice I thought he had caught me looking at him. Thinking of it now, I was only staring in an attempt to make sense of the maze of contradictions that his face was. Remnants of boyhood— the wanting eyes of a puppy dog abandoned by his owners and the full lips of a girl—waged a war for possession with rampaging signs of adulthood—a stubborn, ingrown stubble and an almost cruel and painfully sharp jawline.

Every couple of minutes his hands would slip into his pocket and he would change the song on his Walkman. Or was he rewinding to the same song. I saw him take the book I had earmarked for my next picking. Did I see a glint of excitement in his eyes, a naughtiness, as if he had a toy in his hands? He sat on the ground, leaned on the racks, and flipped through the pages feverishly at some places, and slowly at some, humming constantly. I wasn't as much arrested by his cute-boy-gone-rogue vibe as much as I was by the throbbing bass of his grave, coarse voice, which seemed like it had broken only yesterday. It felt like someone holding a heavy-duty concert speaker to my chest. THUMP. THUMP. A little later, this gorgeous boy calmly ripped off the hardcover of the book—an easy hack to smuggle books out of the library. He tucked the book into the waistband of his jeans at the back and casually walked towards the exit. I must have been really distracted because he bumped into me on the way out.

'Sorry, Advaita.' His voice went straight to the pit of my stomach and made it rumble as if a million caterpillars had just finished their metamorphosis into aggressive, fluttering butterflies. It only settled later when I realized he knew my name. I had never seen the boy before, he wasn't in my class, and he wasn't even a family friend's friend. He was a stranger. That snuffed out the butterflies in an instant.

9 August 2002

I could talk to Di about this, but she always says, 'Boys are useless and we should never talk about them.' After Vibhor Gupta left her, Di had taken a radical anti-boy stance, which is unfortunate because BOYS is a great concept (it's romantic love that's nonsense in my opinion, not boys). Boys are great till they are not. It's the greatest joy to see groups of seven-year-old boys frolicking around, giggling and laughing and jumping off stairs and kicking balls and falling over each other. They are brats but respectful towards their sisters and mothers, more than they are to themselves or their own kind. They grumble but do what they are asked to do; they have a strict moral code about what's wrong and what's not; they clean up well and are cute without measure. What's not to love? Then what happens in those eleven years after which they become unbearable at eighteen? How does one fall in love with these annoying, disrespectful boys? Thank god in the Vaid house it is forbidden to fall in love, the sheer existence of it is denied despite Mumma's and Papa's love story. Should I go into the story? I have only the sketchiest details . . . but what the heck.

It's hard for me to imagine Buaji as a young, sprightly woman full of life and hope and dreams and a working heart, but it's said that she was once exactly that. A fourteen-year-old girl, bright in studies, someone with a spring in her step and a naughty twinkle in her eye. Some say she was the splitting image of Divya Di, and was deeply loved by everyone. I have seen old pictures of her and I can testify to that part of the story. She really was beautiful.

The month when the incident happened and the chronology of events and the characters change every time the story is told, but over the years I have picked out the common narratives in all the stories and made one of my own.

It was January and freezing cold, and Dadaji, along with his brothers and their wives, was out sitting by the fire which Dadiji kept alive by throwing little twigs and stoking it from time to time. Papa was then seven and in Dadiji's brother's arms, while Anil Tauji was rollicking with the other kids. No one saw how it happened, but eyewitness accounts categorically state that it was no one's fault. The fire was dying down and Dadiji had bent over a little too close, poking at the dying embers, when her *pallu* fell over and burst out in flames, engulfing her in a second. She screamed and howled, and while everyone understandably stood frozen, Buaji foolishly and bravely ran to her, and pulled the sari off Dadiji. As people watched in horror, Buaji tripped and the sari wrapped itself around her. The fire, which had spared Dadiji, now burnt through Buaji's skin, melted her tissue and charred it to the bone by the time Dadaji and his brothers managed to extinguish it.

Papa tells me he can still sometimes smell the ungodly stench of human flesh burning in the courtyard.

'Is Ma okay?' Buaji had asked when she was being taken to the hospital.

Papa, who was too small for his memories to be reliable, says that Buaji hadn't shed a single tear, not then and neither when she was in the hospital recovering.

Things changed swiftly. She came back home with a splotchy, scalded scar tissue running from the top of her neck to the wrist, with the right side of her body reduced to a battered, burnt battlefield. Revulsion followed, people turned away their eyes in pity and shameful disgust, making Buaji realize that she was no longer what she once had been. Mirrors were painted over at the behest of the doctor. Not long after, she dropped out of school and then stopped leaving the house altogether. Dadaji and Dadiji, both racked by guilt, did everything they could to not make her feel different, but there was little they could do. That fire was the inflexion point of Dadaji's and Dadiji's relationship with Buaji; their love for her multiplied many folds, and often became unreasonable. Family heirlooms and jewellery were sold, savings were exhausted, and Dadaji worked himself to death to pay for the reconstructive surgeries that took place in Delhi. But nothing helped much, and it was Buaji who put a stop to the futility of the exercise.

The realization that she would never get married had also struck home.

In an exceptionally unreasonable moment, Dadaji made Anil Tauji and Papa forsake marriage because he knew that the day they got married, conversations around Buaji's marriage would fly fast and thick.

Tauji forsake love and marriage and family, but Papa deceived everyone when he dared to find love and happiness in Mumma. Drama followed, but that's a story for another time. With Anil Tauji and Dadiji spending their lives blaming themselves for what happened to Buaji and cringing pitifully every time they saw her, and Papa having broken her heart, it was only Dadaji who saw beyond her scars and became her everything: friend, family, father. They were complete in themselves.

'I will only be your daughter,' Buaji used to tell Dadaji. 'No one's wife, no one's mother. I am okay with that.'

But soon after, Fufaji walked into Buaji's life and agreed to marry her without a rupee in dowry, giving Buaji a chance at normalcy. Buaji fell in love with the man and got married within a month. Buaji's wedding day is the only day Dadaji has ever cried. The pictures of Buaji's wedding confirm that; Dadaji looks a happy but broken man.

What I say from here is pure hearsay and there's a huge chance that none of it is true. Fufaji wasn't the man everyone thought him to be. Marriage for him was just a cover to carry on his philandering behaviour, and what better cover than Buaji, a pity project? It's said that their wedding was never consummated and that Karan Bhaiya and Anshuman Bhaiya were born in a lab and borne by Buaji.

'IVF in older women often results in twins,' says Di, who firmly believes in the story.

So love has had a sketchy history in our house. Even though I never want to stumble into the delusional, romantic aspect of love, I do enjoy looking at boys from time to time. I have heard that boys from Delhi are much better looking, and those from Bengaluru more articulate, from Mumbai more ambitious, and from Kolkata more loving, but for now, Dehradun boys have served their purpose well.

And this boy . . . uff.

But how the hell did he know my name?

11 August 2002

The more time I spend thinking of him the more handsome he gets in my head, and the angrier I get. I know it should only be the latter, but I can't shake off the image of him gazing lovingly at the books. I would have taken him to be a criminal—with an eighteen-wheeler heavy baritone—if he had an AK-47 in his hand, but he had books. He looked more . . . like a poet, an angry one who has not been getting paid for broken words, who gets his heart shattered for nothing. I just had to stop thinking about him. Who had he asked about me? How did he know my name? Isn't that what stalkers do? Wasn't that what Meghnad did? Maybe I'm overthinking this. I know the names of a lot of people too, none of whom know mine. But I need to confront him, contain this before things spiral out of control. And I've just got to stop thinking about him.

Shifting to more important matters, Manish Chachu's back from Saharanpur.

After failing as a medical representative, losing a small fortune in real estate, he has decided to try his hand at the furniture business.

'Your Chachu is too soft for business. He should have been a big movie star instead,' Papa always says.

Chachu was Dadaji's favourite because he was Buaji's favourite, but then he grew too old and too unsuccessful, and dropped out of his favour. It got worse when he kept deflecting the question of marriage. After Papa's debacle of giving Dadaji two granddaughters, Manish Chachu was the only way the *great* Vaid name would survive. But even then, he rarely gets the short end of the stick from Dadaji because of how much Buaji loves him. Born a year after that calamitous fire, Buaji had gotten attached to Chachu quickly; he was the only one who didn't see her as a victim and didn't flinch when he saw her. She literally brought Manish Chachu up. Buaji did everything to make Manish Chachu another Dadaji, but only managed a severely watered-down version.

Last year, the remaining chunk of Dadiji's jewellery was pawned off to save Chachu from the murky moneylenders he had chosen to owe. No questions asked.

'I could have employed more tailors, rented a shop, given the money back with double the interest. Your buaji is blind, she has no sense of money,' Mumma had groused back then.

'She'd rather slit her wrists than help you,' I had replied.

He's a good-looking man, no doubt about that, so much so that till I was eight I was adamant he would be the man I married. I would chase women away from him with a stick. When he was younger, he used to be much kinder to us than our brothers, and we would cling to him. Those were good times.

Manish Chachu is thirty-five, past the so-called prime marriageable age by at least five years. However, despite his advanced age, and his failure to make something of himself, he's still a valued pick in the marriage market. He's tall, he's got Dadaji's good looks and is just as finicky sartorially. Like Dadaji, he wouldn't be caught dead without his fitted, starched white kurta–pyjamas. When Chachu was younger, brash old women would flock to Dadiji with proposals for their daughters, all of which were rejected with an upturn of the nose and a wave of Dadaji's walking stick. They wanted someone richer, more beautiful, less fat. The proposals, once a gush, slowed a little once word got out of Manish Chachu's wretched luck with money.

'Of course your buaji is looking for a girl for him,' Mumma said today. 'With your dadaji falling sick so often, they need the money. Do you think your dadaji's patients pay him anything? Nothing. *Thenga*. Only respect, no money.'

Fufaji and Buaji know most of the older girls in Dehradun and their families by name and the kind of money they have.

'Only a girl can set things right, bring happiness to the house,' Buaji often says these days.

Divya Di and I raise our hands, but they are ignored. By happiness, we all know she means money. Dowry is only bad when women are burnt for it.

'Maybe then they will throw us out if they find a girl rich enough,' Mumma would say. 'They would be able to afford maids then.'

'Why are you sad about it? It will be good riddance if we leave and they forget all about us!' Divya Di would say.

'Where do you think our ration comes from?' I would butt in.

'We will be able to afford it,' Divya Di would be confident. 'You people just don't want to take the risk.'

'I am not sure I want to risk starvation,' I would scoff. 'Di, there's no way we will be able to pay the rent. Or even find a house.'

'Oh, please,' Divya Di would disagree. 'If they ask us to leave, they are not going to make it difficult for us to find one. Get over your victim syndrome.'

Divya Di has always been the most optimistic of us all, egging us on to leave everything and move to Delhi, far from Dadaji's influence, and try to make a living there. She assumes Mumma's customers would magically appear, and she herself would get a lot of work: 'There are people dying to give me small jobs or internships, and scores of modelling assignments await me.'

'Stop talking about his wedding!' Mumma would say. 'Nothing has happened yet.'

That's true. Manish Chachu has been less than enthusiastic about getting married. It was only when he asked Dadaji and Fufaji to loosen their purse strings for his furniture business idea that, he had to give in to their demands for his marriage.

'No one's going to get married to him if he doesn't have a running business, or at least a shop,' Fufaji had argued in front of Dadaji. 'We will recoup everything from the girl's family. Trust me.'

Divya and I have vowed to foil our family's designs.

'Manish Chachu? Do you really want to get married? I never thought you would,' asked Divya Di.

'Everyone has to. Your time is going to come soon,' he said before he picked up his helmet.

14 August 2002

15 August is a big day for Divya Di and me.

What had started as a competition between Karan Bhaiya and Anshuman Bhaiya on one side and Di and I on the other means a lot more to us now.

Mumma gets irritated at how seriously we take this day—the unabashed aggression, the war-like preparation and the whole attitude. But Di and I look forward to the adrenaline rush of winning the kite-flying match, and counting the scars left behind by the crushed glass of the *manja* cutting through our fingers. They are like notches on our belt, badges on our chest, our warpaint. We are undoubtedly the best in town. We haven't settled who is the better one amongst us though. The one time we had decided to fight against each other, it had ended with nine-year-old me wrapping the manja around Divya Di's neck trying to make her concede defeat. Mumma and Papa tell me I could have killed her that day which I took as an exaggeration then, but now I know it could be true. A barely visible scar in the shape of a long smile on her neck still bears testimony to that day.

The year before last we had taken bets and on paper we won 3000 rupees. Imagine that! In one evening! But then no one coughed up any money and the parents of a few kids even complained to Dadaji about Divya Di terrorizing them, and that was that.

Anyway, today is the day we buy our kites and the baddest, sharpest manja in the market. The shopkeepers are not going to save up the delicate kites for a year, so the discounts are crazy. And what's the deal with flying kites on any other day than 15 August? What exactly are you celebrating? A Thursday? 15 August, Independence Day, kites flying high and free, do people not get the metaphor?

But neither Di nor I fly kites for fun any more, we do it to win. It's the day when the Vaid sisters always come out on top.

We were on our way back from the market when we saw a bunch of kids running and shouting, *'Baarvan! Ye Baarvan tha!'*

'Did they really say twelve?' asked Di, stopping the scooter.

The highest number of kites Di and I have cut with a single kite is seven. And that's the unofficial Dehradun record. We had to find out if these kids were telling the truth. We drove behind the kids, eyes on the sky, looking for the kite responsible for obliterating our record.

Within minutes, we spotted it. A shimmering black kite which swooped, glided and cut through the air with incredible decisiveness. Di and I gasped despite trying hard not to be impressed with the whole thing. The next second, Di banged the scooter against a *thela*, a wooden cart full of litchis.

'Go and see who it is,' Di said to me, even as she traded insults with the thela guy.

I traced the manja of the kite and ran in its direction.. A left from the Rispana *pul*, right through Jogiwalla, past the taxi stand, a sharp left from the bus stop, and straight on to the Haridwar bypass.

And there he was, standing on the road, fingers bleeding, tongue rolling in his cheek, eyes stuck on the taut manja, wrists twisting and turning, feet moving swiftly—a veritable kite god! He was good, very good! His handsome face was an example in concentration.

He was the boy from the library. Was I imagining it? No. He was there. Really there.

I had no instructions to go talk to him and so I stood there and watched. To be honest, I was a long way from home, and I was a bit scared about approaching him.

He didn't have an extra kite lying around, no backup plan if he lost this one in the air. Such arrogant confidence he exuded, bordering on the foolish. He didn't exult, celebrate, pump his fist and shout *'Ai vo kaate!'* like an amateur when he won a duel. He would shrug and move on to the new one, his face not betraying any emotion. I sat down and looked at him dominate the field, mimicking the way his wrists moved, committing to memory his tricks; I was both mesmerized and furious. A little later, he finally lost his kite. He wasn't beaten. The weathered manja had just given away and the kite floated away into the mountains, a fitting end to his innings. He picked up the *charkhari*, the spindle for the string, turned and left. I followed him but he walked too briskly and disappeared into the open fields.

I stopped a few kids running after a kite and asked them who he was.

One of the girls said, *'Mai nahi jaanti. Ek–do baar bas basti mein dekha hai.* (I don't know, I have just seen him a couple of times in the slums.)'

My hour-long search for that boy yielded nothing, no one knew who I was talking about (but I couldn't tell anyone that he was gorgeous, or that he filched books from a library, or that he was magnificent with a kite, so I'm not sure if they were talking about the right guy).

On my way back, I found his charkhari lolling about on the roadside. I won't lie, I picked it up and carried it home.

At first I was just curious to see if it was any different from the ones we used and almost even threw it away when I saw it wasn't, but for some reason I kept it hidden.

'Where were you lost?' Divya Di snapped at me when I got home.

I tried to lie but Divya Di knew straightaway that I was fibbing. I spilled all.

'Boys can never be our friends. As for his record, we will beat it tomorrow,' she said sternly.

17 August 2002

It's been two days but my fingers still hurt. Di's are even worse. We didn't even come close to beating that boy's record but we did beat our own using the tips I had gleaned from looking at that boy. At one point, even Buaji was cheering for us, exulting over our every win against the neighbourhood boys. It's in moments like these that I imagine an alternative reality where our relationships aren't strained by miseries and hate, and that fills my heart with so much joy. But then again, as humans, I think cruelty and hatred towards each other is our default setting, and the more time people spend with each other the more chances are there for the mask of civility and decency to slip away . . .

We didn't spot his kite. Why would someone so good chicken out on 15 August, a day when everyone brings out their best? Di isn't thinking about it any more; she doesn't have to until next year, but she sensed that I was caring a little too much.

'Do you like him?' she asked, straight off the bat.

'What! No? I've just seen him twice.'

'Stay away from that boy. If he feels he's getting some attention out of a cute girl like you, who knows what he will he do?'

'I'm not cute,' I said.

'Don't fish for compliments,' she said. 'We don't want another Meghnad on our hands. You wouldn't know how to handle—'

'Shut up and tell me if you're coming with me to Saharanpur tomorrow,' I said. I don't know why I wanted to steer the conversation away from Di bashing the boy. I didn't even know him and yet . . .

'Do we have to go?' she asked, displeased.

'Mumma needs cloth for the lehnga orders. I can go alone if you don't want to'

Divya Di paused for a bit before saying she didn't mind. Unlike me, Di is justified in disliking Saharanpur. But it's not that she hasn't bumped into Meghnad in Dehradun in the oddest of places. Sometimes I feel he orchestrates these accidental bump-ins, and that he still hasn't gotten over Di. Even now he and his friends shout out 'slut' and 'whore' whenever they run into Di in public places.

Just when we think we've seen the last of him and his shenanigans, someone or the other reminds us of what had happened all those years back. Most women in the neighbourhood, the ones who had seen the fullest extent of Meghnad's madness, shamelessly tell us that we let a good boy out of our hands.

But the good boy the women gush about is often found terrorizing other young women.

18 August 2002

It's a two-hour-long boring, dusty ride to Saharanpur. Every time I wish the drive isn't as bad as the last time, but it always is. The bus itself is filthy beyond imagination: paan-stained corners, vomit streaks on every window, all kinds of smells—from people carrying food and vegetables to sell. I usually sleep and drool all over Di's shoulder for the entire two-hour journey.

'We have reached,' said Divya Di and the bus stuttered to a halt. 'We won't waste any time here like the last time. Keep looking over your shoulders. Slim chance that he would be here, but you never know.'

I nodded and we headed out.

The Vaids are master bargainers. We take pride in it! And so what should have been a quick in-and-out stretched to four hours. Di and I were locked in a fierce battle over who could win the better discounts from the seasoned wholesalers of Saharanpur. By the time we finished, it was sundown and we had to shout and bawl our way to the last bus back to Dehradun. We paid the full fare but didn't get a seat.

'So much for saving money,' said Di.

The bus had barely left Saharanpur when a bottle of beer came crashing inside through the window behind us. Little shards of glass crunched beneath our feet. All of us looked outside, scared. We saw a car with a bunch of boys hanging out of the door, shouting, screaming, whistling. *'OYE! IDHAR! IDHAR!'*

Divya clutched my hand in mild panic and my heart leapt up.

Meghnad was on the driver's seat gazing straight at the road, nostrils flared, as if it hadn't been years but days since that incident. He looked drunk; everyone in the car did. He had now grown a menacing beard which accentuated his crooked nose and his doped-out eyes, and looked infinitely more repulsive and lizard-like. Di tugged at my arm, made me sit down and asked me not to look outside. The car followed us for a couple more kilometres; insults were traded between the conductor and the boys—the conductor polite, the boys incorrigible—and more bottles were thrown in. The bus reeked of alcohol. When the car stopped following us, a few passengers looked at us accusingly.

'*Kya hai?*' Di snapped back. 'We don't know them!'

We must have covered just another kilometre when there was a loud bang and the bus spluttered to a halt. A tire had given way. The passengers grumbled, but knew they had no choice, and everyone got off. It was discovered that the puncture had to do with a few iron nails that had been strewn on the road. Wouldn't be the worst thing Meghnad has done. In fact, quite an improvement from last month when he had whipped out a gun at someone who had cut him off in traffic.

As the driver and conductor were changing the tyre, we drank a cup of revoltingly sweet tea at the roadside dhaba.

Then I saw the boy again—the book-stealing, name-knowing, kite-flying boy, washing his hands at the dhaba's hand pump. I double-checked. It was him, no doubt about it.

If anything, his kurta was even dirtier and he was carrying a backpack. Now he was sitting alone in a corner on a bench of the dhaba, writing in a notebook. He didn't look up even once before the conductor called everyone to board the bus.

'There are a few more people boarding, so if you want to go to the roof, feel free to do so,' said the conductor.

People rushed in, and Di tried to push me inside.

'I will take the roof,' I said.

'Why? Mumma will kill us if she gets to know.'

'She doesn't have to know,' I said.

'Fine, I'm sitting inside,' she said and went in.

I followed the boy and a bunch of others atop the bus. The conductor slammed his hand on the side of the bus, and asked us to be careful at the top.

Between him and me sat ten others. Twice I tried walking up to the front of the bus where he sat, but people sat me down, telling me it was too dangerous. The boy didn't turn to look, and kept scribbling in his notebook, which he was struggling to hold on to, his rough, long hair flopping behind his head.

'Oye!' I shouted finally. 'Oye, you!'

The boy turned and looked at me.

'What?' he said gruffly.

'HOW DO YOU KNOW MY NAME!' I shouted back over the honks of the bus.

Without missing a beat, he said, 'Who doesn't know the granddaughters of the respected Dr Vaid?'

He looked away from me.

It was clear to me that he was lying, but I couldn't find the words to probe further, to ask what his name was.

I fumbled for a way to start a conversation but fell short and he got back to his notebook.

For the next hour, I sat upright and alert, to catch the boy as soon as the bus comes to a stop. But when the bus stopped, he just jumped off from the front and disappeared. I felt frustrated.

The boy was gone. *Who doesn't know the granddaughters of the respected Dr Vaid?*

Every time I hear this in my head, I am baffled.

When I first heard it, the meaning was simple. It was a taunt at Divya Di and me, the shameful prodigal daughters. In effect, he was saying, 'Who doesn't know about the infamous, *bigdi-hui* granddaughters of Dr Vaid?

But now that I keep going through the words repeatedly in my head, I feel his stress was on the words *respected Dr Vaid*. As if he was not taunting Di or me, but Dadaji. The word *respected* was uttered with sarcasm, not reverence. Maybe it was said to strip Dadaji of both respect and the title of doctor. And why not? It made sense to me. For us, neither of it was valid. But what could he have against Dadaji?

23 August 2002

There's a puja at Manish Chachu's new shop.

Dadaji and Manish Chachu wore white, starched kurtas, and looked like freshly minted politicians. Fufaji wore the only suit he had, and Papa was in an old shirt–pant, looking like their accountant.

'Why do we have to go?' grumbled Di.

'When was the last time Dadaji paid for our meal?' I asked.

'Keep your mouths shut, don't laugh at Chachu, and don't look Dadaji in the eye,' said Mumma before we left.

Karan Bhaiya and Anshuman Bhaiya had spent a good part of last night and this morning sweeping, washing and painting the shop. About a hundred yards from the Ghantaghar, the clock tower, it was housed in a prime location and had come at a hefty price. Dadaji and Buaji had dipped into the fund that had been saved up for Karan Bhaiya's and Anshuman Bhaiya's engineering studies.

'Now see the kind of *rishta*s that will come flocking!' Fufaji said with glee as Karan Bhaiya and Anshuman Bhaiya fixed the shop board: Vaid's Furniture. Proprietor: Manish Vaid

The pandit was late by an hour and Dadaji grumbled like it was our fault.

Dadaji made Karan Bhaiya and Anshuman Bhaiya dust every corner of the shop again while we waited outside.

My attention was caught by the sound of a motorcycle. I turned. Was this a certain trend? Of seeing him when and where I least expected to? In a cloud of dust, riding a

47

150-cc choking, coughing, angry Enfield, his soiled white kurta billowing in the wind, and a pandit—with paan dribbling out of the corners of his mouth like blood—clinging on to him for dear life, there he was

'Arre! *Pagal*! Who drives like this? Are you a mad man?' cursed the pandit, scrambling off the bike.

'Your god will save you, will he not?' said the boy impudently.

The women of the house who are not supposed to touch the feet of anyone other than their elderly relatives were asked to touch this foul-mouthed, paan-chewing man's. The pandit scrunched his nose, and waved us away without so much as a look, as if we were lepers.

He asked Dadaji, 'None of the women are impure?'

Buaji, Mumma, Di and I shook their heads.

The pandit walked in and after him Dadaji and Manish Chachu. Then the pandit turned around and told Papa in a matter-of-fact tone: 'Your daughters can come in, but not your wife.'

'*Haanji*, of course. It's my fault. I should have remembered,' said Mumma politely and stepped away from the entrance of the shop, her tears barely hidden. '. . . it's my fault.'

'But, panditji—'

'She can come in after we finish the puja,' the pandit interrupted Papa summarily. Then Fufaji, Buaji, Karan Bhaiya and Anshuman Bhaiya walked inside. Papa and the rest of us stood outside, shaking in fury.

'Om Prakash!' thundered Dadaji to Papa. 'You're needed here.'

This was not the first time and yet something breaks inside us every time Mumma is asked not to partake in havans and pujas, the religious ceremonies of the house; this feeling keeps getting worse. We shouldn't even feel bad anymore but . . .

Earlier, Divya Di and I used to be subjected to the same treatment, but over time it has changed. As if somehow Papa had managed to dilute our mother's lower-caste lineage out of us.

'Pitaji, she also should be—' said Papa.

'We can start without you,' said Dadaji.

Papa lowered his head and said, 'Start without me.' Dadaji was fuming.

Divya Di had also just begun to turn away when Mumma held her hand and made her stay. We watched on, our faces burning with shame and anger.

The havan, the sacred fire, was lit, with the men in the front and Buaji at the back.

Mumma whispered, 'I'm OK, it doesn't mean anything.'

I damn well know what these fucking, divisive rituals mean! They are all hogwash, meant for dim-witted people.

Divya Di squirmed in Mumma's grip. Meanwhile, I distracted myself by stealing glances at the boy who'd decided to stay and watch the ceremony. The boy leaned against the motorcycle and stared unblinkingly into the fire. Once in a while he would change songs on his Walkman and then again carry on with his staring business. Twice, he spat on the ground as the pandit's sloka reached a crescendo.

The third time, he walked over to Divya Di.

'This will help,' he said, and gave her his Walkman with the earphones dangling from it. He looked straight at me and said, 'You take one,' and pointed to one end of the earphone. Before Papa and Mumma could protest, he turned away from us and started walking back to the motorcycle. Ignoring Mumma's protests, we pushed 'play', and literally the harshest rock/metal/whatever-it-is-called, blared out of the earphones. The pandit's words were no longer audible, and it seemed like he was the one mouthing the expletives in the song we were listening to. No longer did Di look furious. The song changed and it was no longer metal. It was a song from our childhood—from the movie *Dulaara*; the song '*Meri Pant Bhi Sexy*' had been banned because it had that word 'sexy' in it. It was hilarious. Divya Di and I did everything we could to not break out laughing at the boy's audacious choice. Divya Di smiled at the boy, and flashed him a thumbs-up, and he nodded ever so slightly.

Karan Bhaiya nudged Anshuman Bhaiya and pointed at the earphones in our ears and the smiles on our faces. We didn't take our eyes off the havan, which was now very much tolerable.

'You can come inside now,' said the pandit once the puja was over, and we all shuffled in.

We were now in great spirits.

'You can come inside too,' Dadaji said to the boy.

The boy looked on, not answering, and said after a long pause, 'I don't want to get involved in this nonsense. I was asked to drop the pandit here and take him back. If there's more work, I need to get paid for it.' He lit another cigarette and let it hang from his lips limply. I was correct about *Who doesn't know the granddaughters of the respected Dr Vaid?* His demeanour showed no visible respect for Dadaji.

'Is that how you were brought up?' said Buaji sternly. 'Call him panditji!'

'Does it look like I am talking to you, aunty?' he said, his voice harsh.

Divya Di and I looked at each other, and the briefest of smiles passed between us before Karan Bhaiya stood up and said, '*Saale*, is this the way to talk? *Tameez nahi hai kya*, where are your manners?'

The boy threw the cigarette on the ground and crushed it with his chappals.

'I don't want to cause a problem here,' he said, staring straight at Karan Bhaiya, who was itching for a fight.

Anshuman Bhaiya was sizing the boy up, and perhaps realized that his brother was no match for the calm gruffness of the boy.

'Leave him alone,' said the pandit.

'Didn't you see how he talked to you? To mother?' asked Karan Bhaiya.

'Listen to me, Karan. We will deal with him later. *Abhi jaane de suar ko* (Let the pig go),' said Anshuman Bhaiya cautiously.

The boy stood there unmoving, staring unblinkingly at Karan Bhaiya, unaffected and supremely arrogant. And then, he stepped forward, his feet sure, his eyes focused. I knew how this was going to unfold. The boy would walk within sniffing distance of Karan Bhaiya, wait for him to take the first swing, take the hit boldly, and then watch Karan Bhaiya nurse his bruised knuckle; he would then smile, light another cigarette, have a long, satisfying puff, and blow it all on Karan Bhaiya's face; finally, he would let go a swift uppercut and knock Karan Bhaiya out. He would then stamp on his face while holding Anshuman Bhaiya by his neck.

None of that happened.

He came to me, and calmly fished out the earphone from my right ear and then Di's. He wrapped them around the Walkman meticulously and put it all back in his pocket.

The boy took out the key of the Enfield from his back pocket, dropped it in my hands, and said, 'Ask your Fufaji to drop the old man home. Ask him to be a little useful.' He turned and left.

25 August 2002

Dehradun is a small town. Gossip, rumours, scandals spread like wildfire and no one knows that better than us. Di tells me it's not so in the big cities, where people hide behind locked doors, and don't trust their neighbours. Trusting one's neighbours has not got anyone anywhere, especially if you have the ones we do.

So in a neighbourhood, and in a town like ours, people were really curious about this boy everyone had seen, but knew zilch about. The Enfield was from a garage near the pandit's house.

These are the recorded testimonies of the people who had talked to him.

He has been here a few times. He always sits at the computer at that far corner. He wipes his browser history before he leaves, so I don't know what he looks at. Never talked to him. Looks like a goonda, so I never tried. He's always a little angry. Don't know where he's come from. My business is not to ask questions.—Suresh Uncle, Gupta Cyber Café

He's not that good-looking. No, never bothered to ask his name. He calls me bhai, and I call him bhai.—A boy from the garage

Tall guy? Wears kurtas? Heavy voice like someone drove a scooter over his neck? Haan, haan, I know him. Nice boy. Pays after every peg. No trouble ever. Though a little scary. Doesn't talk much, stares at

his drink all the time he's here. Not a word to anyone. Looks like he has a broken heart. Don't know his name though. Why would I ask a customer his name?—Chachaji, owner of a bar on the highway

The boy is pretty good-looking. But he always looks angry, doesn't he? Always sketchy about his past. Must have run away from somewhere.—Another boy from the garage

Aren't you Om Prakash's daughter?—Neeraj Uncle, owner, Neeraj Sweet Shop

Have seen him with those boys of the slum a couple of times. He talks little. Heard from somewhere that he had done something big in Delhi. Had to run away and come here. How long? Some say a year? Before this he was in Ghaziabad. Comes here often waiting for a call. Never calls his parents, that's strange no? Beta, why are you asking? Aren't you Vaid Bhaisaheb's daughter?—Suman Aunty from the PCO booth

He definitely did something in Delhi. Otherwise why does he hide his name? I asked him once. He didn't bother to answer. Looks like a loafer though. Don't talk to him. Doesn't look safe.—Suman Aunty's son

I told him once or twice to stop smoking. But there's a lot of anger in him, so he has to smoke. What about the anger? Do you think I will ask him? Who knows what he has done! I don't want to get into that.—Rajesh, corner paanwala

All of this threw up a picture of an angry, heartbroken boy who had run away from Delhi after something big had happened to him, and found succour in Dehradun in loneliness, cigarettes and the occasional drink. But what was he doing with that book in the library?

29 August 2002

This morning, the guy from the garage called. The boy had come to pick up a bike, their cheapest, Yamaha RX100, and paid twice the rent for the day, plus security.

'You didn't ask his name? What kind of a business are you running?' I asked. 'Do you know where he went?'

'Sahastradhara I think,' he had answered.

On a stupid and reckless whim, I took the scooter out and drove to Sahastradhara, the only picnic spot my school knew. As kids, we weren't allowed to take a dip in the sulphur-rich water or even sit on the rocks, which were slippery and weepy. I was parking my scooter when I spotted him. Perched precariously on one of the weeping rocks, the biggest of them all, the water meandering and gushing around him. Shirtless and wet, he sat there, eyes towards the sky, calm but taut. I shouted and it struck me again that I didn't have a name. *OYE!* I shouted. My *Oyes* didn't reach him.

Exhausted with all the shouting, I sat there waiting for him to swim to this side. He was now lying down, lost in a world of his own. Then after what seemed like hours, he got up, and jumped into the shallow pool. He was not seen for what seemed like a long time. Then he came up gasping for air. Water snaked down his body in little rivulets, navigating its way through his rigid musculature. His body seemed like a starved version of Michelangelo's David. He had the muscles, the sinew, the nerves that snaked on his arms, but was lankier, maybe even more defined, maybe even more perfect. Ugh! You could put him in a lab to study muscle definition.

I got up, and in the light of this specimen, I became acutely aware of how my thighs wobbled as I stood up. He dried himself off with a cloth, and slipped into his jeans and a black T-shirt which hung loosely on him.

'Hey!'

'Yes?' he said, his eyes boring into me this time, his voice reverberating inside me.

'Don't you remember me?'

'Advaita Vaid,' he said, walking away from me with a cold look, a far cry from his helpful self that day. He lit a cigarette and took a long, hungry drag at it.

'Thank you for that day,' I said, smiling politely.

He kicked his motorcycle to life, without sparing a nod. Desperate to keep the conversation going and a wee bit curious, I said, 'What did you mean by what you said that day? Granddaughters of the respected Dr Vaid?'

He didn't react again, and I was pushed into saying, 'You can't talk about girls that way.'

'I didn't.'

'You were taunting us, Divya Di and me, I am not daft.'

'I didn't talk about any girl in the manner you're accusing me of.'

'Then who were you talking about?'

'You're smart enough to discern,' he said, kicked the motorcycle to life and drove away.

'HEY!'

He was already far away.

For the next hour and a half, I chased him down all through to Dehradun, extracting every bit from my two-stroke engine. After a while, it felt like he was mocking me—he would slow down, making me feel I was covering ground, and then speed up again. Later, he parked his motorcycle near Tomato Soup Walla, a misnomer because he sells chicken soup too. This was where Di and I had caught Karan Bhaiya and Anshuman Bhaiya being bad Hindus and slurping on soup floating with chunks of chicken.

'What do you want?' he asked.

His words were like a jackhammer on my skull. What did I want from him? I couldn't have just said that he intrigued me, and I wouldn't mind having a conversation with him. How lame would that have been? So, like a headless chicken, I fumbled and stammered.

'Arre? You can't just mock my Dadaji and walk away,' I said.

He looked at me and said, 'I won't apologize for what I said about him.'

'That's rude. I don't know what you have heard about my Dadaji, but it's unwarranted. Tell me who said what to you?'

He looked at me as if I had asked him something ridiculous.

'I am not leaving before you tell me who told you what. I won't stand for this rumour-mongering,' I said, and leaned back into the chair.

'You're seriously going to sit here till I don't tell you?'

'Yes.'

'Suit yourself.'

Fifteen minutes passed and while he read through the newspaper, hardly blinking, I grew restless. He was also sipping his soup, and spewing smoke out like a goddamn chimney. Must be nice to be rich enough to support such an expensive, filthy habit.

I should have gotten up and left, but I stayed put. I had overcommitted to the cause and I would see this through. I could be stubborn too. What kind of granddaughter would I be if I didn't squash 'rumours' about my Dadaji?

'Are you always this sullen or is it just your voice?' I asked.

He stared at me again, saying nothing, just those painful eyes looking at me as if it was me who had done something wrong.

'I wanted to give you this for that Walkman thing you pulled off for us. Here, take it,' I said.

'What's this?' He opened the polythene bag and held the kurta in front of him. The briefest smile came on his face, but he said, 'I can't take this.'

'It's made for you and I got into a lot of trouble getting it for you. Keep it or dump it.'

He put the kurta back in the polythene bag and let out a feeble 'thank you'.

'You're welcome,' I said. 'But that doesn't mean I have forgotten about your rumour-mongering!'

He rolled his eyes irritably.

'You know my name. The least you can do is tell me your name. You look like an Aditya, are you? Wait, wait. You're Samir, aren't you? Or Rehaan?'

'Pick any of them.'

'OK, I will do that, but what's like your real name? The one your parents gave you.'

'Raghu Ganguly,' he said, catching my gaze, and smirking pitifully. 'Used to be a proud Hindu, a Brahmin like your grandfather and your buaji.'

'Why are you smirking? Look, whatever anyone might have told you it is not true.'

'Is that correct?'

'Absolutely!'

'Did he not celebrate what happened earlier this year? Give a fiery speech against Muslims at the Mohyal Convention in July? Ask for all Hindus to unite and drive the Muslims out of the country?' The last of his words were angrily spat out.

'Look, I hardly know you and you can't just—'

He grumbled, 'Did he or did he not?'

'He did.'

Earlier this year, thousands of Muslims, and a slightly lesser proportion of Hindus had been cut down to pieces. Both communities had raped each other's women, impaled infants on tridents and swords, and burnt down neighbourhood after neighbourhood. It is said that the broad-chested chief minister was complicit, but everyone knows that—like in the case of most riots in India—nothing is going to happen to him. The support he had, explicit and implicit, from Hindus all around the country was overwhelming. Dadaji had been at the forefront in Dehradun, giving fiery anti-Muslim speeches at gatherings, droning on about the need for Hindu households to stock up on crowbars, swords and axes in case the war spills over to their state.

'We should slowly flush them out from this country,' Buaji had said.

Dadaji had said, 'They too must have joined the war against us Brahmins.'

Mumma told me later that Altaf and Iqbal were too scared to come to our house since they had heard about Dadaji's speech.

'I got to go,' he said and folded the newspaper.

'But . . . but what does that have to do with you?' I asked.

'People like . . . like your grandfather destroyed my life.' He slammed the table.

1 September 2002

Things have moved rather quickly, and Manish Chachu's shop is already yielding rich dividends. Only yesterday, Manisha Chachu, Fufaji and Buaji went to three houses, two on Rajpur Road, one on Turner Road, and met eligible girls. Manish Chachu had gone through the proceedings with his head hung low, with the interest, if you may, of a dying man. Two of them were in their thirties, *mangliks*, but wealthy and servile, and the last one was, in Buaji's words, 'unbearably ugly and had studied too much'.

'How dare they think I would give Manish to such a witch?' Buaji had said once they left this girl's house.

But within twenty-four hours, Buaji changed her tune and seemed to be smitten with the girl she had found to be a monstrosity. This was because some rumours had reached her ears. There was talk of how the girl had run away, gotten married, but the man had left her within two months and she had returned to her mother's house with bruises on the face, a fractured hand and a shattered heart.

'Her parents will do everything to get this marriage to happen. We can ask for anything,' she would have said in her conspiratorial tone to Fufaji and Dadaji.

'What about Manish? He will say yes?' Fufaji would have asked.

'Leave that to me. I will handle Bhaiya,' Buaji would have said.

And I imagine that Dadaji would have kept quiet, knowing Buaji was the more discerning one.

I haven't been able to get his gorgeous, face, his words, his pained eyes, his gravelly and yet soft voice, and his supposed hatred for my grandfather and his ilk out of my head. I stay awake and think of all the things that could have happened to Raghu Ganguly for him to say what he had, and that pointed in one and only one direction. He had been in love with a Muslim girl and that the relationship had fallen apart—as it usually happens—because of their religions. Like any self-respecting sleuth, I asked around to check if my story held.

4 September 2002

After a long time, Divya Di has snagged some print catalogue work and she has been working on it for the past few days. Buaji and the others have turned up their noses more than once, but the money she will bring in will help the household, and so they haven't done anything drastic. So I had to head out alone when I got the news that Sumitra Bali of Rajpur Road was on the shortlist for Manish Chachu. She needed to be saved.

I saw Sumitra Bali at Paltan Bazaar buying ice cream bricks. Were they expecting visitors? Or were they as wealthy as Fufaji and Buaji hoped they were and were having ice cream every day?

She was far from how Buaji had described her. 'Ugly' was the last word I would use for her. 'Powerful', 'decisive' and 'strong' came to my head instantly. Tall and straight like an arrow, she stood out from the others in the bazaar. In a sari with not a single pleat out of place, her chin up, shoulders exuding confidence, and her strides long and purposeful, she looked like she had stepped straight out of a world-changing board meeting.

She was surprised to find me sitting on her Scooty. She couldn't place me at first. When she did, her demeanour changed—shoulders drooping, eyes downcast, a polite smile pasted on her face.

'You can't get married to my Chachu,' I said. 'Go home and tell your parents that this can't happen. Make up any excuse, OK?'

I could understand the shock on her face, so I had to explain.

'You know, we Vaids are very proud of the way we look. We are all fair, tall, and strong-boned. Pucca Aryans, except our mother, of course. But you . . . I know you're a Brahmin too but you're what we call shit-faced. You are brown and I wouldn't want my little brothers and sisters to be dark and unappealing like you. Are you getting my point? Manish Chachu himself had wanted to say this, but he sent me. Go home and do what I just told you to. We can't have another person looking like you in our house. Or—'

'Or?'

'Let me just say your presence at our house wouldn't be taken kindly. And given your history, I don't see your parents jumping to your rescue either. Or would you rather be chased away from another house?'

Sumitra, unfazed by my threats, said, 'What will you do to me that hasn't already been done before?'

'You have no idea,' I stumbled and stuttered, my plan of scaring her off crumbling to pieces.

'Your Chachu will rape me?'

'I . . .'

'Or your buaji will ask for money?'

'Sumitra . . .'

'Or Fufaji and Dadaji will scald me with the tea I make for them?' she said, her lips quivering in anger, the ice cream in her hands slowly melting.

'Umm—'

'Why? Don't you have any other threats to make?'

'I haven't even started!' I protested, still trying to stick to the plan to scare her away from the horrendous trap she was about to find herself in.

'Then why are you doing this, Advaita?' she asked.

'Look—'

'I am not scared of you, Advaita. You're a child.'

'I'm not a child!' I snapped.

'You want ice cream?' she asked.

'No!'

'You're so cute, Advaita.'

Of course I wanted some.

Sumitra was already sitting next to me, slipping the paper cover off the ice cream. Then she scooped it with a plastic spoon, had some of it herself and then offered it to me. I ate it begrudgingly, deciding not to enjoy it too much.

'It's nice, right?' she asked as I savoured it. 'You want more?'

I did, and so I nodded, and she gave me the brick and the spoon. She had seen right through my charade, my empty threats.

'Your Chachu is a nice man. I can see that,' said Sumitra. 'Your buaji and Fufaji are devils, but I don't see how they can be worse than my own parents.'

'But—'

'I know what I am getting into, Advaita.'

'I'm sorry for what I said. You're really beautiful.'

Sumitra smiled for my sake. I'm sure my words meant nothing to her. Over the years she would have heard too many times from too many people that she's dark, *saanwli*, poor-looking. It bumped uselessly against her thick skin.

'Don't say I didn't warn you.'

'Thank you for that,' she said.

'How bad has your life been to think of my family as an escape plan?'

'That's what your Chachu also said. But all misery is relative, isn't it? Can't lose hope, can I?'

We both laughed at her misfortune. Later, she let me drive her Scooty. She's a nice girl. I like her. I vowed to protect her.

She dropped me back to Paltan Bazaar, and before she left, she thanked me for describing her as beautiful.

'I believe you,' she said, smiling, her perfect, pearl-like teeth gleaming. Then she called me just as I was leaving, 'Hey?'

'Haan?'

'Does your sister know about your Chachu and me?' she asked, her voice glum.

'Why?'

'She used to be my best friend in college,' she said.

It's strange that I have never heard her name from Divya Di.

Divya Di looked like she had seen a ghost when I told her whom Buaji had picked for Manish Chachu. Her entire body shook with anger, and she paced around the room as if looking for something to punch. It looked like she would have a seizure.

'WHY THE HELL DID NO ONE TELL ME THIS BEFORE!'

'Who is Sumitra—'

'THAT GIRL IS A BITCH! SHE'S A LYING, CHEATING WHORE!'

'Di? Calm down—'

'Don't you dare tell me to calm down. That woman was my best friend and was fucking Vibhor! She was my friend, helping me pick gifts for Vibhor and fucking him!' Angry tears flooded her eyes.

She continued, 'She had the gall to keep in touch with him even when Meghnad drove him away from the town. She eloped a year later.'

'Vibhor Gupta wasn't a good guy, Di.'

'You don't know him, Advaita. WHO KNOWS, SHE MIGHT HAVE FUCKED EVERY MAN IN DELHI!'

'Look at what he did to Sumitra. The way I see it, you saved yourself a lifetime of pain.'

'You won't get it. That woman is the absolute worst. If she comes to this house, I will punch her in the face!' she said and stormed off.

Frankly, I don't want to get it. If Divya Di and the boy (if what broke him was love) are what you become when you fall in love, I don't want to feel it. Why invest so much in an emotion when all it gives you is unbridled pain? There are enough miseries in the world, why add another one?

6 September 2002

We all heard it from our house.

By the time we, along with our neighbours reached the accident site, there were thirty-odd people looking on, shocked, and frozen in their places. Blood, fire and the stench of burnt flesh filled the air. Karan Bhaiya was the first among us to break through the ranks and rush to where the toppled bus burnt. Screams that barely sounded human filled the air.

Amidst all this, I heard Raghu's unmistakable voice— deep, husky and authoritative. Divya Di and I jostled our way to the front. Three ambulances screeched to a halt in front of us. Raghu, covered in blood, Karan Bhaiya, Anshuman Bhaiya and other men extracted one person after another from the mangled bus which had collided head-on with a truck. They loaded people into ambulances. More men and women joined in the rescue operations after they got over the blood and guts that had spilled on the roads. Those who watched from the side were crying too, perhaps imagining the mortality of their own selves.

I saw Raghu pacing around, holding his head, crying, bawling, trembling. And then in a flash he ran, jumped over the road divider into the moving traffic, and stood in the middle of the road waving down cars, pointing to the accident on our side of the road. A few cars swerved away, narrowly missing him, not sparing the dying a look lest they have to live with the guilt of not stopping for the rest of their lives. Raghu picked up a rock and threw it at a car which had been trying to steer clear of him. A man and a woman stepped out, shouting curses. Raghu punched the man, and pushed the woman away, and charged to their car. Then he drove the car over the divider and towards where the dying lay.

'Everyone! Inside!' he shouted.

People swung into action. The injured were pushed up inside till there was no more space to spare.

'Advaita! Don't!' shouted Divya Di.

'I know the shortcuts!' I screamed as I ran towards the car.

As Raghu started to drive away, muscle memory from years of catching buses kicked in, and I opened the door and jumped in.

'Hold on.' He stepped on the accelerator.

'Look at me,' I said to him.

For the next fifteen minutes, I guided him through the narrow alleyways, the shortcuts of Park Road and Turner Road and Clement Town, and we reached the hospital before the other ambulances that had left the accident scene. The ward boys came running to us as soon as he slammed the brakes.

Raghu stood there as the ward boys got to work. He watched till the last person was unloaded on to a stretcher, limbs flopping around uselessly. He stared unblinkingly at the splotches and pools of blood where once the bodies lay, his boyish eyes pools of tears, his hands trembling by his side. He looked broken. Lost. Defeated.

'We need to leave,' I said when the last of the bodies were taken away.

He turned towards me, eyes bloodshot and lips quivering. He moved his mouth, but the words wouldn't come. Little rivulets of tears streamed down his cheeks as he pointed to the bloody mess.

'Brah . . . Brahm . . .' He stuttered.

'They will be OK.'

He turned away, irrevocably wrecked. He slumped to the ground, and buried his face in his palms. His body heaved and jolted vigorously.

'We should go,' I said, helping him up.

'But she . . .' He pointed to no one, just blood and gore.

'There's no one there, Raghu.'

'She was . . . she was right there . . . she was . . . I loved her and I couldn't save her . . .' Then he looked at himself, the blood on his body, and panicked. He started to hysterically pat the blood off himself.

I had to hold him and drag him out of there. He was lost, his body out of control, his eyes staring uselessly ahead. He trudged behind me at first, shuffling and stumbling, falling over twice, but once we were out of the hospital compound, he broke into a run. I had to let go of his hand. After ten minutes, he was still running, sprinting away from me, saying things under his breath.

'STOP!' I shouted but he didn't seem to listen.

I tried to keep up, but my lungs closed up and I stumbled over. He was still running away, a blur to my muddled brain. He didn't slow down, my screams didn't seem to reach him. If anything, he ran faster every subsequent second. I hobbled behind him as he ran distractedly, barely missing vehicles. Then he got on the Splendor motorcycle he had hired today. In a moment of recklessness, I hopped on too. I tried to talk to him, shouted in his ears to stop, told him that we could talk, but he rode on.

* * *

Jharipani waterfalls, that's where he drove us to in two hours, with me clinging on behind like a little monkey.

Overgrown men in VIP briefs and women and girls in soaked salwar kameezes scampered around, clicking pictures. He took his drenched kurta off. He stepped out of his pants and slipped into the water, navigating the crates of cold drinks kept there to cool.

I sat and saw him disappear to the far end of the waterfall. I have tried standing right where the water hits the ground during picnics with Mumma and Papa. The water slaps your chest with a ferocity you are not prepared for, and soon enough you bend—the pain's too much. He stood there unmoving, the water thwacking him violently. Other men and boys, exhorted by their egos, tried to walk to where he stood, and failed miserably. When he walked out, looking less shabby, he sat on the rocks and lit a cigarette.

For a second I wanted to give him a piece of my mind, but he was still shivering, the cigarette and his fingers shaking. I bought an 'I Love Dehradun' T-shirt from a boy selling them nearby and offered it to him to wear.

'Huh?'

He was surprised to see me there, but he took it and wore it. The tears were gone, the smouldering look was back, but there was still that vulnerability in him. And anger and pain, pain and anger.

'Should I leave?' I asked.

He didn't answer. He caught my gaze and tears trickled down his eyes again. Did that mean he wanted me to stay? Hoping to comfort him, I reached out and held his hand. Within seconds, he retracted his hand and looked away from me. I would have asked him what was troubling him, but his pain seemed beyond words or repair, so I just sat there and watched him smoke.

'Did it remind you of something?' I asked. 'The accident? The blood?'

After a while he said softly, 'Death.'

I toyed with the question for quite some time before I asked, 'Raghu? What's in Delhi? What did you leave behind?'

He turned to me, in horror or anger or surprise I wouldn't know, and then got up and started walking away.

'Raghu? Maybe I can help. Talk to me.' I said and followed him like a pesky stray dog. 'Raghu? What was that you were trying to tell me? Brahm . . .?'

He didn't stop.

'I can help,' I said.

He turned towards me and snapped, 'You can't help. No one can. No one fucking can . . .' The last words were warbled. He looked at me and said, 'Thank you, but don't try . . . stop.'

The anger, the pain in his voice, shook something in me. I couldn't ask further. I watched him walk away.

I came back home, alone.

16 September 2002

Buaji had insisted on a low-key wedding. I was there when it was proposed to Sumitra's parents. They were served food and water which they refused politely as girls' families do. Twice I saw Divya Di and Sumitra look at each other and then away, the tension between them palpable. I had insisted Divya Di stay away from home but she wasn't one to listen.

'You know your daughter,' said Buaji, sympathetic yet hissing. 'We don't want to do a big affair and then field questions about her previous relationship, about her purity. You know this better than me, don't you?'

Sumitra's parents and Sumitra listened with their heads hung low as Buaji told them what she expected in the wedding. Buaji was treading her ground softly, slowly ramping up. Manish Chachu, the protector, watched on silently.

Fufaji took over. 'We will do a court wedding. No reception. Of course, our relatives have been waiting to come to Manish's wedding, so we can't let them go empty-handed. That would be shameful.'

Buaji looked apologetically at Sumitra's father for an answer and he jumped in, 'Surely. We understand. Just tell us what you need from us and we will try our best to accommodate everything. We will do the best we can. We don't want to disappoint the family.'

Dadaji, who had been watching the proceedings silently like a vulture, nodded at Buaji, who slipped a note in front of them. Sumitra's father took the paper, looked at it and then at his wife, who didn't even bother to look at the paper, and nodded. They were in such a hurry to dispose of their daughter.

'The girls should go inside,' said Dadaji, looking at us. 'Take her too.'

I linked my arm around Sumitra's and we walked to our room; Divya Di followed. Karan Bhaiya was sent to shut our door.

'What number do you think was on that paper?' I asked Sumitra.

'More than my parents can afford.'

'Won't you ask?'

'I don't want to be slapped around,' she said.

'Had you been slapped when you most needed it this wouldn't have happened,' grumbled Divya Di.

'Di? This is not the time for this. I had asked you not to come,' I said sternly.

'You don't tell me what to do,' said Divya Di.

'I saved you from that man. If anything, you should be thankful to me or you would have been standing where I am,' said Sumitra.

'How do we know it wasn't your fault? Who knew what you had been doing? *Haan*? Who knows how many people you have slept with in Delhi?' alleged Di.

Sumitra's eyes burnt in anger and pain.

'Divya Di, we are not going to blame her!'

'I will always blame her, Advaita,' she said and looked at Sumitra. 'So, what happened? Who did you find?'

They looked at each other as if they had not shared lovers but as if they had been lovers themselves and broken each other's hearts. Their anger, love and disappointment with one man choked the small room. Suddenly the door was opened and in came Mumma. She led Sumitra out, and her teary face suddenly brightened and the crease on her forehead smoothened, her body no longer firm with rage. She was seamlessly slipping into the role of a wife.

'Let's go outside,' I said to Di as I followed Mumma and Sumitra.

The *rishta* was finalized. As we all left the house, a bunch of hijras were already outside, singing songs of weddings and love and heartbreak. No one knows how they come to know of festivities and then come asking for money. Whether they seek out happiness or sadness, no one knows. Given the fate nature has dealt them, I would bet on the latter. Sumitra's family had presented a gold necklace, and there was now talk of selling it and getting the wall of the house repaired.

Divya Di was in the living room, walking around like a grieving ghoul.

19 September 2002

Saturday. I was on my way back after delivering Mumma's wares to grumbling aunties when I saw him at the bus stop. I had been thinking so much about him lately that for a second I thought I had conjured him out my thoughts. I slowed down my cycle and followed him. He ripped off little pieces of paper with a scale and stuck them on bus-stop poles, electric poles, and car windows. He waited around for people, picked them out at random and passed the chits of paper. Most of them threw them away before reading. I stopped to read the crisp handwriting:

Sad? What's One More Week?
Let's talk. Sundays.
013-3343447
10 a.m.–6 p.m.

At first it sounded like a prostitution advert seeking sad housewives seeking an outlet for their repressed sexuality. I imagined him in a dingy one-room kitchen near ISBT, waiting for libidinous women with his legs apart, naked, waiting to rub the humdrum of the boring lives of these women out of their inviting vaginas. It was only later that it struck me and that made me feel rank stupid. It was so obvious who he meant it for—it was unmistakable.

Curious still, I dialled the number. It was the number of a PCO at the outskirts where I had seen him flying kites.

'You're saying he comes here every Sunday?' I asked the man at the PCO.

'Every Sunday on the dot. For eight hours he's just sitting there staring at the phone. Doesn't eat, doesn't drink, doesn't even talk. That boy's a little strange, but he pays me more than I expect, so I don't know.'

'You have no idea why he comes here? What sort of people call him? Nothing?'

The man at the PCO started to laugh. 'Beta, it's been a year that he's doing this. Not one person has called. Do you think this has something to do with *pyaar ka chakkar,* love? Is he waiting for a girl's call? I'm telling you these Bollywood movies are making *aashiq*s of our well-meaning boys.'

'No.'

22 September 2002

I had waited for today. I called the number first thing in the morning. It didn't even take an entire ring for him to pick the phone.

'Hello?' I said in a voice as far as possible from mine.

'Hi,' he said, his voice softer, sympathetic and without the heavy tenor.

I imagined him in the PCO with a handkerchief muffling the sounds of trucks and buses passing by, and the man in the PCO looking on surprised to see him actually taking a call.

'I needed to talk to you,' I said.

'I can give you the numbers of professional suicide helplines if you haven't tried them out,' he said politely. 'If that hasn't worked for you, we can talk here. About anything that you would want to.'

'I am not sure I can talk on the phone. My parents are here,' I said, struggling to keep my fake tone in place.

'We can meet at a place of your choosing,' he said.

'Where can you see me?'

Without missing a heartbeat, he said, 'FRI. Morning? If that's OK with you? At nine, or you can choose a time.'

'Sure,' I said and cut the call.

The absurdity and desperation of Raghu's entire operation kept me awake the entire night. I was seriously intrigued now. What was he trying to do?

23 September 2002

I reached FRI at eight-thirty, but he was already waiting. I hid and watched him as he nervously swept the place clean, and plucked and arranged flowers as if preparing for a date. He switched places thrice before he chose to sit. His knees shook, and he rubbed his hands anxiously. It was precisely at nine that I stepped out from behind the trees and walked towards him. He got up when he saw me, at first with a rehearsed smile, then with confusion, and then hate and anger. In a flash he was on to me, his frothing, furious mouth a hair's breadth away from mine. I stumbled backwards, once, twice, and found his hand firmly clutching mine.

'What do you think you're doing here?' he barked, the mellowness of his voice now gone.

I think that's what he said. I could barely hear him over the thumping of my own heart. In those few seconds that he was screaming, foaming at his mouth like a rabid dog, I felt he would slaughter me, break my rib cage and crush the life out of my beating heart.

'IS THIS A JOKE TO YOU!' he shouted.

I heard these words. I heard them repeatedly, but I felt too paralysed to answer. I gazed into his eyes and failed to look away even when I wanted to. There was too much of everything. The little capillaries were too red, the pain too much, the fury unabated. What had I moved in him? What did I break? He waited and then his clenched fists went limp. He turned away and walked into the trees.

'RAGHU!' I shouted, but he was gone.

24 September 2002

The TV has been on for hours now.

I was serving Dadaji his third cup of tea when I saw Manish Chachu preparing to sneak out again. This was the third time in three days. He had made a smooth shift from his starched white kurtas to white shirts and jeans.

It was no secret that this was all for Sumitra. Buaji has encouraged Manish Chachu's efforts. She's already collecting prospectuses of engineering colleges in Delhi and Bengaluru, and marking out their fee structure.

Only yesterday I had seen them at the newly opened coffee shop near DIT, their hands close but not touching, and their lips moving softly, like they had always been in love. They make me think that maybe love could be arranged too. But it wasn't just me who had been noticing this, Di had too, and hadn't taken it lightly.

She has been snapping at everybody and everything for the past few days, finding reasons to fight with me and Mumma. Only yesterday, she'd hauled me up for not trying hard enough to earn more money. 'When was the last time you went to type at Suresh Uncle's? Haan? You were telling me about teaching eighth-standard students? What happened to that?'

'Di? I went yesterday! And there was no work! And you were right there when Buaji said that I should not be going to people's house to teach—'

'Excuses!' she snapped right back.

'You know they are not!'

'Of course they are!'

'Di—'

'Go, run some more around that boy,' she said and then suddenly grabbed me. 'Don't be stupid, Advaita! You know that sort of thing helps no one! Not us definitely! You shouldn't be wasting your time staying at home, you need to get out. Do you get that? Or do you want us to rot in this house forever? Are you just waiting for that boy to be the knight in shining armour?'

Fighting back my tears, I said, 'No!'

'Your actions say otherwise. Where were you yesterday? And the day before? And the day before that?'

'Nowhere!'

'Get your act together and stop obsessing over that boy. Do you hear me?'

She left before I could ask her if it was that bad to have something else to think about other than where the next thousand rupees would come from. If it was that horrible to have a friend to talk to. I don't remember the last time Divya Di or I had a person we could call a friend. It's true that we are knit airtight as a family and there's nothing that we need to hide from each other, but then every conversation we have is riddled with our miseries and tragedies.

Sometimes do I want to talk to someone who wouldn't have heard stories about Di, me and Mumma and Papa? Of course. What's so wrong in wanting that—to be part of those giggly groups of boys and girls who go and watch movies together, eat chow mein, and talk about how to bunk classes?

Maybe Raghu could take that place. He doesn't care where I was from, or what my family had been through; he doesn't pity me or think of me as dodgy, so what's the big crime in wanting to be friends with him?

26 September 2002

It's pathetic that these days I am not able to sleep. What's even more pathetic is my insensitivity towards his idealistic enterprise of talking people out of their wretchedness (which, I should add, has helped no one up till now). I have been toying with the idea of apologizing to him, but Di is probably right. I shouldn't delve into this any more. Whatever had happened to him in his past in Delhi has broken him, and I have enough melancholies of my own to care about someone else's. Despite that, every time I close my eyes, I can see him sitting alone in that PCO for hours on end, staring tragically at the phone, willing it to ring, to get a call that's never going to come. Who had he failed to save that he's been driven into this madness? How deep is that hurt? And how many lives will he have to save till he gets over it? Or am I reading it all wrong? Did he kill someone? He doesn't look like a killer, but he could have indirectly caused it, no? That should be enough reason for me to maintain as much distance between us as possible.

27 September 2002

We were sleeping when we heard a few men shouting outside. It was too early for fights about parking spaces and broken boundary walls.

'You stay right here,' said Mumma when she saw me getting up.

'Nothing doing,' I told her and followed her outside.

Dadaji and Buaji were already outside, holding their heads, murmuring among themselves. The entire neighbourhood—Shekhawat, the lecherous, drunk uncle who threw the biggest *Mata ki Chowki*s, Chibber Uncle, who along with his wife, had chased away their daughter-in-law in a mere two weeks, Nandi Uncle, whom everyone suspected had another woman in Meerut—was in our courtyard. The loudest of the voices was Shekhawat Uncle's. He was calling out Mumma's name.

When Shekhawat Uncle saw Mumma, he strode towards her and said, 'You don't know what kind of people are coming to your house! And that too a house with girls!' He pointed at her a half-broken cricket bat stained with what seemed like blood.

Shekhawat Uncle, who has whistled at both Divya Di and I in the past and yet remains Dadaji's close friend, waved a stick and shouted, 'Altaf! Saala, *deshdrohi*, betrayer. We should have killed him.'

'What happened to him?' asked Mumma, staring unwaveringly at the splintered and bloodied bat.

It's a story everyone wanted to tell, or at least their versions of it. Within an hour, there were at least four, I counted. The first (narrated by Nandi Uncle) was that someone had overheard Altaf sympathizing with the Muslim terrorists who had mercilessly mowed down eighty men, women and children while they prayed at the Akshardham temple in Gandhinagar.

The second (narrated with more vigour by Datta Uncle) was that Altaf's cousin had been part of the operation.

The third (narrated by Patnaik Uncle) told of how Altaf wanted to repeat Akshardham in Dehradun, and how he wanted to spill Hindu blood this Eid.

The fourth, and the most vicious, was narrated by Shekhawat Uncle.

'We heard that he had swords and kerosene in his house. Why would he have that? And money, more money than he should have. Where do you think that came from? Saala, we have taught them the right lesson,' said Shekhawat Uncle, and the other men grunted in approval.

Dadaji patted Shekhawat Uncle's back and thanked him for catching the bastard in time.

'Bhabhiji, anything could have happened. You know how these people are. They rape and kill without mercy,' said Shekhawat Uncle to Mumma. 'Now I would like to see him try, with his brains spilled out on the road.'

Mumma tried to swallow and barely kept herself from breaking down. Her nails dug into my arm deeper with every story, every detail of how they had bludgeoned him close to death.

Shekhawat Uncle continued, 'He wouldn't dare to work in this town any more. *Police mein hamare bahut Hindu bhai hai, baaki vo samhbal lenge* (We have enough Hindu brothers in the police, they will take care of the rest.).'

'We should have burnt the entire slum down,' said Datta Uncle.

'Time *aega*,' said another person in the mob.

Of all the men, it was only Manish Chachu who had a different opinion. He talked of 'proof', 'justice', 'law', 'freedom', but these words were washed away in the general vitriol. He was the only one in our family (and the entire colony) besides us who didn't think talking to Altaf and Iqbal soiled their soul. There were times he would drop Altaf and Iqbal to where they lived, and like us, he probably knew that there was no way these two men could be terrorists.

'You don't know them,' said Dadaji sternly to Manish Chachu, who walked away.

While the men kept talking about the incident repeatedly, I held Mumma and took her inside the house. Without a word, she went to the terrace and started to cook.

Neither of us believed a shred of what those people had said about Altaf. He was a kind man, kinder than my own blood. He must be at least ten years younger than Mumma, about Manish Chachu's age, and yet I had seen him scold Mumma harshly every time she pricked her finger. He used to wince at the sight of Mumma's blood. To accuse him of terrorism was absurd. What do they know of the dresses he used to stitch from wasted cloth for Divya Di and me every Diwali when we were small? My dresses were always better than Di's and Di often accused him of favouritism. That's the only thing he was guilty of. THIS. IS. SO. UNFAIR.

28 September 2002

This morning, Mumma gave us two packed lunches and an old, tattered purse with 5000 rupees in it. It was almost all the money we had saved.

'Find out where Iqbal is, give him this and tell him we can give more if he needs it. Ask him where Iqbal is. Divya, go with her,' said Mumma.

'You should come, Mumma,' I said.

'I can't,' she said, giving us directions to Altaf's place. 'When you go there, tell whoever you meet whose daughters you are. They will point you in the right direction. Tell Altaf and Iqbal I'm sorry.'

Divya Di and I were at the bus stop when Manish Chachu came spluttering towards us in Dadaji's scooter. 'I will drop you, come, sit,' he said.

'Do you know where—'

'I know,' he said.

We hopped on to his scooter and he drove us to the shanty in which Iqbal and Altaf lived.

'Are you going to come?' asked Divya.

He stared at the rows upon rows of houses—if they can be called that—breached into each other, a heaving, groaning mass of asbestos and tarpaulin sheets, and asked us to go ahead.

The stench and the mud and the number of people were overwhelming. My insides threatened to come up my throat. I stifled the feeling when I saw Di marching from house to house without a shadow of discomfort on her face. She asked around and people kept sending us deeper into the maze. It was strange to know that being Mumma's daughter was a privilege and anyone we asked invited us inside for a cup of tea. It took us a good fifteen minutes to find Altaf's and Iqbal's shanty. We knocked and waited. It was quite some time before the door opened.

It was Raghu. He quietly stepped out of the way. He didn't look surprised; it was as if he had expected me.

Iqbal got up. 'Di?'

He folded his hands and welcomed us in. We entered with our heads bowed, ashamed. It felt like we too had been a part of the mob.

'Sit, sit,' said Iqbal.

Raghu dusted the ground and put two stools for us to sit on. The room wasn't big enough to take a fifth person; we were so close we could hear each other breathing.

'Tea?' Raghu asked us.

'Why are you asking? Just make *naa*, bhai,' Iqbal told Raghu. He looked at us and said, 'Di, you shouldn't have come here.'

'How could we not?' said Divya Di.

'How is he?' I asked.

Altaf was in the nursing home. Iqbal asked us not to go there.

'They hit him repeatedly on his fingers, grinding them to dust,' said Iqbal softly. 'They didn't hate him or us enough to kill him. They wanted to douse his spirit, make him a cripple. That's what they wanted. If the Hindus—' He stopped himself.

'Why did they pick Altaf?' asked Divya Di.

Iqbal didn't have an answer to that. Raghu poured us tea in three little tumblers.

'*Achhi nahi ho to batana* (Let me know if it's not good),' said Altaf. 'Otherwise, no one makes tea like bhai does . . .' he said softly and tears welled up in his eyes.

'It's perfect,' said Divya Di.

'It is,' I chimed in.

There was not much to say after that. We finished our tea and assured Altaf that we would be there for anything he would need from us. We made hollow promises that Altaf would be OK. But no matter how hard we tried, he refused the money, but took the food gladly.

On our way out of the slum, Divya Di asked, 'What was that boy doing there?'

'I didn't know he knew them.'

We gasped for air as we exited the place and found Manish Chachu right where he had dropped us. 'I couldn't simply leave you here,' he said. 'Come, I will drop you home.' We followed him to the scooter. 'How's he? Altaf or Iqbal?'

'Altaf,' I said and told him what Iqbal had told me.

'Which hospital is he in?'

'Boudhiyal,' said Divya Di.

29 September 2002

Mumma's better now. Grief is the luxury of the rich. Mumma has thrown herself headlong into work again. Dadaji has forbidden Muslim tailors inside the house, their religion reduced from a badge of honour in the profession to an abomination. Yesterday Mumma chased away a hack of a tailor for spoiling Sumitra's lehnga, and has now gotten down to doing most of the stitching herself. Her eyesight is not as it used to be, and it pains me to see her working for hours, hunched over a piece of cloth. But whenever I offer to help, she gets furious.

Instead, she told me to double-check Sumitra's measurements for the lehnga. 'Come back quickly, OK? This lehnga is taking me forever to make,' said Mumma, as I was stepping out.

It should have been a quick in-and-out thing at Sumitra's, but it took three hours and some. I was fed, loved and cared for. In those moments I felt how boys must feel with their mothers fussing over them; they showered me with such attention that I could not really handle it. After I had been forced to down three gulab jamuns, I was allowed to take Sumitra's measurements. She led me to her room, a concept that had always fascinated me, a room for yourself, for your things and your secrets, for all things you.

'Your mom cooks wonderfully,' I said.

'One tends to get better if one does the same thing all one's life,' said Sumitra, her comment uncharacteristically acrid. Then she asked, 'How's Divya taking it?'

'Not well.'

'She has met me twice.'

'What?! What—'

'She asked me to walk out of the wedding. I don't know what to say to her. She's refusing to reason.'

'I will talk to her.'

'Do you think she will listen?' she asked and smiled weakly. We both knew the answer to that.

'Shall we start?'

As she twisted and turned, I took her measurements. I asked, 'It must be hard to put on an excited face in front of my family, isn't it?'

'It's not harder than what I have been through,' she said. 'I know what I did to your sister was unforgiveable, but I really loved that man. And he could make everything seem right, even abusing me. He was good at making me feel as if everything was my fault.' She shook her head and stared at her fingers. 'After every rough night he would apologize, promising on all my unborn, unconceived children that he would never repeat it and yet . . . '

In the next hour, I become a ledger of Sumitra's welts and bruises, a journal of hurt and pain, a chronicle of her heartbreaks.

'Does it always end like this?' I asked.

'For women, yes,' she said and forced a smile. 'It's a pity god didn't make us of clay and wax. Would have been much easier to adjust and fit in, and mould ourselves to the ways the world wants us to.'

'And you can't slap plasticine too, it wouldn't help,' I said and we both laughed, sadly and angrily, if that was possible.

When I got back home, Manish Chachu was wringing the water out of his kurtas. He insists on washing and drying his own clothes, despite Buaji's constant opposition to it.

'I needed to talk to you, Chachu,' I said.

Chachu looked at me. 'I know you talked to her.'

'She's a nice girl, Chachu.'

'I won't do what her previous husband did to her.'

'If you do?' I asked.

Chachu promised me he won't.

2 October 2002

Di lied through her teeth. Delhi assignment, my foot! Mumma bought it hook, line and sinker, but I didn't. Not the modelling agency she has supposedly signed up for, not the three music videos that were promised to her, and not the agent who has promised her big things. They were all lies, one after another! Mumma, in her happiness over the future of her daughter, couldn't shake the flimsy ground Di had created to not attend Sumitra's wedding.

'I will tell Mumma it's all a lie. I know you have been meeting Sumitra and telling her to walk out of the marriage.'

Di didn't react.

'She will believe me if I say this. If not, I will make Sumitra talk to Mumma,' I said.

Di didn't look up from the *Filmfare* she had filched from the salon.

'I will come to Delhi with you then. See what this agency is about and how many music videos you have been offered. You shouldn't have a problem with that.'

Di flipped a page nonchalantly, stopping at the Shah Rukh Khan centrefold. She then tore it off and kept it in her pocket.

'How long will you run? Sooner or later, you will run out of money, won't you? Delhi is a harsh place. Who will you turn to if you get into trouble?'

'Who do we turn to when we get into trouble here?' she asked.

'But you can't go—'

'I'm going, Advaita. It's done. Nothing you or Mumma and Papa have to say is going to change my decision. You should know better than trying to convince me,' she said. And added with a smile, 'When has that ever worked?'

I softened within a matter of minutes, and my intention to bully her into changing her plans swiftly turned to cajoling and crying. 'What will I do here alone? When will you come back?'

My fears weren't allayed. She took me into her arms and kissed my forehead. 'You wouldn't understand my pain, Advaita. You're too young. You don't know what it feels like to have your heart broken,' she whispered in my ears.

'If it means leaving your only sister alone, then I would rather not fall in love at all!'

'Many have tried and failed to not fall in love,' said Di.

'I won't. Why the hell did you fall in love if that meant losing your sister? I would never do that! That's incredibly selfish of you,' I said.

Di chuckled.

'What have you told Buaji? Dadaji?' I asked.

Di hadn't, and for the first time, I wished that Dadaji had won.

Buaji and Dadaji were told. The news had been slipped to Karan Bhaiya and Anshuman Bhaiya who relayed the information with the requisite anger.

The thought of an agency, of her being in a music video, of making a mockery of her *khaandani* izzat, but most of all the mere thought that our family would be known through the name of a woman, was profane.

'She's going nowhere,' said Dadaji while we all ate.

Dadaji and Buaji assumed that this reaction of an upturned nose, a light warning would be enough for Di to know that it was an unimaginable thing to hope for. But neither Divya Di nor Dadaji stepped back from their positions and by the time it was evening, the conversation around Divya Di's audacity to even think she could go to Delhi had reached a fever pitch.

From what I could hear through the closed door, Mumma and Papa were being lambasted by Buaji for their failures in raising us. Mumma and Papa maintained that they didn't know anything and expressed shock at their daughter's decision to move to Delhi.

'We didn't know she was up to this,' said Mumma. 'I will make sure she doesn't step out of the house.'

It was ironical considering Di wasn't home in the first place. Papa stayed quiet for most of the conversation, acted upset and disappointed in his daughters. It looked like Divya Di would have to run away from the house if she decided to not change her mind.

'Talk her out of it,' said Dadaji to Papa.

The ultimatum was delivered in a low tone, as if deciding what to eat for lunch, and that's what made it ominous. The punishment—whatever it might be in Dadaji's head—wasn't to be taken lightly.

Papa said, 'If she has something going for her, she has to leave. She can't rot in this house any longer.'

'Of course,' murmured Mumma.

Divya Di was briefed about what had happened in the evening. She listened, and with every word, her face grew harder, her skin paler. We played down the happenings, knowing that every word we say would only weigh her down. Not enough to keep her here but enough to keep her awake for nights.

Divya Di and I lay down on the roof, but sleep evaded us. I searched in vain for words that could tell her how devastated

I would feel when she was no longer there, when I would be left alone in this cesspool of toxic relationships. She had no words to assuage my pain.

'Who will I talk to when you leave?'

'Why? Whatever happened to that guy?' asked Di playfully.

'I haven't seen him in days.'

'Whatever you do, don't fall in love.'

'I'm not mad. I have enough problems already, and so does he.'

'What's his deal though? Every time I have seen him, he looks like he's just had his heart broken or like someone has died,' she joked.

Di and I stayed up for the rest of the night, stared at the stars, and played our favourite game—What if We Had Money.

7 October 2002

It was a shock to see him on the terrace. He stood there standing with his arms crossed in front of him. I wanted to whisper-shout at him to leave before any of the neighbours caught us, but I couldn't manage the words.

'Your chacha shouldn't be marrying that girl,' he said, point-blank, straight as an arrow. 'He's in love with someone else, not a girl.'

'What?'

'Altaf's struggling for every breath and he's getting married to someone else. Ask him to be a decent man and cancel the wedding,' he said and stepped forward. 'He needs to or I will make it happen. I won't repeat it.'

'Raghu—'

'Tell him.'

Before I could wrap my head around what he had said, he had already walked away.

'Raghu!' I called out.

He stopped and turned. My head was scrambling to put in perspective what he had just said to me. True, Karan Bhaiya and Anshuman Bhaiya had an effeminate classmate who is said be in love with boys, and that boy has had a tough time about it. He's been called hijra, *chhakka* and what-not. Di tells me that Bombay and Delhi are full of such men, even women, but here, in Dehradun? And Chachu? How can that be? He seems so normal.

'There must be some mistake. Manish Chachu . . . he's a womanizer. It's a known fact. How can he . . . and Altaf—'

'WHY WOULD I BE LYING?' roared Raghu. 'Love's not something to be trifled with.'

'You're lying.'

'I am not here to convince you, Advaita. The choice is yours,' he said and rushed off.

8 October 2002

But the more I think about it, the more it seems plausible. However, Chachu is nothing like the men who are supposed to fall in love with other men. He doesn't have a love for garish clothes, neither does he throw his hands around like there's a crick in his wrist, and nor does he sway while he walks. Nothing I had seen in the movies about homosexual men resembles Manish Chachu.

And yet when I told Di, her reaction was subdued, as if she always expected it.

'Imagine when Dadaji gets to know of it,' she said with a twinkle in her eye.

She got me thinking as well. The possibilities were endless with a secret like this. We could blackmail Dadaji out of his money if he had any left, buy our freedom and run away. But who's going to believe us? And what's the proof? But why would Raghu lie? Why would he even come to me with something like this? He could have kept quiet and let it be.

'Let Sumitra have him. She deserves someone like him,' said Di, refusing to discuss this further. 'If he has pulled off this sham for all these years, what's a few more.'

'And what happens to Altaf?' I asked.

'Manish Chachu and Altaf should have known that their relationship would never come to fruition. It's their fault,' said Di.

How quickly we become selfish, don't we? Divya Di, Mumma and I had felt like our hearts had been ripped out of our chests the day Altaf was assaulted. It hasn't even been a month and how drastically our positions have changed! Di and I have been to Iqbal's house twice to give him food, prayed for him, and yet now we were thinking of leveraging Manish Chachu's and Altaf's dirty secret for our gain, or even use it to exact revenge from Sumitra!

9 October 2002

Manish Chachu returns home from work at eight every evening. That's a bit late for a fledgling business, some would say. But in hindsight, everything about Manish Chachu can be questioned. His disappearances, even his general happy demeanour despite his repeated failures at making something out of his life. But you don't think like that, do you? Things like these don't happen to you, they happen to people around you.

I had decided to find out the truth on my own and today I tailed Manish Chachu after he shuttered down his painfully empty shop and headed in a direction different from home. Had Sumitra been a swine, a bitch, even remotely unlikeable, I would not have done this. But not only is Sumitra immensely likeable, unfairly treated—the way women usually are—it had also started looking like a test. As if Raghu was watching me with a telephoto lens, peering in, weighing my goodness.

And so I followed, wanting Manish Chachu to stop at Neeraj Sweet Shop, buy some samosas and bun tikkis and turning back, proving Raghu wrong.

Manish Chachu didn't stop anywhere and drove straight to Boudhiyal Nursing Home where Altaf was still battling his injuries. The hospital was packed with the dying and the scared, so hiding wasn't hard. Iqbal and a couple of his friends from the slum welcomed Manish Chachu at the reception and led him to the room where Altaf lay. Before long, Iqbal and the other men filtered out of the room, leaving Manish Chachu alone with him. Amongst the men was Raghu who carried a prescription in his hands and listened intently to the doctor. I turned on my heel and left before he could see me.

He must have seen me because he caught up with me in the parking lot and confronted me, 'What are you doing here?'

'I wanted to see if you were lying.'

'Come with me,' he said.

Without saying anything further, he held my hand and led me all the way to the back of the hospital, past the dumping shed and the water plant. He counted the windows and said, 'That one. Come.' He scaled up the skirting and helped me along.

'There,' he said and pointed at a heavily grilled window.

It was a small room, barely 10 by 10, and on a rickety hospital bed lay Altaf. Manish Chachu sat at the edge of the bed, crying softly but continuously.

'Now do you think I'm lying?' whispered Raghu.

Between sobs, Manish Chachu would run his fingers softly on Altaf's face and whisper in his ears. In his hands was Altaf's hand and he apologized for not being with him. It was hard to watch. Raghu pulled me back down.

'Hmm?'

'You were not,' I said. 'But why can't you tell Manish Chachu? You seem to be friends—'

'I am not his friend. I know Altaf and Iqbal and a few other boys,' he said.

'Even if I do tell Manish Chachu, he's not going to do anything. If he meant to, he would have done it by now. No one stands up to Dadaji,' I said.

'So you would rather have your chacha celebrate his wedding when the man he loves is dying.'

I felt cornered. 'Hey! Look, it's not in my hands, OK. Stop being unreasonable. You don't know how my family works.'

He rolled his eyes. 'I know very well how families work. Stop being a coward.'

'Who the hell do you think you're calling a coward?' I asked, furious.

'Was I not clear enough?'

'Why do you care anyway?' I snapped.

'Because I do. Because the man dying inside is . . . friend,' he stated loudly.

'Then go and tell him, why don't you? Because this clearly is super important to you!'

'Maybe I will, you coward, go and live your life with your tail tucked in,' he growled, stepping close to me.

'Says the guy who ran away from everything!'

'Shut up, Advaita. You don't want to go there.'

'Why? Now you want me to shut up, huh? Master of fucking secrets! Should I meddle into your business? Why don't you tell me your damned story, huh? What happened there, huh?'

'SHUT UP,' he said, his angry eyes burning a hole through me.

'Why? Why should I shut up? And who's going to believe a single word you say anyway!' I scoffed.

'YOU NEED TO STOP TALKING.'

'No, I won't!'

'FUCK—'

His voice stopped abruptly. He looked away from me and at the ground. Like me, he too realized we had crossed a line that we shouldn't have. We both breathed heavily, our faces flushed. Slowly, our anger abated.

'I'm sorry. I shouldn't have shouted at you,' he said.

'Yes, you shouldn't have. I shouldn't have either.'

We stood there awkwardly for a while, not sure where this conversation would lead us. Finally he said, 'Do you want tea?'

I wanted to storm off, tell him that poking into my family matters was none of his business, but I wasn't angry any more and I remembered the tea from the other day. He fetched the thermos flask and poured me a little in a cup.

'You're not going to have any?' I asked and he shook his head. I continued, 'Raghu. It might be pointless even if I tell anyone. Your intentions might be noble, but it will all come to naught. Dadaji and Manish Chachu will brush it away, call it a bare-faced lie. Altaf and Iqbal can't risk running into trouble again, can they? It's good for everyone that it stays hidden.'

'What about the girl?' he asked.

'She . . .'

'The least you can do is tell her,' he looked at me, the bravado, the anger and the pain gone from his eyes. I could only sense a sorry desperation writ large on his face.

'I will try to tell her,' I said, not wanting to disappoint him. 'Can I ask you something?'

He nodded.

'What does their love mean to you?'

'What kind of a question is that?'

'Whom did you lose?' I asked.

'No one.'

'It's not about no one. It's not for no one that you left Delhi and are loitering around here, smoking yourself to death, waiting for calls to come, murmuring to yourself that you couldn't save someone. There was someone, wasn't there?'

He sighed, and after a long pause, his lips moved ever so slightly, and he said as if talking to himself, '. . . rahmi.'

I said her name under my breath. Brahmi.

'What happened to her? Is she—is that why you run that suicide—'

'I should go now,' he said, as if realizing he had shared something he hadn't meant to.

Raghu took the cup from me, screwed it back up on the thermos and left.

Now as I write this, I can't help but wonder what would have happened to this girl, Brahmi. Strange name. There are some obvious conclusions that I have made in my head, but I don't want to write them down lest they come true. With every passing day, it seems ridiculous that people bother with love. When has it ever done anyone any good?

10 October 2002

The last few days haven't been kind to Mumma. With no other tailor to help her out, work's been piling up.. She's past the age for doing everything herself and the struggle is all too visible. To make matters worse, no matter how hard she tries, she can't hide how devastated she is about Divya Di moving to Delhi.

I helped her deliver the suits this morning. For the most part she had been silent, going through the motions like a zombie. To lighten her mood, I insisted we stop at Singhwal's Chaat Korner before we went home.

We were digging into our second tikka when I started to probe about Manish Chachu's supposed philandering, his alleged affairs with Dehradun women, and why he had stayed away from the question of marriage all these years.

Mumma looked at me with surprise and then with anger. Both of us were shocked that the other knew. But I had just been told. How long had Mumma known about Manish Chachu's homosexuality?

'Stay out of it, Advaita,' said Mumma, sternly.

She knew.

She said, 'Who told you? Who else knows about this? You can't tell anyone.'

'Mumma, how long have you known about this? About Manish Chachu, about Altaf?' I asked, shocked.

Why would Mumma hide this from me?

'What they were doing was disgusting. I warned Altaf to put an end to it and I thought they had. Iqbal himself told me that it was over,' said Mumma. 'I had told him he would get no work from me if it continues. I thought . . . they had got over it. Iqbal even told me that Altaf's parents were looking for a girl back in his hometown.'

'You can't get over homosexuality—'

'Don't talk like that. It's a disease, nothing that can't be cured. Dadaji himself has cured it. Karan's and Anshuman's classmate? They say he's gotten a lot better,' she said with a firmness that couldn't be fought against. Not even telling her that the boy probably had his homosexuality beaten out of him and was not cured by sweet pills.

'What about Sumitra?'

'What about her? Once he gets married, he's going to mend his ways. Everything is going to be all right. You don't have to meddle in it,' she said impatiently.

'But Sumitra—'

'She will do what all of us do. Live with it. That's what women do,' said Mumma, getting a little angry. 'She shouldn't have gone with that boy to Delhi in the first place. Didn't she know that he wasn't a nice boy? Now what options does she have? She was a good student. She could have made something of herself.'

'Bu—'

'I don't want to hear another word regarding this, Advaita. If one word of this reaches anyone, you don't know what will happen,' she said irritably.

On our way back, she said, 'Learn something from the mistakes that Sumitra had committed. Your didi told me you have been spending a lot of time with that boy Raghu. I am warning you—'

'Mumma—'

'Listen to me. Have I ever stopped you from doing anything? But he doesn't look like he's got a future or a plan. I wouldn't have said so if it were any other boy. If you want to fall in love-shove, then find someone who deserves you, not any random boy on the street. I know how all these boys are. They see a girl in need and they—'

'He's not like that.'

'You're already defending him,' snapped Mumma. 'Just remember that all men are pigs. Except your father.'

'Mumma, I don't feel anything for him.'

'You should have just gone to a better college and found a job,' Mumma said, shaking her head.

'With 42 per cent I was never going anywhere.'

'Don't be smart with me, Advaita,' she said, and then with a tinge of sadness and desperation, she added, 'I wouldn't want you to end up like Sumitra or your sister. Be careful.'

11 October 2002

When I got to Sumitra's house, she was cleaning her cupboards. Neat stacks of clothes lay on the bed, on the ground, and on the table. I felt a pang of jealousy piercing through me.

'Like something?' she asked.

I shook my head.

'It's all yours,' she said and held my hand. 'I reckon we will have to alter a few clothes, but most of them should fit you.' She picked a dress and held it against me. 'This looks so pretty on you.'

'Dadaji won't allow me to wear this,' I said.

'We will find a way—'

'Sumitra Bhabhi, I needed to tell you something.'

'What happened?'

I paused for a bit and went over my decision again. I kept hearing Raghu's words over and over again. I told Sumitra everything without pausing, not wanting to change my mind or tone things down. Sumitra heard me out, and I could see her heart slowly breaking, her eyes a little clouded, her hand on mine a little lighter, the veins in her forehead throbbing.

'No one knew?' her voice quaking in fear and anger.

'Mumma does,' I said.

'You should leave now,' she said.

'Sumitra, we should talk about this.'

'JUST LEAVE.'

She got up and I got up after her.

'Sumitra, can we please talk about this?'

'I need to be alone,' she said.

As I left the house, the fear of what would happen if Sumitra tells on me and my mother abated, and a certain sense of reckless abandon took over. Probably this is what goes on in the minds of foolish men who take a bullet to their chests for a society not worth saving.

When I got home, Mumma sat Di and me by the table, held both our hands, and told us, 'It's going to be OK.'

She knew I had told Sumitra, and that it could change our lives.

'You shouldn't have,' said Di. 'She deserved what was coming to her. You're foolish to have put us at risk for her.'

15 October 2002

Five days have passed since I told Sumitra about Manish Chachu and Altaf, and nothing has happened. The marriage hasn't been called off, the stitching of the clothes is still going on at breakneck speed, and the cards are still being distributed. It's only going to make things worse when the wedding is actually called off.

We have spent hours and hours talking about what would befall us when the news breaks. Papa's still in a haze of disbelief that his brother could be a homosexual. Unlike Mumma, he doesn't think of homosexuality as a disease and knows of its permanence.

For the past two days, I had been asking about the whereabouts of Raghu to tell him that I have done what he had asked me to. To be honest, it was also a pretext to see him. It's quite incredible that Raghu goes to everyone's houses and the hospital, but no one quite knows where exactly he lives.

'Raghu Bhai doesn't talk about himself. It's only with Altaf that he spends hours talking. God knows what they kept chattering about,' Iqbal had said when I asked him about Raghu's address. The others in the room shook their heads.

'He does make great tea though. Best in Dehradun!' added Iqbal.

I concurred.

'Do you know about the girl he left behind in Delhi?'

Iqbal shook his head. It was nice to know that I was not the only one who knew nothing about him.

I heard Iqbal shout just as I was leaving the slum, 'Advaitaji!' Beside him was a young boy of thirteen. 'He lives in the colony. It skipped my mind that Raghu Bhai teaches him mathematics and science. He knows where he lives. You know, right?'

'Can you please tell me?'

The boy nodded enthusiastically and hopped on to my cycle. 'How far is it?'

'Twenty minutes,' said the boy cheerfully.

I queried after forty minutes when my legs started feeling like jelly. 'How much further?'

'Just twenty minutes,' he said.

'That's what you said when we left.' The boy giggled shamelessly. 'So he teaches a lot of children?'

'No, just me and a few more kids. No one wants to come this far. Their parents don't allow them to,' he said.

'Do you pay him?'

The boy nodded. 'Although Ammi hasn't paid him the last two months. Raghu Bhaiya says it's OK and that I can pay him the next month. There!' He pointed. 'That's his house,' he said and jumped from the cycle. 'I can go back on my own!' He sprinted off.

Needless to say, Raghu was surprised to see me knocking at his door.

'A boy you teach showed me the way,' I said to explain.

'Come,' he said unsurely.

It was the ground floor of a house whose construction had been stopped midway. Raghu was using just one room.

There were a bunch of mattresses lined on the floor, a few too many for a single boy's use. There was no television or fridge or cupboard; his clothes were stacked in a bunch in the corner of the room. He apologized for the darkness.

'The house is cheap. There's no electricity or running water. No one wanted this place,' he said. 'Do you want something? Tea? Water?'

It wasn't as much a house as just bricks cemented atop each other.

'Don't worry about it,' I said.

He looked considerably less tense, less angry than I have usually seen him. It felt like he was at *home*. Then he lit a kerosene stove and with deft movements put the tea on the boil. His movements were too quick, too precise. Soon he poured the tea into two disposable cups and gave one to me.

'How long have you been living here?'

'Been a while,' he said and swiftly changed the topic. 'Did you call off the wedding?'

'That's not a decision I have to make, is it?' I said. 'I told Sumitra. The ball is in her court. What she decides is up to her.'

'Thank you.'

'It was the right thing to do. I wouldn't have been able to live with it had I let things be. Of course, Mumma and Di think differently. Di has her own reasons, and Mumma thinks it's the fate of all women. Anyway, how's Altaf? What are the doctors saying? Does he need—'

'He's not getting better.'

'Mumma prays for him every day,' I said.

We didn't say anything to each other for a bit.

'What do you teach?' I asked to cut through the awkwardness.

'Mathematics and the sciences. IIT aspirants. People who want to be doctors.'

'Here? How many?'

'Six, not many want to travel this far. And I get by so I don't need more,' he said.

'Are you an IITian?'

'Never went to college. You want more?' he asked and I nodded. He poured a little from his cup into mine. I didn't tell him it was the best tea ever.

'Raghu?'

'Yes.'

'I know nothing about you and you seem to know quite a bit about me, about my family. I have the right to know how. Can I ask you?' I said.

'Altaf would talk about you often,' said Raghu.

'He would talk about me?' I asked.

He added after a bit of hesitation. 'Yes.'

'What else do you know?'

'Why is it important how much I know?'

'Just . . .'

'Whatever Altaf knew.'

'But why would he talk to you about me? Of all the things he could have talked to you about, why me?' I asked.

'I would ask.'

'Why?'

He paused for a bit, as if weighing if he should tell me, and then said, 'You reminded me of her.'

'Her?'

He didn't answer. It felt like he had already given away more than he intended to. I didn't want to probe, but the words just bubbled out of me unhindered.

'Brahmi?'

'Can we not talk about it right now?' he asked, almost taking a pleading tone.

'Do I look like her?'

He shook his head.

'Then?'

He didn't answer my question.

'Who did you leave behind in Delhi?' I asked.

I saw his eyes grow intense. 'I am not comfortable talking about it,' he said, his eyes now bloodshot.

'I get that,' I said and then to lighten the mood added with a smile, 'If I ever manage to leave this city, the last thing I would want to talk about would be Dadaji or Buaji.'

I chuckled and he smiled a little.

'Did I just see you smile? Wow. That's a rarity,' I said. 'You know what they say about smiling, don't they? *Hasa to phasa*?'

'Your taste in movies is really bad,' he said, trying hard to not smile.

'Says the guy who has *Dulaara* songs on his playlist.'

'Only the best.'

'I should go now. We have a little Dussehra celebration in our neighbourhood,' I said.

He walked me to the door, but it was pouring buckets.

'There goes your celebration,' he said. He got me his umbrella—rather, a big, old tent. 'How good are you at cycling while holding an umbrella?' he asked.

'I have never tried.'

'Come.'

He walked beside me, holding the umbrella over me while I cycled. We both thought the rain would end and he would walk back but it worsened.

'You can go back now,' I said when we'd travelled some distance.

He acted like he hadn't heard. Thick ropes of water were slamming against us, and we were wet to the bones. And yet, he dropped me two lanes away from my house.

'I need the umbrella back. Leave it on the terrace, I will pick it up.'

'Hey?'

'Yes?'

'Does this make us friends? Because all this while I feel like I have been trying to put a label to this.'

'You should know that I have been unlucky for my friends.'

'I can live with that. You can't possibly make my life worse.'

I cycled back home with my friend's umbrella.

17 October 2002

The umbrella was still lying on the terrace.

I had stayed put at the house, hoping to bump into him again, but there was no sign of him.

Had our blossoming friendship been nipped in the bud? It's quite stupid how my brain has prioritized issues. My eyes have been stuck to the roof of Shekhawat Uncle's terrace, looking out for that moderately friendly Spiderman. There was no sign of him. Didn't we have a moment? I thought we were friends. I should stop thinking about him.

I should close this diary right now and go about helping Mumma. God knows she needs it.

18 October 2002

OK, I have the umbrella. I should go return it to him. That's reason enough, right? Moreover, what could I possibly lose? With the sword of a called-off wedding hanging over us, could anything be worse? I must see him again. Why am I writing this diary again?

19 October 2002

I waited outside, peering in. Three young boys were sitting around. Raghu was listening to them intently, and sometimes smiling. He should do that more often. For the first time, it didn't look like the burden of the entire world was on him.

'How long have you been waiting?' he asked when the students left and he saw me at the door.

The smile was gone, the tension back on his face. There was something off about him.

'I thought you would want it,' I said, handing over the umbrella.

I was about to turn and leave when he invited me in. On the mattress were heavily earmarked books on inorganic chemistry, trigonometry and calculus. He didn't talk. He distractedly cleared the area for me to sit.

'Did you always want to teach?' I asked.

He gave me a cup of tea from the thermos. 'It's hot,' he warned. 'No, I didn't.'

'Then? Is someone from your family a teacher?'

He sipped his tea as an awkward silence hung around us, and I moved on knowing he wouldn't answer. Sooner or later, he would open up if I just continued to chip away at him.

'Why didn't you come to get the umbrella?'

'It didn't look like it would rain,' he said.

'You're not a good liar.'

He looked at me, tears pooling at the base of his eyes. 'Altaf died. They buried him yesterday,' he said. 'They couldn't save him. Your chachu was there the entire time.'

'But, but—'

I gasped for words. He watched on, not knowing what to say.

'Mumma would have told me! How can she not have told me!'

'Why should she have? What would she have told you anyway? That the man your chachu loved is dead now? That there's no problem any more in him getting him married to whichever girl your family chooses?'

The room suddenly seemed gloomier. I felt choked. The darkness, the gloom, and our long shadows wrapped around my throat and squeezed it. Flashes of Altaf came rushing to my head. His smiling face. The toffees he got for me. His kind eyes. His deft fingers.

Gone, he was gone.

It didn't seem real. A few minutes passed or an hour, I don't know, but the tears eventually stopped. I told myself he had been freed from the suffering he had endured in that hospital room, that he was in a better place. I told myself all the lies you do when someone dies.

'Altaf's family didn't claim his body. No one came down from Aligarh. They knew . . . they knew that he had a man in his life. Your chacha paid for the funeral. Talk to him, make sure he's OK.'

'I'm not talking to anyone!' I cried.

'We had to drag him out of the cemetery. He . . . he was shattered.'

I nodded, thinking about Manish Chachu and his detached demeanour in the past few days. I had kept a close eye on him to discern if he had been told anything by Sumitra. Not a furrow on the brow, not a forced smile, his homosexuality had made him an artist, an actor and an effortless performer.

I didn't know what to say any more; I didn't know why I sat there for the next hour, eating Raghu's namkeen, drinking his tea, sobbing silently.

25 October 2002

Sumitra came to our house unannounced this morning.

'Is your chacha home?' she asked me, her voice firm. I nodded, my heart in my mouth. This would be the beginning of the end.

'Are you sure you want to do this here?' I asked, unsure of how Manish Chachu would take it.

I had been looking for cracks in Manish Chachu and had failed. True, he used to disappear for long periods of time, but that was nothing out of the ordinary. Even now he always left his room smiling, his hair, clothes, and forehead without a crinkle. No matter how hard I try I can't conjure up an image of Manish Chachu flailing around, howling and screaming, being pulled back by men, preventing him from jumping into the grave his lover was being lowered into.

'Sumitra beti? Here, suddenly? You should have called. We would have made something for you. Are your parents comings too?' asked Buaji.

'No, they are not. I just needed to talk to . . . him.'

Buaji frowned.

'Should I call him? Is something wrong?' asked Buaji, her voice cold as steel.

'I would rather go to his room and talk,' she answered.

Buaji nodded angrily and said, 'Sure. Of course. Now you two are getting married. His room is your room only. Go, go, give him a surprise.'

Sumitra had already turned towards Manish Chachu's room before Buaji could finish.

Buaji turned to me. 'Make tea and go to Manish Chachu's room. Don't leave till the girl leaves. And tell me what they talk about. You hear me? Don't leave the room till she leaves. Did you see the gall of the girl? Wants to talk to him alone. Huh,' she said, her eyes glowing in anger.

I made them tea, arranged the biscuits, and killed as much time as I could before I entered the room. A heavy silence was being punctuated with the soft sobs of Sumitra.

'Keep the tray and leave,' said Manish Chachu without looking at me.

I stood there, feet stuck to the ground.

'We are fine,' said Sumitra. 'You can go.'

'I can't—'

Manish Chachu snapped, 'What do you mean you can't?'

'Buaji. She . . . she asked me . . .'

'Just give her an excuse. Sumitra and I are talking.'

'I can't.'

'ADVAITA!'

'Stop, Manish,' said Sumitra. 'It's not her fault, is it?'

'THEN WHOSE IS IT?' he said, more desperate than angry, the cracks now showing, slowly getting wider.

'So, what happens now?' I asked.

Manish Chachu looked at Sumitra for an answer. She sighed and wiped her tears.

'Everything stays as is. The marriage proceeds. I'm sure about it and we will never discuss this henceforth. No one has to know. Can we all do that? Manish? Can you do that, Advaita?' asked Sumitra.

'You don't have to do it for me,' said Manish Chachu.

'I'm doing it for myself,' answered Sumitra.

Just then Buaji, who must have been dying to know what was going on, walked in, and asked if we needed to eat something.

'No, I must leave now,' said Sumitra and got up.

'What did you want to talk about?' asked Buaji with a smile on her face. 'I'm asking because in our family nothing is really private. We don't have the culture of talking behind closed doors.' She clasped Sumitra's hand lovingly.

Sumitra said, 'We were actually talking about what surprise we can give to both families on our wedding. We were thinking of a dance performance. It will be nice, no? He was a little shy, but I have convinced him about it.'

Buaji smiled and kissed her fingers and touched them to Sumitra's chin. 'Ah, my thoughtful *nanad*. So sweet of you. Advaita, why don't you drop her till the gate?'

The instant we were out of Buaji's earshot, Sumitra said, 'He's a nice man.'

'But he's . . . he's a homosexual.'

'How often do women marry for love?' she said. 'And I will find other ways to love him, and to be loved back.'

'This isn't right.'

'I believe getting married to a homosexual man isn't the worst thing in the world. Trust me, I have been there. Everybody finds some way of being happy, don't we?'

She revved up her scooter and left.

Later in the afternoon, Divya Di said to me, 'Seems like the music video contract and my Delhi trip is happening after all.'

A part of me wished Sumitra had created a big scene and walked out of the wedding, throwing a spanner in Di's plan of abandoning us.

26 October 2002

It's embarrassing how little I know about Dehradun's rains. I was drenched by the time I reached Raghu's house. My body burnt with shame when I changed as he waited outside.

'Give them to me,' he said as I clutched my drenched clothes, *all* of them. 'Do you want them to get dry or no? Carry an umbrella next time, will you?'

I let go.

There was a second-hand inverter and a wire heater in the room now. Much to my shame, he spread out my clothes in front of the heater, my bra staring me right in the face.

'Tea or something stronger?' he asked, seeing me shiver.

Have you heard of peer pressure? Yes, I crumbled. I had never tasted alcohol before.

'Here,' he said, holding out a glass of whisky.

It smelled vile, but it didn't taste as bad as I thought it would. Just like one of Dadaji's homeopathic concoctions, even a little sweeter. It warmed me up quite quickly.

'You didn't have to open a new bottle for me,' I pointed out.

'I don't drink alone.'

My limbs felt loose, and my brain all muddled.

'Are you sure you want another one?' he asked after my third.

'I drink often,' I lied and poured myself another one, and insisted he too fill up his.

I should have stopped then, but I didn't and I remember only sketchy details of what we talked about. Every word I said was under the heavy influence of alcohol and perhaps delivered in the diction of a roadside drunk. At some point I asked him why he was such an uptight ass. He had laughed and told me that I needed to drink lime water, and just like his tea, his lime water was incredible too. I had told him he should be a chef and he had laughed again. Was he drunk too? Not long after that, I had started bawling my head off and he had to comfort me. Of what I remember, he was warm, affectionate and patient.

'Iqbal must be thinking of us as such bad people, no?' I cried. 'I should go meet him. I should go meet him right now! Why are you not moving? Let's go! Come! I need to see him right now!'

He held my hand firmly and made me sit down. 'He has left Dehradun.'

'What? Why? How can he . . .' I leaned into the wall sadly. He brought me another lime water and I slowly sipped on it. The alcohol started to wear off, leaving me tired and groggy. Despite that, I didn't stop talking.

'Unlike you, I don't have an Altaf to tell me anything about you. You're the definition of a closed book,' I said.

'. . .'

'I keep making stories about you in my head, you know.'

'Tell me one,' he said.

'You will laugh at me, Raghu.'

'I won't.'

'OK, here's one. Are you ready?'

'Hmmm . . .'

'Shall I start?'

'Of course.'

'You were a brilliant student, like crazy brilliant, the ones who become examples for teachers to give to younger students, like very driven, hard-working and things like that. But then one day, you fell in love with a girl . . . named Brahmi. Am I warm?'

'It's your story. Don't ask me.'

'So you fell in love, and you fell hard. Your life changed! Oh my god! That girl was beautiful, almost as handsome as you are. You both were perfect. Two happy people who made the perfect couple in school! Everyone looked up to the two of you. But then, your parents didn't like that. I can tell that happened because you always scrunch your nose like you smelled something bad every time I talk about family. You told her that you couldn't be with her and she . . . killed herself. You know, that's why you sit in that PCO waiting for calls.'

I waited for his reaction.

'Again, it's your story, not mine.'

'What I can't figure out is, what is it about friends and friendship that you dislike? Why are you averse to that? Like I'm sure Iqbal and Altaf counted you amongst their friends and would expect things from you, but you don't. Like, even if I hound Iqbal now, he wouldn't know a lot about you, would he? Why is that?'

'You're the narrator.'

'Look at you. Look at your face. The sadness, it's contagious. How long has it been? A year? Two? Three? How long will it keep hurting you? How long would you take to move on? What happens from here?' I asked.

'Your story, you tell me.'

'Umm . . . let me think. Umm, yes! I believe that your healing process has started. It has started with meeting me! My friendship will heal you. I think it has already started. Earlier you used to turn your nose up when you saw me, and now look at you, you look forward to it! Don't tell me I'm wrong.

I have seen how your house is suddenly cleaner, and so are your clothes. You have bought another white kurta besides the one I gave you, haven't you?'

'OK.'

At this point I tried standing up and the world spun. He made me sit and steadied me. Another lime water had magically appeared in front of me. Apparently, I was still woozy.

'You know what? You know what?' I said, giggling.

'What?'

'I think you will fall in love with me! And then you will be all better.' I ran my fingers over his face. I continued, 'But . . . but . . . don't do that. I have no time for love. You know that, right? Love's a waste of time, I have learnt. It's the absolute worst thing that can happen to anyone. Look what has happened to Mumma and Papa and Di, even Manish Chachu, and then there's you. It has a 100 per cent failure rate. Will you fall in love with me? Is that what's going to happen here?'

I don't remember his answer because I passed out on the mattress. When I woke up, my clothes were kept in a neat stack near me. He was smoking outside. I changed hurriedly. When I left his house, I didn't know what all I had said. It's only coming back to me now and I wish the earth would open up and swallow me.

30 October 2002

Today is the day Di's leaving for Delhi. The right words escape me. Divya Di had maintained a surprisingly low profile ever since Dadaji had reacted adversely to the idea of her leaving for Delhi. Mumma and Papa had been doing everything to collect money for Di's stay in Delhi. While Papa cried openly at nights, Mumma held back her tears.

Di had insisted that she had her own money saved up, but we all knew she would run out of it within two months. With the savings we had, at least she could be there for six months and not go hungry to bed. No matter how hard she tried, we could all see her cracking. The senselessness of what she was doing was slowly dawning on her as well, but every mention of that bolstered her decision, and worsened that festering wound.

Sometimes she would let it slip out, 'Modelling is not the only job there. There are scores of young people working.'

'You don't have a college degree,' I had pointed out.

'I will buy one,' she had said.

Our breakfast was lavish and we had it in secret. Aloo puri from the bania who sits near the mandir. Di and I were allowed to polish it off. Mumma and Papa lied to us that they were already full. Mumma then gave strict instructions to Papa to not come home before seven in the evening to avoid suspicion. He hugged Di, cried, and walked out with a sorry face, his shoulders drooping.

Di and Mumma fought all afternoon on what to pack and what not to.

'I'm keeping this, what's your problem?' said Mumma.

'There's no space in this room, can't you see? Throw some of these things away and you will have more space for yourself.'

'You're leaving. How much more space do you want to leave us with?' said Mumma.

'Mumma, that's—'

'You will want all this later, I'm telling you, and then you will regret throwing them away,' said Mumma.

'I am not going to regret not having ALL my books from the seventh standard. Mumma, I have taken what I need. Please, please, let me throw these away.'

She tried pulling the books from Mumma's hand.

'NO,' said Mumma. 'You can go wherever you want to, but you're not getting to throw these away. I will find space for them. You don't have to worry about it.'

She scooped up everything, dumped it in the cupboard and locked it. Then she stormed out of the room.

'I don't see the point,' said Di to me.

'Isn't it obvious, though?'

As the time of departure neared, we lost our voices, our hearts shrank, and we all sat in the room looking listlessly at each other. To dispel the gloom, Di suggested we all play Ludo. And so we did. Papa won most of the games, cutting turns and pieces at will. Mumma came inside thrice to ask us to keep our voices down.

'You're going to come there soon,' said Divya Di to me later.

'And then we will call Mumma and Papa?'

'Yes.'

'And then we will go to India Gate on Saturdays.'

'Bangla Sahib on Sundays?'

She nodded.

Mumma and Papa talked amongst themselves and pretended not to hear us.

The last bus was at 10 p.m. She left at nine. Raghu picked her up on a borrowed scooter. Mumma had been less than enthusiastic about the last part of the plan, but there was no one else we could trust. We have all spent the last hour looking at the wall clock with half a mind to handcuff Divya Di to the bed.

She's gone.

1 November 2002

My blood boils writing about this.

Di would have done something about it. She would have picked up the steam iron and smashed Buaji's head with it. It's hard to imagine she would have stood doing nothing like I did, like a goddamn fool watching it unfold.

Buaji twisted Mumma's arm and then slapped her like she wasn't a grown woman but a child. For a moment, Mumma's eyes flashed with anger that I hadn't seen in her before, but when Buaji asked her to lower her eyes or leave the house, she lowered her eyes.

'Enough!' Dadaji had said ironically because he was the judge and Buaji the executioner.

'We didn't know she would run away,' said Papa to Dadaji.

Dadaji smiled, a disappointed, pitiful smile, shook his head and said, 'I can't believe you're my son.'

He left leaving Papa burning in shame. The three of us—Divya Di, Mumma and I—understand each other's pain, hold each other's hands and say the right things, but we have never figured out what to really say to Papa. There's a line Di often used to describe Papa and it's true.

'They never let him be a man, a person, only a cripple.'

Except for Mumma, who saw the goodness or had pity on him—we will never know—we see him that way too. Papa overplays the basic emotions—he smiles too much, he laughs too loudly, and weeps like a baby. Even if you ask him what he likes, his stock answer for the last two decades has been, 'Whatever the three of you like,' accompanied by that silly smile.

'I shouldn't see Advaita out of the house before nine or after five. If I see that happen, she can stay outside and so can you and your wife,' Buaji said to Papa. She turned to me and said, 'And no one should know that she has left the house. We will say she's studying in Delhi. Do I make myself clear?'

Buaji stormed off. Fufaji glared at us till we slunk back into the room.

14 November 2002

The wedding has been crunched and fitted into a one-day affair. The dowry money, instead of being wasted on food, the pandal and what-not, will be credited to Dadaji's and Buaji's accounts.

Mumma and Papa had done most of the running around for the wedding, but they have been threatened with consequences if anything goes wrong. They listened, head bowed, and went about their work. The talk around where Di had suddenly disappeared has already reached a fever pitch. Some say she has run away with a boy, others believe she's part of a prostitution ring, and so forth. We have stuck by our story. She has gone to Delhi to do a computer course which guarantees a job. We have pasted smiles on our faces and sold this with all the confidence we could muster. Di, who had been calling the local PCO every day, told me she wouldn't call today. I really miss her.

'Go, check on your chachu. See if everything is fine. I haven't seen him since morning. Your buaji is going to shout at us. We have to leave in a bit,' Mumma told me.

It took Chachu ten minutes to get to the door.

Chachu's room has been cleaned, plastered and painted over. The cupboard has been rearranged to make space for Sumitra's clothes. On the bedside, though, two empty bottles of alcohol are lolling about. I took them and wrapped them in a newspaper and dumped them outside the window. Manish Chachu lay splayed on the bed, looking outside, lost.

'Careful, Chachu. Don't give it away today. Shave and look happy. You chose this relationship.'

He didn't spare me a look, grumbled, and looked away and out of the window.

'I'm not answerable to anyone.'

'Of course you are, Chachu. My sister is not here because of this wedding. The least you can do is not mess it up.'

A little later, he emerged, like the brilliant actor that I have known him to be, dressed in a resplendent sherwani.

The evening was packed with rituals that Manish Chachu and Sumitra went through like a couple in love, while I was asked strictly to stay away from the envelopes of money that were kept in a bag.

'Will you stop following me around? For god's sake!' I said.

Karan Bhaiya and Anshuman Bhaiya laughed and said, 'We have been told to keep an eye on you. Can't help it that you're such a petty thief.'

Fortunately, a few girls from Sumitra's side of the family distracted them from me. There were a few boys who watched me while I ate, but they promptly looked away when told by their mothers that my father was a pauper and I wouldn't get anything in dowry.

'The paneer is good. I like it.'

'Huh?'

I turned around to see a man looking on lecherously, a twisted smile playing on his face.

'Meghnad,' he said. There was no alcohol at the wedding and yet he reeked of it. 'I am sure you remember me, don't you?'

'I don't.'

'Your sister and I were in a relationship till she . . . you know what she did with that man. Vibhor Gupta, was it? Of course, I did it with your sister before he could, but no one touches my girls . . . that poor guy had to leave Dehradun.'

'Are you a guest?' I asked, looking over his shoulder for escape routes.

'We are good friends of Sumitra's parents, business partners actually. They were supposed to open furniture showrooms with us here, but then they backed out citing money troubles. And here they are, throwing this big wedding!'

'It's not really big,' I argued.

'It's big for them,' he said. 'Anyway, Advaita. I have always loved your name. The way it feels on the tongue.' He put his hand on mine, I retracted mine immediately.

'Where's your sister? People are saying all sorts of things.'

'She's doing a computer course in Delhi.'

'But I heard she has gone there for a music video? Or has she gone back to that man, haan? Sumitra's ex-husband, isn't he? I know people in Delhi. Wouldn't take long for me to find out.'

My heart thumped.

'She's gone there for a computer course.'

'You really think anyone here believes that? Your buaji has been saying that like a fucking parrot,' he said and chuckled.

'What do you want?'

'I just want to talk. Is that too much to ask for from the sister of the girl who once loved me, huh?'

He leaned into me.

'She never loved you.'

He ignored that. 'So when are you thinking of getting married, Advaita? You don't want to get too old, do you? Or do you have a boyfriend like your sister?'

'I am not that kind of girl,' I said. Over time, you learn to say such things.

'Yes, you don't look like your sister. I should have known how feisty she was the minute I saw those . . .' He cupped his hands and then put them back in his pocket. 'Nice wedding, though. And you look great! See you around.'

'Bye.'

He got up to leave. 'But hey? Let me know if you get any news of your sister and that man.'

I anxiously waited for him to leave the wedding which he did soon after he handed over a thick envelope to Buaji. Buaji embraced him like he was her long-lost son. During the *varmala*, the garlanding ceremony, he fired his gun in the air. Some people scuttled away from him, others encouraged him. He kept reloading and shooting till the pandit asked him to stop.

'What was he saying to you?' Mumma came running to me.

'Nothing.'

The *fera*s, the ceremonial circling of the sacred fire, like always, were supposed to be at the unearthly hour of 2.30 a.m. I was caught snoozing twice, so Karan Bhaiya was asked to ferry me home. I could have asked for nothing more. My body had given up and was crying for sleep.

But as it always happens, I was wide awake once I was home. Within minutes I was restless, thinking of Meghnad and Vibhor and Divya Di. I wanted to be anywhere but home. The scooter was right there. At first I was scrambling to get out of my lehnga and then I changed my mind. Raghu should see me in this, I thought, and hurried out of the house. If anyone sees me, I would just tell them I was trying to find my way back to the pandal. Not that it would have spared me a beating, but I wasn't thinking clearly at the time.

'What are you doing here? And in this?' he said when I reached, pointing at my clothes.

The couple of extra seconds he took for the next line were quite reassuring, flattering even.

'You look beautiful.'

'The food was great at the wedding, the tea wasn't. Also, there was this other person who was there whom I don't really like.'

He asked who it was, and like always, I spilled everything out to him like a child. How is it that I'm always the one telling everything?

'I missed my sister today.'

'Of course you did,' he said. 'But wasn't there an embargo on stealing envelopes?'

'How do you know . . . oh, Altaf. Never mind. I wish she were here. We could have danced a little at least.'

He nodded.

'What are you nodding like that for, Raghu? I say something like that and your reaction is just sympathetic nods.'

'What do you expect me to do?'

'You're the only friend I have here. With Di gone, you're the only person I can talk to, and if you don't share things with me I will keep feeling like I am an imposition. You're not my psychiatrist.'

He must have felt guilty because he didn't say anything for a bit.

'What do you want to ask?'

'Do you miss your family too?'

'Every day.' He shook his head and stared at his fingers. 'Not what they had become, but what they were. They loved me very much. And I loved them.'

'More than you loved Brahmi?'

The long silence that followed was the sign for me to stop prying. He sensed my stubbornness and steered the conversation away.

'Was your chacha happy?' he asked.

'He acted well enough.'

For the next hour, we ate the dal–chawal he had made, drank his tea, and talked about nothing at all. He made me not miss Divya Di any more, and I saw him smile more tonight than I have in all previous days combined. I felt . . . content, happy, however you might want to put it.

When I left his house, I felt lighter, my feet floating a few inches above the ground.

Di was wrong. Maybe there's a boy who's not all that bad after all. And he's my friend—Raghu Ganguly.

15 November 2002

To think of it, from all that the businessmen and politicians of the country have stolen from us, the Vaids needed just twenty lakh rupees. Just twenty lakh out of the hundred crore they stole! They wouldn't even know it's gone.

Why I am talking about money is because this morning the cheque that Sumitra's parents had handed over to Dadaji after much delay bounced. For the first time, Dadaji and Buaji lost it with the Balis. Earlier this morning, Dadaji and Buaji had banged on Manish Chachu's door, demanding that he send the girl away right then.

It had swiftly become '*the girl*' from Sumitra 'beti' within the course of an hour.

Sumitra and Manish Chachu have spent an inordinately long time locked in their room during the last ten days, trying to sell the newly married thing too hard.

'What's this?' Buaji had demanded from a groggy Sumitra, waving the cheque in her face.

Sumitra had squinted at the cheque and acted innocent. 'I don't know, Di.'

'Oh! You don't know? How naïve! No one in your family knows anything. All of you are lambs, aren't you?' said Buaji 'You wouldn't mind if I take your jewellery, would you? I will return it of course.'

'Yes, sure,' said Sumitra and smiled politely at Buaji.

'Where are you going, Di?' Mumma asked.

'To the jeweller,' said Buaji and shot a look at Sumitra who stood there like a cow, unknowing and coy. Buaji and Fufaji promptly left the house with Sumitra's jewellery.

Karan Bhaiya and Anshuman Bhaiya looked sternly at Sumitra Bali, the girl who was going to rob them of their dream of going to a big city, to a big engineering college with lots of girls and fun things to do. It was pleasurable to see them scared and angry. They were like leashed, hungry dogs ready to pounce, but waiting for their master to give the order.

Mumma whispered in my ears, 'I noticed the jewellery at the wedding, it's fake. The Balis have no money.'

All I could think in that moment was what Meghnad had told me. There was truth in at least one thing he said.

Mumma continued, 'Buaji is not going to take this lightly.'

16 November 2002

We were sitting like we owned the place and the Balis were standing with their heads hung low. Not Sumitra though. She had shouted, cried, fallen at Buaji's feet seeking forgiveness for her parents, tried to tell her that it was an honest mistake, but Buaji was not in any mood to forgive her.

'Will you eat something?' asked Sumitra's mother.

Buaji threw the bag of jewellery on the table.

'YOU LIED TO US!' she shouted. 'And you have the gall to ask us if we want to eat at our bahu's house?' Buaji was so angry she could barely talk.

'We . . . we are sorry,' said Sumitra's father. I wondered if he was sorry that he had cheated Buaji out of her rightful dowry money or that he had chosen to allow Sumitra to live. He seemed to have aged since the wedding. He knew this day had to come when his subterfuge would be caught and his daughter's fate, his family's honour would hang in the balance.

'Sorry? You're sorry? Do you know what you have done, huh? My brother . . . my brother could have married any girl in Dehradun and now he's stuck with your ugly daughter. Do you have any idea what our relatives called your daughter?' Buaji spat on the ground.

'Do you know what will happen now?' Buaji asked Sumitra's parents, who just stared at the ground, probably hoping the earth would open up.

'Didi, let it be—'

Buaji glared at Mumma, and shut her up. 'The mistake that we did with you won't be repeated again.'

She looked at Sumitra's parents and said sharply, 'Pitaji wanted to come here himself . . . with your daughter, leave her here to rot, but it's only I who stopped him. I told him we should give you a chance to mend this.'

'How can we mend this? Tell us? We will do anything,' said Sumitra's mother, now weeping and pleading.

'Sell this house!' said Buaji arrogantly. 'It will give you enough to pay us and for whatever the two of you need for yourself.'

Sumitra's parents looked at each other and then at us.

'It's mortgaged,' said Sumitra's father and then added in a pathetic tone. 'But don't worry . . . I have some money coming in. I promise I will pay what you need. Don't send her home. She will do whatever you ask her to do in that house, but don't send her home.'

Seeing Sumitra's parents begging with hands folded, I thought they deserved what was coming to them.

Buaji rubbed her forehead with her palm, and tried her best to not burst in anger. Calmly, she asked for the property papers to check if they were lying. Seeing them being ordered around like that in their own house no longer broke my heart. Why couldn't they live with their daughter happily ever after? Wouldn't Sumitra have been the most grateful child had they decided to do that?

Having had enough, Buaji got up abruptly.

'Are you going to send our daughter back?' asked Sumitra's mother, horror on her face.

Buaji didn't say anything and just turned to leave. Before she stepped out of the house, she looked at Karan Bhaiya and Anshuman Bhaiya, and said, 'Take what you like.'

And while Mumma and I followed Buaji out of the house, I could sense Karan Bhaiya and Anshuman Bhaiya prancing around, stripping it of everything valuable.

On our way back, my mind had been playing flash-forward of all that Buaji could do with Sumitra. I kept thinking if we were the kind of family which burns its brides. There was no reason to think otherwise. Families who do that don't look very different from ours now, do they?

When we got home Buaji went about her day like nothing had changed, as if her plans of resurrecting the household on the back of a marriage hadn't been derailed by a lying, cheating Sumitra Bali. Every time Buaji picked up a bottle of water, shifted the chair, or handled a scissor, it would be flung at Sumitra. It's another thing that Manish Chachu has been backing Sumitra, and Buaji wouldn't dare do anything in front of him.

But I also know that it's just a matter of time.

25 November 2002

These past few days have been tough for all of us.

Sumitra seems to have had the light knocked out of her eyes. Something has died inside her, something Mumma, Papa, Divya Di and I strive our hardest to preserve—hope. Manish Chachu has been taking care of her, but it doesn't seem like it's helping. What's worse is that often I can't tell what she's thinking. She smiles and goes through the paces like everything is normal, but there are moments when she's just staring out of the window, her eyes dead and her limbs limp with hopelessness. God knows what will happen when Buaji comes up with something else to trouble her with.

But she's not the only one Buaji is taking her anger out on.

Buaji has been constantly haranguing Mumma. She keeps accusing her that she knew everything about Sumitra's lies beforehand and it was all her ploy to bring more misery to the house.

'You people can sniff our money anywhere. Don't I know your *jaat*?' she said on the day the jewellery was declared fake.

Buaji has made threats to throw us out of the house and stop supporting us financially now that she has Sumitra to do the work. Mumma has spent days bent in apology because we need the money for the medicines Papa has been prescribed. Papa's back has been troubling him, the discs slowly giving up after his years of hobbling around. The doctor has told him he can no longer avoid taking medication. In the long run, he would need an operation but I don't want to think about that.

Karan Bhaiya and Anshuman Bhaiya have been meting out their own brand of petty and childish humiliation to us. The water tank is drained out after they take their baths, they make sure the toilets are extra filthy and the floors damp and muddy. They watch me and laugh as I scrub the floors and wash the dishes and trudge around like a zombie.

'There's no engineering college for you any more. I hope you know that, right? There's no longer money for that,' I said to them this morning and watched their faces fall.

Karan Bhaiya had walked away when Anshuman Bhaiya said rather ominously, 'We will sell you if required.'

'Don't you know what terrible businessmen the Vaids are? Who do you think is going to buy me?' I said angrily.

Anshuman Bhaiya said, 'That's true. Who would buy you anyway! God knows what diseases you carry, Chamarni.' He stormed off.

When Di called today, I told her nothing of this. I know she's floundering in Delhi, I'm sure of that. Had she not been, she wouldn't have been this regular with her phone calls. It's been three weeks and the phone at the PCO rings precisely at 10 a.m. every day. If she were making great strides, she would not have called precisely at that time, would have even forgotten calling and then apologized, and then gushed about the new ad she was shooting for, or the offer for a new TV show. Nothing. There are no music videos, no modelling assignments, no jobs for her in Delhi. It's only isolation and loneliness.

27 November 2002

'Your tea makes everything seem fine,' I told Raghu today.

'Take some for your buaji too then,' he joked.

Mumma might not like Raghu—or any of the men that are around me—but she too had fallen in love with Raghu's tea, even scolding me yesterday for not getting enough for her.

'You know what we should do, Raghu? We should open a tea stall. I'm telling you, it's an incredible idea. You will be the talk of the town,' I squealed.

'What makes you think I would want that?'

'Fine, fine, you remain in the background. I will be in the front for it. I'm telling you there are thousands waiting to be earned. What wouldn't the people of Dehradun do for a decent cup of tea? And yours is like a drug.'

'I'm sure your buaji will love the idea of you selling tea on the street.'

'She won't like the idea of me doing anything,' I said.

This isn't the first time he has shot down a business opportunity of mine. Of course, I'm not serious about the tea-stall idea. What I am aching to propose to him is opening a coaching institute with him—from class five to class twelve—with a focus on IIT and medical exam preparation. It's been on my mind from the day I saw him teach the kids, all of whom seemed to love him and enjoy what they were doing. That could change the landscape of IIT–medical coaching in Dehradun. Back in my school, out of the entire lot only a couple of students had a shot (they failed) at these entrance examinations because unlike Delhi, there are no good teachers here. Makes sense too, why would you stay in Dehradun and teach when you can charge thrice as much in Delhi and Kota?

But I know he will shoot this idea down. Anything that requires him to be part of a give-and-take relationship makes him anxious. Stepping out of the wormhole he's buried himself into will require him to open himself to a lot of people, something he doesn't look ready for. He keeps telling me he doesn't want to be responsible for other people, to be tethered to them, and that he's happy the way he is. Only I know he's not happy with the way things are. He's become used to a certain sense of sadness and gloom.

I switched the conversation and told him about Sumitra, knowing full well he would go on a tirade on how screwed up families are, and he did.

'Now you feel accountable for Sumitra, don't you?' said Raghu. 'You feel like saving her.'

'Of course I do,' I said. 'What's wrong with that?'

'You could have saved yourself had you not had any relationship with Sumitra in the first place. Her pain wouldn't have been your responsibility.'

'Raghu, stop being a jerk.'

'That's how you save yourself further pain. You welcome it.'

'By not being responsible you mean if tomorrow something happens to me, you would just sit here and do nothing?' I said and immediately regretted it for being too harsh. 'I didn't mean to say that. But you can't go about life like this, can you? You have to have some relationships, don't you?'

He had chuckled sadly and said, 'It didn't quite work out the other way, did it? Everyone I loved, everyone I felt responsible for . . . they didn't hold up their part of the bargain and neither did I. I don't want to set myself up for failure again.'

'So if I see you in trouble tomorrow, you expect me to sit around and watch. Is that what you're saying?'

'I would expect you to do everything in your capacity, but I wouldn't be angry if you don't.'

That angered me. I would have wanted him to chide me if I ever failed to come to his help.

But then in the past few weeks I have seen enough of him to know that he has not chosen to be miserable, and that he tries to shake off his misery, but fails. Every laugh of his is punctuated—he stops abruptly, as if he remembers something, and then starts laughing again, more softly, as if he's scared of his own happiness.

There are mornings when I reach his house before he's awake. I watch him through the window struggling to sleep, writhing and sweating, and then getting up with a start. If you ask him, he says it's nothing. I'm not a fool. There's certainly something wrong with you if you stay up nights staring at empty walls, a lone candle lit in the corner, and then get nightmares every morning.

But I try not to probe—he's my friend.

That's why I don't push my real idea on him. But as much as I care about his anxiety, I do think it could be his way back to normalcy. The only time of the day he's truly happy is when he's teaching those kids. He laughs then.

29 November 2002

I finished my errands and returned home to see an SUV parked outside. It blocked the entire lane.

I wondered if it was Sumitra's parents' car, and that they might have finally got over their money troubles and were now in a situation to pay Dadaji and Buaji. My smile vanished when I saw Meghnad lounging with Fufaji and Dadaji in the courtyard. He turned to look towards me when Dadaji did. His eyes followed me till I was inside the house. That man never failed to disgust me.

'What's he doing here?'

'Some business with your dadaji,' said Mumma, trying to stop the conversation.

'What business? He deals in furniture, Dadaji gives out sweet pills. What's the connection?'

Mumma and Papa looked at each other.

'What? Tell me?'

Papa said, 'Mumma thinks he's either going to buy this house or the clinic. That way Dadaji and Buaji will have enough money for Karan's and Anshuman's studies and for them to get by.'

'And what about us?' I asked.

Mumma didn't have an answer. All those years ago, it was out of revenge and anger that Dadaji had made us crawl back into this house after Anil Tauji's death. Over the years, they had successfully broken us, obliterating any chance of us emerging from poverty. We are now only irritants, and they have lost interest in exacting their revenge. We come cheap and maintain the house for them. We are nothing more than pesky maids, and they might not bat an eyelid if it comes to throwing us out. They don't need us any more.

A sense of relief and horror gripped me. The victim–perpetrator relationship in our house is so set it's hard for us to imagine what else exists.

But where will we go? Where will we live? Will we have enough money? What if Papa's back gets worse? In moments like these, I'm reminded why it was never easy to just get up and walk out of this house.

It isn't nostalgia, it is about survival. No matter how cruel Buaji is, no matter how hateful Dadaji is, they would never let us starve in this house. On a rainy day, we won't find ourselves on the street, thrown out by a fickle-minded homeowner. But there's no predicting Buaji's behaviour. Who knows if she's still done with us? Every time I watch her run her hands through her scars, I am scared about an outburst coming our way.

I went to the terrace to eavesdrop on the three men but could only hear them laughing. After Dadaji bid him goodbye, Fufaji and Meghnad hung around his car and drank. He took Fufaji on a drive later. They were both wobbly when they left and I prayed to the gods to do whatever is best for the rest of the world.

10 December 2002

Di didn't call today. I waited at the PCO for an hour. When she didn't, I called the number she usually calls from and got told off by the man on the other side. It was bittersweet; maybe she had finally got work. Today was the day I thought I would unload on Di the full update of the injustices. Seems like it will have to wait another day. I wonder what she's up to in Delhi. Has she got a modelling assignment? Would a director have spotted her at a coffee shop and given her work? Of course that's possible. She has a striking face. Dehradun or Delhi, she had to catch someone's eye sooner or later. Or better still, has she landed an acting job? But I have heard the movie business is murky. It will be so much better if she lands a TV soap. Those women are wildly popular. They make tens of thousands of rupees cutting ribbons during the Navratras.

I was playing Divya Di's' and my favourite game— dreaming of the day we have money—when Papa came and sat next to me.

'Modi is going to win, isn't he?' he said, trying to start a conversation, flipping through yesterday's newspaper.

Like the past few days, he seemed nervous and tense. Our future hangs in the balance. God knows what's cooking between Meghnad and Dadaji. It's going to change the course of our future.

'Papa? Things are going to change around the house, aren't they?' I asked.

He nodded.

'What's going to happen?'

'Beta, with your dadaji not getting enough patients, and clinics springing all around us, your bua was counting on this wedding. All's come to nothing now. She got nothing. Nothing,' said Papa, shaking his head. 'They lost money on the wedding overall. It's now up to Manish to turn it all around with the shop.'

'You don't believe that will happen, do you?'

Papa shook his head. 'As I always say, my brother is superstar, not a shopkeeper.'

Papa always makes me laugh. He chuckled with me.

After a long pause, he said, 'Beta. What I wanted to tell you was that you should . . . you should take care of yourself if anything happens. Go to Delhi, stay with your sister.'

'What do you mean if anything happens?'

'If we don't have a house to live in,' he said.

'You think they are going to sell the house?'

'I know for sure, beta,' he said.

'How do you know?'

'The painting is going to start tomorrow. The painters came today to take the measurements. And you know your dadaji doesn't have the money for it. Meghnad is paying for it. If they give us a little from the sale, you should take it and go to your sister and start a life there.'

'Where will you go?'

Papa was hesitant, but when I persisted, he said, 'Your Mumma has friends in the *basti*. She will talk to Iqbal and see if we can find a room there.'

Angry tears sprung in my eyes. 'You're not shifting to the slum!' Images of those inhuman conditions in which Iqbal lives flashed in front of my eyes. 'I'm not going anywhere without you and Mumma!'

'We have lived a good life. We will be fine here. You have your entire life in front of you. You can't just keep living here. *Hamara kya hai* (What happens to us is not important),' said Papa.

'I don't want to talk about it, Papa. And anyway, there's nothing to worry about. Di didn't call this morning, and you know what that means.'

'She has found work?'

'That's the only reason I could think of,' I said and beamed, and Papa seemed to lighten up. 'Papa? If there was one person you could be, who would you be?'

He sighed, waited, thought, and said softly, 'Milkha Singh.' He waited to see my reaction and then laughed out aloud. It was a joke he often cracked but looking at him now, it didn't feel like a joke. We never knew what he wanted, or if he did ever feel capable enough to want something of his own.

On our way back, he said, guiltily, 'When I get old, I want one of those push-button wheelchairs.'

12 December 2002

The perpetrator had been Buaji but the rest of us had let it happen. We were equally at fault. Isn't that what they say? The bystander should bear as much guilt? Sumitra had been asked to clean the septic tank this morning and we all let it happen.

'You can't make her do it. She's just a child!' Mumma had protested.

'If she can run away with another man and be a bare-faced liar, she can clean a septic tank!' Buaji had snapped.

'Let me help her at least,' Mumma had begged.

'We eat from your hands. Is it not enough that you get to do what you were always supposed to do and then touch our food?'

Sumitra was to clean three months of piss and shit. Every six months it takes three men two days to clean it up. Manish Chachu wasn't home, or Buaji wouldn't have done so.

I was scolded for going upstairs to see how Sumitra was doing. It crushed my heart to see her on the floor retching into the bucket of faeces she had hauled out of the septic tank. She had forced a smile and pretended like it was no big deal. Mumma had fashioned a protective coat out of polythene but that really was of no use.

The smell was ghastly and had spread through the lane. Two neighbours complained, a few expressed concern about Sumitra's health, and some others moved to their relatives' places for the night.

Even Shekhawat Uncle shouted from across the boundary wall, 'Arre, just get the jamadars to do it. They will do it quicker. Why trouble the entire neighbourhood?' His suggestion fell on deaf ears.

The workers who had been working in our house watched on in horror, not quite understanding what was happening. One of the painters even asked if he could help and was promptly chided by Karan Bhaiya. Karan Bhaiya and Anshuman Bhaiya had been appointed caretakers for the repairing and painting job at home and they had been exceptionally cruel to the workers.

Mumma had scolded Anshuman Bhaiya yesterday when he waved a slipper at one of the workers. She said, 'You're not paying for this! It's that man's money.'

'So what? It's my house!'

Mumma hadn't argued further.

Buaji was doing to Sumitra what she had done to Mumma, stripping her off her dignity and breaking her spirit. But not everyone was as strong as Mumma.

'That woman is going to kill the poor child. Can you go check on her again?' asked Mumma.

'Karan Bhaiya is standing guard,' I told her.

Sumitra had been at it for a couple of hours when Manish Chachu burst through the door, past Buaji and Fufaji, pushing Karan Bhaiya out of the way and taking the bucket of filth from Sumitra's hand. Sumitra couldn't find the physical strength to say anything to her husband and crumpled into his arms.

'She's not going to do this!' declared Manish Chachu and carried her away to the bathroom, his clothes now soiled.

The jamadars were called to finish off the work while Manish Chachu washed and dressed an exhausted Sumitra. Mumma was asked to help the workers.

'They are your brothers anyway,' Buaji grumbled.

Buaji sat outside Manish Chachu's room and said, 'Look how he's behaving. It's not even two days and he's already under the spell of that lying, scheming bitch! Doesn't he know what that woman did to us?'

'Why can't we ask Manish Chachu to divorce her?' said Anshuman Bhaiya.

'She should have died in that septic tank,' said Buaji.

Wouldn't that be convenient? Is that her go-to plan to get rid of the women she doesn't want in the house? Did she want that for Mumma as well?

In the evening, Manish Chachu asked for tea and biscuits for Sumitra. I had some tea left over in the flask that Raghu had given me. He let me inside. Buaji watched on, fury consuming her.

'How's Sumitra doing?' I asked.

'She has a bit of a fever. Pitaji refused to see her,' Manish Chachu replied.

17 December 2002

For the past week, Mumma and I had taken turns to sit by her side and sponge her forehead to bring down the temperature. Manish Chachu had helped us out in the kitchen, much to the chagrin of Buaji, who wished she had died before watching her brother cook when there were three-able bodied women in the house.

Despite the jibes, Manish Chachu made sure Sumitra ate well. He made her take her pills on time, escorted her to the washroom, bathed her, clothed her, and cried softly for her when she slept.

For the first time, Manish Chachu hadn't failed at something. If I didn't know that Manish Chachu was a homosexual, I would have said they looked like a couple in love. Yes, as Sumitra had predicted, he'd found something to love in her.

'Didn't I say that marriage would cure him?' said Mumma tearfully yesterday. I didn't bother to correct her. Happiness is a rare thing and if a few white lies can help maintain it, why not! Screw truthfulness, honesty and other platitudes.

There's another truth I would like to believe, and Papa backs me (Mumma's not too sure though). Along with all the pills and the syrups and the injections, there was one other factor that helped in Sumitra's recovery—Raghu's tea. Every morning for the past five days, two thermos flasks of piping hot tea were kept wrapped in towels on the terrace waiting to be picked up. It would see all of us through the day.

I had not met him all this while; he would arrive at odd times to drop the flasks and pick them up. At the peak of her fever, Sumitra would ask for the tea and a biscuit, and nothing else.

'Thank your boyfriend for me,' Sumitra told me today.

'What? No! Why would you say that?'

'You spend a lot of time with him, don't you? Manish tells me he has never seen you around like that with anyone else.'

'No, nothing like that' I said.

'Don't act smart with me! I'm your chachi, be straight with me,' she said with a smile.

'No, Chachi, I'm not in love with him.'

'He seems like a nice boy. You might want to consider what you feel for him.'

'Can we please change the topic? Here's an alternative. Manish Chachu. Can we talk about him?'

'What about him?' she asked.

'Mumma thinks you have cured him of his homosexuality.' She laughed.

'He has been really sweet, hasn't he?' she asked.

'I don't expect that of the Vaid men, Papa being the exception. Mumma and I were both shocked to see him run around for you like he did.'

'I know. He took me by surprise too. I think . . . I don't know how to put it . . . that we have fallen into friendship instead of love. That sounds corny, but that's what it is. We just skipped the part where couples have a sex life and ended up being good friends.'

Having not done it ever, talking about boring or interesting sex lives always makes me confused.

'What if you find another man attractive, you know? Someone who can love you? Someone who can be more than your best friend?' I asked.

Sumitra chuckled. 'Maybe he will have to be as nice as your chachu and then we will talk.'

'That sounds about right.'

'So this Raghu guy? Is he your best friend?'

'I will get back to you after I ask him.'

'I will wait,' she said. Then she asked hesitantly, 'Advaita . . . How's Divya doing in Delhi?'

'Umm . . . she's lying to me,' I said.

'Why do you say that?'

'Something is up, but she's not telling me. She didn't come to the phone for days in a row and then today she tells me it was nothing. How could it be nothing? It just means that either she's on to something and she doesn't want to jinx it by talking about it, or whatever she had been working on has fallen apart and she doesn't want us to know.'

'I hope she's safe.'

'You rest and don't worry about her,' I said. 'It's Divya Di, she always takes care of herself.'

18 December 2002

I asked Raghu the question that had been burning through me. That was the first thing I told him; I didn't bother thanking him for the tea, for being there. Like a dolt I simply asked him, 'Are you my best friend?'

He looked at me strangely for a bit, weighing what to say.

I tried to clarify, 'I'm asking because you seem to do a lot of things that best friends do,' I said. 'You're sweeter to me than you are to others. You share with me things you wouldn't share with anyone else. Apart from your students I am the only person who has come here, so clearly—'

'Advaita—'

'Before you say anything, I have to say I started from my house debating whether you are my best friend or not, and of course you are because you're my only friend, but in all probability you would have been my best friend even if I had a few others. So if I am not yours, I would be sorely disappointed.'

'You are.'

'No, not like that. Not like I'm your only friend and that's why.'

'Otherwise too,' he said.

'Are you sure you're not making it up?'

'I'm not.'

'You're not saying this because I would keep asking you over and over again?'

'No.'

'Are you absolutely certain?'

'Yes.'

'Why are you not smiling then?'

'I thought it was a serious matter for you,' he said, clearly exasperated.

'It is, but like a happy, serious matter.'

'You know why I make you tea? So that you drink it and shut up.'

So I do have a best friend and his name is Raghu Ganguly. Yay!

19 December 2002

Divya Di was rather excited today. She told me she's coming into money soon.

'Just wait for a year! And then see what I do,' she said.

When I asked her about the details, she sidestepped the topic and asked me about Raghu instead.

'Have you kissed him?' she asked gleefully.

'Do you kiss all your best friends?'

'I kiss you all the time, so yes. Also, don't give me that stupid line. You two . . . you're together, aren't you?' she said.

'Why is it that everyone asks me the same thing? First it was Mumma, then Sumitra and now you!'

'It's because you have never had a boyfriend! You were too clingy towards all of us to have one. So it's kind of unfair to us that you would leave us for a friend and not a boyfriend.'

'Feel free to feel what you feel, but he's just a friend and that's it.'

'You don't find him hot? Attractive? You don't feel like kissing him or anything? You're old enough to do that, you know that, right?'

'Didn't you ask me not to fall in love? To stay away from Raghu?'

'Maybe I changed my mind.'

'I haven't. I don't love him.'

'How are you so sure?'

'I just am.'

'For someone who's never felt it, you're unusually sure,' said Di. 'So tell me. When would you know that you're really in love with a boy?'

'When I am ready to leave you for him. Not only you, but Mumma and Papa, everyone, and be with him no matter what. Isn't that what Mumma and Papa did? Or you did with Vibhor? You chose to be with that person regardless of the consequences, didn't you? You know what would have happened if anyone knew about Vibhor Gupta and you. You would have had to leave all of us for him, and you were ready to do that. I am not ready to do the same for him, not even close.'

'I hope it's never put to the test,' she said. 'I am glad you have someone there. But what about Raghu?'

'What about him?'

'What if he falls in love with you? As annoying as you are, one can easily fall in love with you. You don't really give people a choice that way with your puppy face and your adorable cheeks,' she said.

'You're probably right,' I chuckled. 'But no, he's not going to fall in love with me. He's . . . he's still too devastated by whatever had happened in the past. There's no way he's falling in love with me or anyone for that matter.'

'I hope that's true. I mean, the two of you are happy with whatever equation you decide to keep.'

'Oh! Did you know Altaf used to tell stories about me to Raghu? He told me Altaf thought of me as his little sister. That's cute, isn't it?'

'As I said, it's hard not to love you,' she said.

25 December 2002

Christmas. A festival for rich kids.

We celebrated it every year in school by decorating trees, making Santa Clauses out of glaze paper and cotton, decorating the class in red and white, and what-not. The richer kids even went a step further and celebrated it at home, exchanged gifts and made a big deal out of it. Just a thought, if their parents had so much money, they could have just kept it in an envelope outside my home and been my Santa! But since it was a legitimate festival, I went to my newly appointed best friend Raghu's house because it seemed like a best-friend thing to do. He was mopping the floor when I got there.

'Busy,' he said, his voice muffled by the handkerchief on his mouth. Then he placed a stool in the middle of the room and started cleaning the fan. He asked me to fill up a mug with water and add detergent to it. For the next half an hour we cleaned the fans, the panes, the stove and the skirting, wringing all the festivity out of me.

'It's not Diwali, you know,' I said.

'I wouldn't have known had you not told me.'

'Someone's in a bad mood today,' I said. 'I just came here to see if you were bored, and that too during a festival.'

'Ah. Merry Christmas to you too,' he said.

'It's a good Christmas,' I said.

'They are not selling the house?'

'No news about that. Manish Chachu and Sumitra feel they would have known if that were a possibility. But you never know. Buaji and Manish Chachu haven't been talking. But there's good news! I think my sister will start making money soon. Looks like she's finally making some progress.'

'Brilliant.'

'You should meet my sister. You two would have been perfect for each other.'

'I have met your sister,' he said.

'Ummm . . . Oh. . . yes, forget I said that,' I said. 'I just . . .'

'Is there something you want to tell me?'

'I am only telling you because you're my best friend or I wouldn't—'

'Advaita?'

'Yes?'

'Can you stop doing this *best friend* business? It's slightly infuriating now. We established that and we don't have to keep reiterating, do we?'

'But it's nice to say it.'

'For the past week I have heard it a million times from you. I am done.'

'There could have been a kinder way of saying that, but OK . . . so? What was I saying? Yes! So the thing is, Sumitra and Divya Di both asked me if you were my boyfriend and I told them you're not. They believed me, but Di was concerned that you might fall in love with me because apparently I am worth falling in love with—'

'You're exasperating, Advaita!'

'What! I didn't even say it. My sister did.'

'I don't care who's saying, it's not happening. You are and will always be my . . . '

'I will be what? Complete it!'

'Shut up.'

'Complete it!'

'No.'

'Do you mean best . . .'

'Don't say it.'

'Best . . .'

'Don't.'

'Best . . .'

'Someone please kill me.'

'Best friend!'

'Ugh.'

I laughed seeing him squirm.

'You're impossible.'

And that's when I noticed a little cake box right next to the stack of books.

'What is that?' I asked.

'I might have got you a cake,' he said.

'You did? That's so lame.'

'I know.'

'You should have baked one for me if you really had to make an impression,' I said, accepting a piece of it.

'But then, I'm not in love with you, so this is all you get.'

'There's something else for you too,' he said and fetched a little rectangular box. 'This is because you keep writing in your diary all the time.'

He opened the box for me. It was a fountain pen, an expensive one, not like the plastic ones I have. I felt it in my hands. It felt heavy, substantial.

'This is so sweet!'

'Go ahead, try it,' he said. 'I filled it with ink.'

I wrote his name and mine. The pen glided smoothly over the paper. It was wonderful. I had half a mind to ask him how expensive it was.

'If someone had given me this pen when I was younger, I would have been way better at my studies!'

I hugged him. 'Thank you! I want to say thank you, *best friend* but I won't.'

'I am glad you like it,' he said, uncharacteristically shy.

'By the way, I've also got something for you.'

'You didn't have to.'

'What? You thought only you could be thoughtful? Here, open it. And please tell me you like my gift as much as I like yours.'

'Is it . . . a diary?' he asked, frowning.

'Yes! Similar to the one I have!' I said. 'You have no idea how therapeutic it is. For you especially it would work wonders.'

'Advaita—'

'And you know, one day if you feel like telling me everything from your past, you can just give me the diary and I can read it. You wouldn't even have to tell me and I would know.'

'Would you give me your diary to read?' he asked.

'Try and ask,' I said.

'Still, I can't take this,' he said, handing it back to me.

'Why?' I said. 'If you don't take my diary, I won't take your pen.'

'I used to write one,' he said, his voice suddenly serious. 'Wrote it for an entire year. It . . . I . . . can't do it again.'

'Why did you stop?'

He didn't have to answer.

'Brahmi?'

'It had all the reasons I needed to live, the people I deeply loved, but when . . .' His voice trailed. 'I stopped after she was gone.'

'Maybe you will find other reasons? And then you can write . . . '

'OK, I'll take it,' he said and kept it aside. He forced a smile. 'Thank you.'

I knew it will eat dust for a while and be forgotten like bad gifts often are. But I took heart from what it meant. He won't fall in love with me, I will never be reason enough for him to change his life, just like he won't be for me. That sounds sad, the way I put it.

'But you have to admit, Raghu. No one would have done what we did for each other today and that makes us . . .'

'No.'

'Best friends!'

31 December 2002

I was so furious I could have killed a man. Karan Bhaiya and Anshuman Bhaiya peeked into my room every now and then, like guards of a fortress, taking their responsibility of keeping me in the house rather earnestly.

'Didn't I tell you? We would sell you if the need arises,' said Anshuman Bhaiya.

'And don't blame us for it. If you elder sister wasn't the way she was, it would have been her neck on the line.'

'What nonsense are you two talking?' Buaji scolded them. 'And you, Advaita, get ready and put on some make-up. Sumitra will share hers.'

A boy was coming to see me this evening.

When I stormed out of the room and cried out in desperation, Dadaji shouted, 'Go back to your room before I get up from here!'

'At least tell me who's the boy—'

Dadaji got up and raised his stick in the air. Papa dragged me into our room before it escalated further.

'Why is this happening, Papa?' I asked.

'I don't know, beta,' he said in a defeated voice.

Mumma looked on helplessly as she picked out clothes for me to wear.

'If anything, they should get Di married off earlier! Why me!' I protested. 'I'm not going to go through with this, you know that. I will run.'

Mumma and Papa looked at me sternly to let me know that I had to keep my voice down, and I did. They didn't specifically ask me not to run away which meant that it wasn't off the table.

'Just get through the day,' whispered Papa in my ears. 'You can make a decision later.'

But the quieter I got, the more I understood the consequences. If I run away from this marriage and this house, Buaji is not going to sit around and support Mumma and Papa. They would throw them out. They would have to go and live in the *basti*. Or would they stop them from doing that? Make them pay for Divya Di and my transgressions?

Buaji asked me to look my best and be on my best behaviour. 'Act like a girl and don't tell them that you go to college every day.'

'What if they ask me if I am in love—'

Buaji stepped forward and almost raised her hand.

'Look, Advaita, don't make me lose my temper today. You think both you girls are very smart, but you aren't. Both of you are stupid. All these years we have supported my bhai and your mother. I know you think of me and your dadaji as some sort of villains. But just know that we are your family and we love you. Whatever we do is for you to be happy—'

'Buaji, you call this happiness?'

'What else is this? What else can women expect? You think that this is not enough for you after your mother married my bhai? Don't you think your mother would have been happier had she married within her own caste, her own people? My bhai would have had the same respect in our society and would not have been a langda who married a Chamar. This is what happens when women want more. Look at your didi, look at Sumitra. We don't talk just for the sake of it. It's because we have wisdom,' she said and ran her fingers over my face lovingly.

'It's not that I don't love you. You're my brother's daughter, but I do wish you were brought up differently. That you had been taught to stay in your space. Get married to this boy. This will be the best for you. And I promise, I will take care of my bhai and your mother. That's my word to you. They will have a happy life. We will take care of your sister too if she comes back and apologizes to us. We know you talk to her. What is she doing there, haan? There are dime a dozen girls like her in that city. Call her back and ask her to apologize before she has to turn to begging or prostitution.'

Before leaving, she held my hand and said, 'We are not angry any more at how your Papa destroyed this family. We have forgiven him. I promise to make everything all right, beta. We don't want *paap* on our heads, Advaita, the day you get married, Dadaji will sign an affidavit giving a fourth of this house to my bhai. I will personally deposit the money in my bhai's and your mother's joint account that's going to take care of them for a few years at least. We are all thinking of you.'

She hugged me before leaving.

While Sumitra draped the sari around me, I kept hearing Buaji's words in my head over and over again, and that slowly broke my resolve. They will take care of Mumma and Papa . . . Maybe it wasn't a hollow promise; an affidavit transferring a fourth of the house in Papa's name and some money in a joint account.

The man I was to marry was late by an hour, and he was Meghnad Mohyal. He looked at me from top to bottom, smiled, and then introduced himself to me as if we didn't know each other. He came with his parents, his elder brother and his bhabhi. He sat leaning back on his chair, his legs apart, staring at me, while his parents talked about how hard-working and sincere my two brothers were, and how they were expanding their business all over Dehradun and even in Delhi. Mumma and Papa listened to everything with smiles on their faces, and like me, tried hard not to show their emotions. Meghnad's mother came up to me, inspected my face, and then cast the evil shadow off me.

'She's so beautiful,' she told Mumma and Buaji.

His father said, '*Dekhiye ji*, listen, what we feel is what happened in the past should remain in the past, shouldn't it?' Grinning widely, he looked at Meghnad and said, 'Why are you so quiet? Aren't you happy with this alliance? Our Meghnad is a shy boy.'

Meghnad, that bastard, sat up and smiled like a nervous schoolboy. He said, 'If it's okay with her, then I'm OK with it too. Can I talk to her alone?'

Buaji replied before anyone else could, 'Of course!'

Meghnad walked to one corner of the courtyard where our bathroom was. I followed him.

He pointed to our common wall with the Shekhawats and said, 'This is where that uncle lives, right? The man who used to eye you and your sister. Is it not?'

'How do—'

'I will see what to do about him later. I will do that for you.' He smiled. 'How do you like the work that's going on around here? Good? I have also given the workers instructions to make another bathroom on the terrace. Nice tiles, big mirror, hot water on the tap, the works.'

'Why would you do that?'

'I want to take care of my wife's family. That's just the kind of man I am. Too bad your sister never saw it.'

'What else are you giving Buaji?'

Meghnad started to laugh lightly. He said, 'Another question?'

'You're giving something, aren't you?'

'I offered to fix this house and then buy it at a premium. No one would give that rate for this ruin. But you know, my father is a generous man. He will let your dadaji, buaji, those two pesky brothers of yours, and even your mumma and papa live for as much time as they want, free of rent of course. Think of it as a wedding gift. Or a New Year's gift.' His eyes glinted with madness. 'Just know that I will be taking care of your family. You father will not have to worry about his back problem. He needs a surgery, I heard,' he said and crept closer to me. He held my hand and brought it close to his lips. 'Advaita? I see us together. You too should start seeing it that way, jaanu. We are meant to be. Should we go inside? They are waiting . . . for us to agree to this wedding.'

I followed him.

Inside the house, we sat next to each other. Our silence was taken as affirmation. The grown-ups all got up and hugged each other. Meghnad touched my parents' feet.

'Such an auspicious start for the new year,' Meghnad's mother said and kissed my hand. She then slipped an ornate gold bangle on to my wrist. My family, including Mumma and Papa, held my hand up against the light and marvelled at how heavy it was.

Meghnad leaned towards me and said, 'You should lose a little weight, jaanu. Ask how your didi maintains her figure.'

Meghnad's parents handed over a thick envelope to Buaji before they left. We didn't get to see what was inside.

Mumma dragged me inside the room, the tears finally springing in her eyes, and asked me, 'What did he say? Why did you not say anything?'

Papa came in and bolted the door, 'You could have asked for time.'

I cried.

And as I cried I wondered if it was such a bad thing to happen if I could work around it. I could slowly fall out of Meghnad's good graces, maybe withhold intimacy, be boring and inaccessible, and wait for him to be smitten with someone else, to inflict himself on another unsuspecting, helpless girl. He would eventually tire of me and leave me, and let me be with my parents, good riddance. This could be worked out.

I can be with Meghnad.

These tears are stupid. This is what I always wanted—to get money. This is everything I need. My hands are shaking. Is this my fate?

2 January 2003

It was cold. I had stayed up the last two nights, buried under blankets and hugging Mumma, and yet it felt cold. The news told me this morning that North India was in the clutches of a cold wave that has killed many. The notion had struck me in the middle of the night more than once. What if . . . what if I'm found dead, cold, shrivelled, my heart the size of a raisin the next morning, and then I had thought about Mumma and Papa and pushed it out of my head.

Raghu listened intently as I told him that I would get married to Meghnad, get my parents the money they needed, and eventually make Meghnad leave me. By then, Divya Di too would have made something of herself.

'Saying yes to him is not a plan,' he said frowning. 'That's suicide.'

'It's not—'

'ARE YOU OUT OF YOUR MIND?' Raghu shouted.

'Listen, Raghu, it's the only way—'

'Fuck this way. How long do you think it will take him to be tired of you, huh?'

'I have not thought about that,' I said.

'What if he's abusive? WHAT IF HE HITS YOU? Have you thought about that?'

'Raghu, calm down and think clearly. It's the best I can do for my family, OK?' I said, a little angry. What does he know about these things? He can live his useless life for as long as he wants to without thinking of the consequences of his actions.

There wasn't much to talk about after that. I left telling him that I needed to talk to Di.

I had asked Mumma and Papa not to tell Di about my wedding. I asked her only about the money she was going to earn.

'Why—'

'Just tell me, will you?' I asked, trying the hardest not to snap at her.

'But it will take time. I have signed up with the Super Elite Modelling agency. Since they are paying for the portfolio and everything, I won't get much the first year. They will keep most of it, but when the one-year contract ends I can do as much work as I want on a freelance basis and all of it will be mine. All the big models are from this agency. You name one and he or she's from this place. They groom you to be the best,' she said.

'Fine.'

'Is something wrong?'

'No,' I said. 'Just a fight with Anshuman Bhaiya. He told me you were going to fail . . . and I fought with him.'

'Are you sure you're fine?'

'Yes,' I said. 'I need to go.'

I cut the line.

5 January 2003

This morning I found a glimmer of hope in the cesspit I have
found myself in. Things weren't as bad as they seemed to be. I
had wanted to know when the wedding would take place. And
today, it slipped from Karan Bhaiya's mouth that it wouldn't
be before November since the house was getting renovated.
Apparently, Meghnad's family is embarrassed by our house.

'You seem awfully excited to get married!' mocked
Anshuman Bhaiya and then said, 'By the way, if I were a girl,
I would too. Have you looked at his cars? He has two Pajeros,
two! His father drives a Mercedes. You've got so lucky you
have no idea.'

'I wish you were a girl then,' I said.

'He also gave us watches,' he said and flashed his wrists
at me. 'Fastrack. Anshuman Bhaiya checked the price at the
showroom. Three thousand each!'

'You should sell them and get something better,' I said,
pointing at the watch. 'But do you really think they would
wait till the renovation is over?'

'Of course, Ma's not mad. After what happened with
Sumitra Chachi, she's not going to believe anyone, and
Meghnad's father is a pucca *haraami* (bastard). Everyone
knows. Why do you think she's selling it at almost double the
market price? Even if they throw us out, we will have enough
to buy a smaller house.'

6 January 2003

'COME TO DELHI RIGHT NOW!' Divya Di shouted.

'Listen to me, Di—'

'I DON'T WANT TO. You're not getting married to him. NO WAY!'

'Did Mumma and Papa tell you what he's offering?'

'Are you a prostitute?'

'Well, Buaji thinks *you* are.'

'Whatever! Advaita, no matter what he offers, you're not going through with this.'

'I'm getting married to him, not sleeping with him. Think for a minute, Di, without shouting at me. Mumma and Papa will finally be able to buy a house, have some money. Do you know what that means for them?'

'Money earned by this is worth just ashes, Advaita!'

'Maybe you will come into money, maybe you will not, who the hell knows, Di? What should they do? Run to Delhi and live where? Do what? How will we even buy a new sewing machine? And for whom?'

'So you will pimp yourself out? We were not brought up for this!' snapped Di on the phone.

'You need to stop saying that.'

'Over my dead body! You will be here in Delhi by November. I'm telling you, I won't take this.'

'WILL YOU SHUT UP AND LISTEN TO ME! The best thing right now is for you to pursue your modelling career. If one year later you manage to be something, I can just run, right? Didn't you tell me that half of Delhi's big models are from your agency?'

Di was crying now. I could make out since she wasn't able to muffle her sniffles.

'I called you to give you some good news . . .'

'And I gave you one, didn't I?' I said. 'But what's yours?'

'I am getting my passport made. I've got work in Dubai,' she said softly. 'Tell Mumma and Papa not to worry. I won't be wearing a swimsuit, only saris.'

'That's awesome!' I squealed. 'THIS IS SO GOOD! THIS IS AMAZING! That's mental. You will get to sit on a plane. How cool will that be? Will anyone be around who has a camera? Click lots of pictures, okay!' I was hyperventilating.

'But they aren't paying a lot this time . . . and it means nothing now.'

'Di? Hey? Hey? Don't talk like that. Don't be the one who cries, OK? I'm the crybaby, you're the strong one. Didn't you say this is how it all starts? So see, it's all started. I need to go now, Buaji wanted me back home by four.'

'Don't go.'

'Please, Di. Don't make it tougher for me,' I said and cut the line.

Meghnad was at home waiting for me. Buaji ushered me into her room as soon as I entered and chided me for looking the way I did.

'Where were you? He's here to take you out. Do you know how long he has been waiting?' she asked.

'Take me out? Take me out where?'

'To lunch. You should feel lucky that he's so doting. Other men don't bother. Just quickly get washed up and be ready,' she said, and even pointed me in the direction of the bathroom she used.

I hadn't been inside for even ten minutes when she banged my door and asked politely if I was going to take longer. When I came out, she used the perfume she herself rarely uses on me.

Then she put on a fake, stern smile and told Meghnad to drop me back before sunset. My eyes darted towards the clock. Two hours with this man!

The second we stepped into his Cielo, modified and bent and dented out of recognition, big fenders, tinted glasses, blue lights, he asked if we could watch a movie together. When I told him we didn't have enough time for that, he told me he wasn't planning on watching the film but me. I cringed and my throat went dry and I contemplated how hurt I would be if I jumped out of the car. In my head his hands were already on my thighs, clenching, unclenching. What he would do in a movie hall would be much worse.

'I can't go to a movie with you,' I said. 'I am not allowed these things. Buaji is quite strict, especially because of what Di did with you.'

'Don't take that *haraamzadi*'s name in front of me,' he grumbled.

'I don't want people to talk about me like you do about Di. I'm sure you wouldn't want that either,' I said as coyly as possible. 'We aren't married yet. Even being seen like this with you wouldn't go down well with Dadaji. Buaji must have given you permission because she didn't want to disappoint you, but I'm sure she doesn't like this.'

'Whoa, calm down. I just, I just thought we would spend some time together, jaanu. Oh c'mon! Don't cry now. Fine, fine, we won't watch a movie today.'

I nodded.

'Where do you want to go then? Countdown for lunch? OK, now don't cry. C'mon, god! You and your sisters are poles apart. Your sister would have jumped at the opportunity,' he said irritably.

The more he was bothered with my tears the more they came. By the time I stopped crying and blowing snot into my dupatta and hoping a truck would crush the driver's side of the car, we were at Countdown.

Shyly and after he prodded enough, I ordered American chop suey and a cheese pizza. I kept myself just a brink away from tears, lest he tried something.

I ate quietly for the most part. He droned on about all the supposedly cool things he and his boys—Karan Bhaiya and Anshuman Bhaiya are now part of the group that had thrown bottles into our bus six months ago—go about doing in Dehradun. I acted suitably interested. Taking that as encouragement, he talked about the new car he was thinking of buying, and after fifteen minutes of talking tirelessly about cars, he said, 'You don't understand any of this, do you?'

I smiled like I didn't, and he laughed out aloud. 'You girls are so stupid!'

It wasn't until later that I spotted him.

He was right there, at the corner, almost melting into the wallpaper—Raghu.

I tried not to look at him, but even when I did he was peering into a newspaper and sipping from his mug, lost, unmindful. *Was it a coincidence?* Our eyes met twice, and both times he looked away as if it was nothing. I ate slowly, so by the time we left it was already dark.

'It was nice, jaanu,' he said when he dropped me home.

'I would appreciate it if we meet during daytime,' I said. 'Mumma and Papa aren't really comfortable with this.'

'You worry too much,' he said. 'If anything happens, make them call me, OK?'

Mumma and Papa were pacing around the room when I entered. They were relieved to see me smiling.

Mumma held me through the night.

7 January 2003

Sumitra stopped me in my tracks when I was leaving the house to ask if Raghu was in Countdown on purpose.

The pretext in my head for leaving the house was the usual. I had a bunch of Mumma's clothes with me which might or might not have needed dropping off at a few customers.

'You shouldn't go where you're going,' said Sumitra ominously.

'I need to see Raghu.'

'Listen to me.' She grabbed me.

I followed her back inside the house and helped her stack the vegetables she was carrying in the refrigerator. The grocery bags were heavy. Buaji's deal was already making a fundamental difference in what we ate too.

'Advaita, you can't meet Raghu every day, you know that, don't you?' she said, keeping her voice low. 'What do you think *they* will do if they get to know?'

'How will they get to know?'

'But what if they do? It's not as if you're discreet about this. Stay home. Don't meet the boy, Advaita. It won't end well,' she said. 'If Buaji gets to know, she'll think you're jeopardizing the future of her children . . . you know how vengeful she can be.'

'Oh please, I can't just stay at home.'

'There's nothing that's going to come out of this.'

'Just because you have accepted the way you're living doesn't mean I have to as well. He's my friend and I will meet him,' I said and stormed out.

Realizing I had snapped at her unfairly, I went back and apologized. Sumitra was just looking out for me. How easy is it to forget the suffering of others when faced with your own?

Sumitra didn't choose this life for herself. Instead, she had chosen to run for love, and how many girls find the courage to do that?

An hour later, despite Sumitra's desperate pleas, I was on the bus to Raghu's place. The closer to his house I got, the heavier my feet grew. I wrapped my face with the dupatta and looked over my shoulder at every breath. Sumitra's words had struck deep. Buaji would do anything to keep her product— me—safe from spoilage.

There was tea on the stove waiting for me. He had bathed and shaved off his beard. The razor was still lying upturned on the sink, the towel was drying on the clothes line. Clots had formed on his face where he had bled.

'You look like a different person,' I said. 'Please don't shave.'

'Noted,' he said and poured me a cup of steaming tea.

'It's even colder in your house, isn't it?'

He switched on the heater.

'Do you know that twenty-three people are dead in Bihar from the cold wave? We are a people who let other people die because we won't share our blankets.'

'I sense cynicism.'

'It's not cynicism, it's anger. I am so glad Di is going to Dubai. I hope she stays there forever!'

'She's going where?'

'I didn't tell you?'

He shook his head. I told Raghu about the modelling assignment in Dubai, her possible meteoric rise in the ranks of the elite models in India, and of the painful, slow trickle of money she would get, trying my best to be happy.

'There's still a way out of this Meghnad problem,' said Raghu, noticing the lack of spark in my voice about Di's impending success.

'There's no hope, Raghu,' I replied.

'I am fundamentally against hope.'

'Nothing can match what Meghnad's offering Mumma and Papa. It's literally everything they ever needed,' I said.

'It's not literally everything. They didn't *need* their daughter to spend a lifetime of misery, or by your calculation a year of misery. If they did, they would have been happy, but are they?'

'They are not, but once everyone gets used to the new arrangement, they will realize it's for the best,' I said. 'Didn't Mumma say so? That's what we women do. Adjust, find a corner and make ourselves invisible.'

'Or you can fight from the corner. Something you are good at. You guys are survivors,' he said.

'What do you want me to do?' I said.

'By doing something you have wanted to for months now,' he said.

'Raghu, this is not the time for riddles.'

'Humour me. Why do you talk to my students when they are leaving my class?'

'They are cute kids, that's why.'

'How do you know the school everyone goes to, or whether they go to other tuitions, and if they go, where they go?'

'Curiosity?'

'And why have the number of students doubled since you have known me, their payments dot on time?'

'Because you're good, that's why, and you should get your money. Who works for free?'

'Is that it?'

'Yes.'

'Are you sure that in that diary that you carry you haven't thought even once that Raghu is a useless fellow who should turn this into a business? Get more students in, maybe add a few subjects?'

'No.'

'And you have never thought of suggesting it to me?'

I rolled my eyes and said, 'Why are we even talking about this? Raghu, you need your space and I understand that. I might have thought about it but . . . I knew you were never going to agree.'

'What if I do?'

In movies, there's often an emotionally charged scene where a dead man is violently brought back to life by a doctor by using something called a defibrillator. I have always been fascinated with the word and the concept. Two metal pads urgently rubbed against each other, someone shouting '1000, 2000 CLEAR', and then the dead man flopping every time it's put to his chest and then finally coming back to life. It felt a bit like that. Resuscitation.

'I don't want to be the subject of your pity,' I said.

'I will take 60 per cent of all earnings. The timings of the class will be as per my convenience. I won't charge a lot from kids who can't afford it, and I want all transactions in cash.'

'That's harsh.'

'This is purely business,' he said.

'This is purely business,' I said.

'It's not. I'm only doing this for my . . . best friend.'

I tried my best not to burst into tears.

'Are you serious?'

'Aren't you the best thief in Dehradun?' he said and I laughed despite the tears.

When I left his house, I was tingling all over. There are tons of things we could do with this. An entire city sustains itself on this business, so what's the harm if there one more person does it? This could change everything! All I need to do is hide this from everyone till things fall into place. All I need is a few months.

10 January 2003

Meghnad has fallen into his old pattern, only that now he's richer, more powerful, best friends with my horrible brothers, and has the sanction of his family and mine. In the past week, he has asked my family twice if he can take me out, and both times I had to turn him down.

He had come to my college yesterday and waited for three hours for me. Luckily, I hadn't lied to Buaji about going to college and was actually there filling up examination forms.

When I left college, Meghnad was there, leaning against his car. Before he could suggest wanting to take me to a movie, I gushed and said, 'That's such a surprise! I was about to make Mumma call you home today to make you eat her wonderful food. You don't ever meet Mumma! '

Even Meghnad was a bit taken aback at my happiness to see him. I might have overacted a little bit.

'Some other day? Let's go—'

I interrupted him. 'She always keeps asking me why you don't come home and spend time with her. You know how embarrassing that is for me when she asks why I meet my jaanu only outside? I don't want her to think the same about you, jaanu,' I said, being cloyingly sweet.

For someone who prides himself on how smart he is, Meghnad didn't think twice and got me home and ate with my mother like a dutiful son-in-law.

Mumma, piling more food on to his plate. It seemed like she was attempting to feed him to death, hoping that a piece of drumstick would be lodged in his throat and he would die choking on our living room floor.

He chomped like an animal, wasting my time, but whatever he does won't dampen my excitement. Little did he know of the room we were renting out on the bypass, of what colours Raghu and I were thinking of painting it in, of how we planned to steal a bunch of chairs, tables and a blackboard to set it up like a proper classroom. The students were yet to come, but what do they say '. . . build it and they will come'. Of course, I would be a fool to believe that. We need to be at the top of our game for this to be a success. Raghu started the work on the course material the day we shook hands. We will get the material printed with the logo of our tuition centre on top. The mere thought gives me goosebumps.

When Meghnad left, Mumma took me with her to her room and asked, 'What are you doing, Advaita? What's going on?'

'What do you mean?'

'You sat there smiling at him, lost in your thoughts. There's something on your mind, isn't it?' And then in a tone both hopeful and scared, she asked, 'Are you planning to join your sister in Delhi?'

'No, even better.'

I grinned and blurted out everything about the coaching classes, and waited for Mumma to shriek out in happiness and hug the life out of me.

'What if someone gets to know?' she asked instead. 'It's a small town, Advaita. Who's going to get the students? You don't get customers sitting in a room. And you can't make Raghu go out and get the students. He will be too tired to teach then.'

'Of course I will go—'

'How long do you think it will be before one of Dadaji's patients tells him that their granddaughter came propositioning a coaching institute?'

'I will do it carefully, Mumma—'

'Like I did it carefully?' she said, recalling the time she had decided to diversify into stitching men's clothes too. Even though she did none of the measuring or the cutting or the stitching, when Buaji got wind of it, she took Dadaji's stick to Mumma's sewing machine and smashed both the stick and the machine. She didn't even spare the cloth for the pants and shirts, and burnt them to ashes. It set us back six months.

'Do you think there's enough money in this? Have you calculated how much you can save from this?'

'A lot.'

'Have you calculated the worst-case scenario?' she asked.

She sat down with a pen and a paper.

She estimated our student inflow, average fees and expected costs in her little notebook in her scraggly Devanagri script which Papa had taught her after they'd got married. She didn't speak for a long time. She wouldn't even look up from the numbers she had calculated. Almost a repeat of what I had done when Raghu and I had discussed how much we stood to earn in the worst-case scenario. She spoke, 'Do you trust him?'

'I do.'

'Let the coaching institute be in his name. If you're caught, we can tell your buaji you were working for him,' she said.

'Are you sure that will work?' I asked.

She nodded, excited and terrified and happy.

She hugged me and I felt her chest heave against mine.

'Mumma?'

'Yes?'

'There's something else you should know too. Di had asked me not to tell you till her passport comes.'

She burst into tears when I told her about Di's modelling assignment. Neither Mumma nor Papa had ever expected that their daughter, the daughter of a cripple and an untouchable, would sit on a plane and leave the country.

We kept our voices down for the rest of the night. Our happiness has the habit of slipping through our fingers.

17 January 2003

I AM SO EXCITED!

The room rent has been paid in full for three months (by Raghu); it's been painted (by me and I paid for the paint), and the chairs and tables (stolen) are in place, covered with plastic sheets (stolen by both of us). The notebooks have been labelled with the name 'BCC Coaching Institute', and printed and bound. We've divided the room into two parts—an achingly small office with a long table and four chairs, and a fifteen-chair classroom.

The mood at my home would have been rather different if Di and I were boys. It would have been like an early Diwali. They would have told half the town about Di's Dubai visit and my own plans, distributed sweets and laughed and danced. They would have casually dropped the news of their sons' successes in conversations; the sky would have been the limit. Instead, Mumma and Papa are sombre, unsure, scared. Their words have dried up, and the years of asking us to do what we felt was best for us seems to have come to haunt them. Every few minutes they look at each other, confirming each other's fears. For now, both their daughters seem to be stepping into lives that are uncertain, mixing with people they know nothing about. Is there anything worse for the parents of a typical Indian girl? Their enthusiasm has given way to fear and it shows no matter how hard they try to hide it.

They have tried their best to inspire confidence, to feel happy for me and Di, but they just couldn't muster up the feeling. It's like birds leaving their nest to venture into a shooting range.

Mumma got up and sat near me. She held my hand and ran her fingers through my hair and said what I believe all parents tell their kids. 'Time flies. You grew up too early, didn't you?'

'We should leave for the PCO,' said Papa. 'She shouldn't wait there for long.'

They couldn't control the tears when Di came on the line. They howled and cried, and made her swear she wouldn't do anything wrong. Then they wanted assurance that she would be safe in Dubai.

The few customers who were waiting for their turn at the PCO turned away, seeing a grown man and woman crying.

'Promise us you will be safe. Promise us!'

Di cried her share of tears as well.

On our way back, we stopped at the bun–tikki walla and I ate Di's share. The worst seemed over. Mumma and Papa were more loving than usual. We still couldn't believe she was leaving for another country.

'When can we meet him? This Raghu Ganguly?' asked Papa once we got back home.

20 January 2003

I was sticking newspaper on the window (Raghu told me the room needed a second layer of paint) when I saw the news report. A militant outfit in Kashmir, Harkat-ul-Jehadi-Islamia, had asked Muslim women to quit jobs and get married at age fifteen. Whatever this outfit had declared had found support in Lashkar-e-Jabbar which had issued a similar diktat a while ago and thrown acid at the women who hadn't complied.

'This entire country is like this. If Dadaji could have gotten away with it, he would have killed us long back,' I said.

'You're incredibly brave then, aren't you?'

We got back to work.

Just before we left, I asked him if he could meet my parents.

'Any time they deem fit,' said Raghu, without missing a beat.

21 January 2003

Luckily enough, Meghnad had been busy with throwing someone out of one of his rental properties and finding new tenants.

He has taken to calling me at least twice now, once before I leave for college and once after. Every phone call feels like the twisted cord of the phone wrapping itself tightly around my neck.'

Divya Di must be in the aircraft right now. It's giving me goosebumps to write this. Is it scary? Does it make your stomach rumble like on a Ferris wheel? Would she be OK? Buaji doesn't know or she would have found some way to inflict pain on us. No one in our family has seen what the world looks like from more than seven storeys high. We haven't seen an airport, and planes hovering above make us stop and stare. And there she is, sitting in one, not going to Mumbai, or Bengaluru, but DUBAI! She would have taken the window seat (who would want any other) and would be staring out, smiling, pumping her fists, rejoicing in her new status of being a 'foreign return'. How will I ever match up to her? An international flight, a hotel stay, possible remuneration in a foreign currency—she is on the brink of everything we fantasize about. I am so happy I can cry. In fact I have. It all seems believable now. Now that she's away from this terrible town and terrible country and its terrible people. I feel extraordinarily unpatriotic today, and not without reason.

Harkat-ul-Jehadi-Islamia can go fuck itself!

22 January 2003

There is nothing to feel awkward about it and yet I am. As if what they think of him will reflect on the kind of person I am. Like he's the sum total of my choices in life, of what I have absorbed from what my parents have tried to teach me. I won't lie. It felt like Mumma and Papa were going to meet my boyfriend, my fiancé, the love of my life. Mumma and Papa too were behaving in the same way; they were nervous. The nicer clothes were out and it seemed like an attempt to show him that we were rich. It was all a bit silly and cute.

His room had been scrubbed clean, the books and newspapers tucked away carefully, and the porch swept clean. There were two stools in addition to the two chairs that had been there. The mattress had been folded and kept on the side. Twice, he pointed out that I was fidgeting and that my knee was shaking like a tuning fork.

We waited for what seemed like an eternity.

'You don't look nervous,' I said.

'Should I look nervous?'

Before he could say anything more, there was a knock on the door and he got up. He duly bent down and touched their feet. He pushed the stools forward and requested them to sit. 'Tea?' he asked.

Mumma and Papa looked around the room, questions bubbling in them just as the tea was. They sipped the tea and at first refused the biscuits, but they were Jim Jam, our family's favourite, so they took one each.

'She told us about the business you two are running,' said Papa, his voice sterner than usual. 'We were not very happy about it. But what do I say? Kids do what kids do these days.'

'Papa, what are you saying?'

Mumma interrupted me to let Papa continue his tough-dad speech.

'Let him speak,' said Mumma.

'It will be better if we can talk to your parents before you two do this,' Papa said.

'Mumma, I told you to not talk about all this.'

Raghu shot a look towards me. I had promised him that Mumma and Papa wouldn't ask such questions, and they too had promised.

'Uncle, I haven't seen them in months and I don't intend to. I apologize if that is a prerequisite for us to start the coaching institute.'

Mumma and Papa looked at each other and then at me, and then nodded.

'Just tell us everything that's going on, beta,' said Mumma, her voice now soft and buttery. 'You know, as parents of a girl, we are constantly scared for her.'

And in a rare moment of weakness, or vulnerability, or what should I call it, being human, he said, 'She's lucky to have you. Not many have such parents.'

A little crack. I wanted to reach out and split him wide open, peek into what he was hiding but he closed up again.

After a while, Mumma spoke. 'We will send food for you. Just tell us what you usually eat,' she said.

For the next half an hour, we talked about everything and nothing.

'He's a nice boy,' said Mumma on the bus back home.

24 January 2003

We had been worried sick. She should have landed in Delhi yesterday and there has been no news from her. We had spent hours outside the PCO, taking turns, and yet there was no call, no news whether Di was still in Dubai or had landed in Delhi. Mumma and Papa were in tears most of the time, angry at her and at themselves for letting her take this stupid, stupid step of going to Dubai on her own. We had all heard horror stories of people getting stuck in the Middle East, with their passport seized, the women pushed into slavery, or worse still, prostitution. Mumma was so scared that at one point she shouted, 'No coaching business! Just stay at home!'

So when Di finally called today, they gave her a piece of her mind before she could even utter anything. But midway through their shouting, Mumma and Papa both burst into tears and apologized and asked her if she was all right.

She told us she was stuck because of some misunderstanding regarding her visa, and apologized for going missing.

'They gave me six thousand rupees.'

'Shift to a better PG,' said Mumma before she could offer her the money. 'Eat on time and don't skimp on food. You know what happens to your skin when you don't eat.'

'Mumma. Listen to me.'

'We don't need anything here,' said Mumma. 'Your sister already has three more students enrolled in her coaching institute! Even the classes have started.'

'I have to send something home,' Divya Di insisted.

Mumma kept ignoring her. 'Also I'm making three lehngas! So don't act oversmart, and keep your money with yourself.'

There was no discussion after that about what to do with her money.

Di and I talked formally and awkwardly because the questions we had for each other couldn't be shared in front of our parents. She told me she'd got chocolates and perfumes for me.

27 January 2003

I felt light-headed and thought I would pass out because of the stress. Would he try to kiss me? Would he be the first man whose hands I hold? Would he be the first man who touches me that way? Over the past few days, these nagging thoughts had refused to leave me. If everything failed and I was married to him, without my consent, or with consent exacted under trying circumstances, would every time he . . . sleeps with me be rape?

The clock moved inordinately fast. Having had enough of my dilly-dallying, excuses and ruses, Meghnad had asked Buaji and Mumma permission to take me out for a movie. He had assured them awkwardly that he wouldn't lay a finger on me, which I knew was a white lie. He hadn't told Buaji and Mumma which movie he was taking me to, but he had whispered it in my ears before he left.

'*Jism*,' he had said, his voice lingering at the *s*. Had we not been in the living room, he would have slipped his hand under my T-shirt right then.

I hadn't told Mumma and Papa about the choice of movie or his veiled intention.

Last night, Mumma had desperately suggested to me ways on how to get out of the whole thing. 'You don't have to go if you don't want to. Dip your legs overnight in cold water and you will have a cold.'

'I will have to go,' I had said.

'But he's Meghnad, beta. You know how he is.'

'He's just a boy. Nothing I can't handle,' I said.

Mumma hovered around all morning to see how I was doing.

'When's he coming?' asked Mumma.

'At four,' said Buaji and asked her to make her a cup of tea. When Mumma left, Buaji came and sat next to me. She pushed into my hands what I thought was money, but were two movie tickets instead. Prabhat Cinema. 4 p.m.

'He called me to get the tickets,' said Buaji and then added after a long pause. 'You're a big girl now. So . . .'

'So?'

'He would want things, things that boys want. Don't act so innocent,' she said conspiratorially.

There's no reason why I should have been horrified with this act of Buaji. But I stared at her, stunned.

'Don't let him do everything,' said Buaji, her eyes glinting. 'He will think we didn't teach you anything. Also, say no to everything and then . . . a little . . . just a little . . . you don't want him to think you are . . .'

I didn't slap her though she thoroughly deserved it. Her training of me as an escort was rudely interrupted by the ringing of the phone.

She picked up the receiver and talked with a smiling face at first, and then expressed regret, and then said, 'Oh never mind. Any other day is fine. No, no, don't worry about the tickets at all! Ah, it's fine, beta. Don't worry.'

She disconnected.

Before disappearing into her room, she said as if it was my fault, 'He's not coming. Some miscreant slashed all his car tires with a knife.'

Mumma, who had been listening to everything, came trotting out, smiling, and said, 'There's a god after all, I think.'

I smiled back at her, knowing full well this was a small delay after which he would be back to his despicable self.

'You can't be sitting home. Go, watch the movie. It's on Buaji's expense. That doesn't happen very often, does it?'

'Come!' I squealed.

Mumma and I watched the embarrassing movie together. The steamy scenes made both of us squirm in our seats. We heaved a sigh of relief when the movie ended.

'Aren't you coming home?' Mumma asked.

'I need to go to the institute real quick,' I said.

Raghu was working on his notes when I reached. I asked him, 'Raghu? Did you slash Meghnad's tyres?'

Raghu looked at me for a bit and smiled.

'I wanted to, but your Papa didn't allow me to. It was all his idea. He did it himself.'

30 January 2003

I don't want to jinx it . . . I don't want to jinx it . . . I don't want to jinx it.

Between yesterday and today, three more students enrolled at BCC and paid for three months in advance, taking the total to nine students. I clutched the bundles of money and wept softly.

'It's only money,' Raghu said and then shut his mouth when I threw him a murderous look.

'Fine, fine, let me make you some coffee. I have found a new way to do it off the internet.'

'No, no, once I come back. We need a lot more students to enrol,' I said. 'I'm going to the English–language school to distribute flyers. Put the money in the box.'

'You can take a little with you. Get something for your Mumma and Papa.'

'Absolutely not. We need to get two more heaters for the class, maybe a water dispenser too. Mumma and Papa aren't going to accept anything anyway,' I said. 'Will you be here when I return?'

'I think so,' he said.

When I got back, Raghu was bent over a bunch of books, poring over three of them, scribbling on two different notebooks. These were the books we had filched off libraries and bookstores, books that there was no way any of the students who came to us would spend money on or even understand.

'There's a lot of drivel in these books, just filtering them out for the students,' he said when he saw me.

'But they take notes, don't they?'

Raghu nodded. 'But writing everything down is a distraction. Everyone starts to concentrate on just noting whatever is on the board. Instead, we can just give them this and they can spend more time understanding it.'

I flicked through his carefully spaced and beautifully written notes.

'It's a first draft,' he said like a novelist. 'I am going to cut more stuff that's not needed.'

'This is amazing! This way I can tell the parents they don't have to get these expensive books! Instead, they can pay us for the notes. It will be like a correspondence course.'

'I was thinking of including this as part of the fee—'

'No!' I snapped. 'There's nothing we will do for free. They are getting a brilliant teacher for already too little, nothing else.'

'Harsh.'

'Will these guys have a better future in your hands?'

He shrugged, not wanting to blow his own trumpet, but I knew it was true. It had barely been ten days but the parents are inordinately happy. Never had they seen their kids pick up books on their own.

'Shut up and tell me how I can help,' I said. 'That is, if you need any help.'

'Yes, lots in fact,' he said and pointed me towards a bunch of books. 'Open that one . . .'

For the next three hours, we worked without taking a break, and by the time we ended we were exhausted, and yet we found ourselves smiling.

1 February 2003

It was my fault that it was late by the time I got home. I had just stepped into the house when my arm was grabbed by Karan Bhaiya. Before I could make sense of things, I was dragged to the living room where everyone was waiting for me. The negative energy in the room immediately enveloped me. I stood there knowing something seismic had shifted.

Dadaji got up, and without a word, slapped my father like he was a six-year-old. Papa stumbled and fell backwards.

'Saala, langda!' shouted Dadaji.

Dadaji went back to where he had been sitting. He stared at Mumma, not deigning low enough to hit a lower-caste woman.

'You two knew, didn't you? Your daughter is getting into business without your knowledge? You want me to believe that? Receptionist, my foot!' Buaji growled at Papa. 'That's what's her mother tried to tell me! That she's a receptionist. Which receptionist in the world goes around asking parents to join her coaching institute! Begging!'

It was my turn. Buaji came and grabbed me by my hair. Mumma and Papa moved ever so slightly, but Dadaji stopped them with a furious stare.

Buaji slapped me. 'Look at her! The gall. Look at how she's looking at me!' She then spat on me. 'It's our fault. No, no, it's our fault. There's your other sister sleeping for money, isn't she? Sending you money from there! She was always like that! All you women, the same. *RANDIYAN*!'

'BUAJI!'

'Shouting at me, huh?' scoffed Buaji. My reply had struck somewhere deep. 'This is what we get for keeping your father alive, for trying to give you a future. We are so proud of you!'

Then she grabbed me by my hand and started to drag me towards her room. 'Why are you staying in your room, huh? Come to ours! Throw us out! That's what you want, isn't it?'

Fufaji chimed in, 'Ask her what she was doing with him in his flat.'

Karan Bhaiya lied through his teeth, 'I can't go to college any more because of her, Papa. You should see how they look at me.'

Anshuman Bhaiya joined in, 'We should go teach that boy a lesson.'

'NO ONE IS GOING ANYWHERE,' said Buaji strictly. 'She's going to get married to Meghnad and that's the end of it. I'm not going to risk that, do you get me?'

Karan Bhaiya and Anshuman Bhaiya nodded like puppies.

'As for you,' Buaji grabbed my hair again and said, 'you are going to stay in the room till Meghnad comes and gets you. Do you hear me? You sleep in there, you shit in there, you bathe in there! You don't leave the room . . . and then you go to that Meghnad who will teach you how women should behave.'

She looked at me, her lips twisting into an angry, evil smile.

'NOW GO—'

Her words were cut short by Sumitra whose voice we had begun to forget. 'She will work, Didi.'

'What?' said Buaji, more shocked than anything.

'She's going to work,' said Sumitra again, her voice steeling a bit.

'GO INSIDE,' said Buaji. 'HOW DARE YOU meddle in this, you lying—'

'Buaji. I am not the only one to lie. We have all lied about something or the other, haven't we?' asked Sumitra.

'WHAT ARE YOU TALKING ABOUT?'

'You know,' said Sumitra, and looked at Manish Chachu.

A few tense seconds passed. Silence. Glances were exchanged, fists unclenched.

The more the silence prevailed, the clearer it became that Manish Chachu's secret wasn't just his own. My eyes darted around the room and I realized that it was only the dimwits Karan Bhaiya and Anshuman Bhaiya who hadn't caught on. Manish Chachu stood unwaveringly, looking at no one and nothing. It looked as if Sumitra and Manish Chachu had talked about this. That a day would come when Sumitra would not stay silent and neither would Manish Chachu and that they would use this card against the family. Which shocked me because they were using this card for me.

'What do you mean?' demanded Buaji, her voice a curious mix of fear and anger.

'You know, Didi, what I mean. What we only know, everyone will know tomorrow and Manish will stand by the truth.'

Buaji looked at Manish Chachu and waited for him to catch her gaze, but Manish Chachu stood there, firm and unshaken.

'What is she talking about?' asked Karan Bhaiya.

Buaji gritted her teeth and stared down Karan Bhaiya and Anshuman Bhaiya. Karan Bhaiya and Anshuman Bhaiya looked over at Manish Chachu. Anshuman Bhaiya was the one to realize it first. He nudged his brother and let his hand fall effeminately. Anshuman Bhaiya put two and two together, disgust and disbelief writ large on his face.

Sumitra spoke again, 'I won't speak of it if we go on about our lives. You let her do what she's doing right now. She will tell Meghnad that she's working as a receptionist in that business, and that will be the end of it.'

Buaji snapped, 'Papa will not let that place run. You know what he did to bhai when he dared to break away from the—'

Sumitra interrupted Buaji, her voice firm but polite, 'Raghu Ganguly is a Brahmin name. Even if it were not, I don't think the parents who want their children to enter IIT really care. Things have changed in the last twenty years, Didi.'

I was right, there had been a seismic shift. Mumma, Papa and me stood frozen in our places as a compromise was struck.

Buaji stormed off, saying, 'Let her do whatever she wants to. In a few months, she will be someone else's problem.' She clearly wasn't counting on the tuition centre to be our escape plan. It hadn't crossed her mind yet. For her it was ludicrous that Mumma and Papa would give up their inheritance and an opportunity to start a new life for an upstart, puny business.

We all trudged back to our rooms, still in disbelief.

We are all still awake.

There's pin-drop silence. We are straining to hear the opening and closing of doors.

All I can think of is Dadaji's burning eyes as Sumitra spills the secret.

Would they actually . . . would they. . . I will write it down. Would they kill her? They are disgusting, low-life scum, they would have thought about it, but are they smart enough to pull off something like that?

No, they aren't.

It's too much of a risk. They wouldn't dare.

Mumma whispered later at night, 'This peace will be short-lived. If something happens . . . call your sister, run to her.' She ran her fingers over my face lovingly. 'Your didi is earning enough for the two of you. I see no other option.'

'I won't run. Either I give you what you need or Meghnad will.'

2 February 2003

I had just entered my lane when I saw his car. From close up, I could see his fist was clenched too tightly around the steering wheel, his eyes bloodshot, and his mouth twisted in a snarl. My heart thumped. But it seemed like he already knew about BCC. And why not, he had two of his best friends and chamchas living under the same roof as me. 'Meghnad Jiju, Meghnad Jiju', is all I've heard from their mouths these days. He opened the car door for me.

'Your bua has already given me permission,' he scoffed.

I stepped inside the car, my bag firmly in front of me.

'Has he touched you?' he asked.

'What are you saying?'

'I AM ASKING, HAS HE TOUCHED YOU?!' he said, screaming this time.

'I am not understanding you.'

He slammed his fist on the steering wheel and shouted, 'DO YOU TAKE ME TO BE A FOOL! THAT MAN YOU WORK FOR! THAT TUITION GUY WHO WATCHED THE MOVIE WITH YOU!'

He turned towards me, grinding his fingers against his palm, the muscles of his neck pulsating. I knew I was going to get punched in the face today. That's what men do. Desire us and then leave us battered enough to repel everyone. As I stared at him, I wondered what he would leave me with. A couple of broken teeth? A broken nose? A wrecked spirit for certain.

'You think I wouldn't know? Huh? You don't know how many people know me here! Salaam *tokte hain* (they salute me) the people in half the shops here. I didn't want to believe those people when they said they saw you with a man outside the theatre. NOW WILL YOU TELL ME OR—'

His left hand was in the air, my face smack in the middle of the trajectory. Not even his right hand. A left-hand slap is not just about anger, it's anger and ownership. The aggressor doesn't even care if he gets it right the first time, he can try again. I wanted to swing out of the way, but I kept staring at his hand. For the most part, I wanted to be him. Powerful and fearless. How must that feel?

The hand didn't come down. My benevolent fiancé decided to give me a chance to explain myself.

I scrambled for an explanation. I said, 'When he bumped into me outside the movie hall, I couldn't say no.' The tears came. 'I can't believe you would spy on me or think I could be like . . .'

'Why wouldn't I spy on you? Huh? YOU DARE TO TAKE UP A JOB WITHOUT ASKING ME! You think your brothers won't tell me about your job!'

Those assholes.

Driven into a corner, I did the only thing that works with men like Meghnad—be submissive. I started to cry. Screaming and bawling, my entire body heaving like I was having a seizure. It's not hard to conjure up tears when you're in front of the man who's always a moment away from violence.

'*OYE! RONA BAND KAR KUTTIYA!* (Stop crying, bitch!),' he shouted.

I matched his volume with my piercing cries.

'STOP CRYING, WHAT'S YOUR PROBLEM!'

Between sobs, I said, 'I wanted to make . . . make you . . . proud. Earn some money for you, jaanu.'

'What? What nonsense are you talking about?'

'You . . . you're doing so much for my family, jaanu, and I can do nothing for you . . .' I stammered, crying into my palms.

'OK, just stop crying, Advaita. ENOUGH.'

I blew into the handkerchief he gave me and stuttered to a stop.

'You don't have to do this nonsense, OK,' said Meghnad. 'What the hell do you think my family will make of it? I'm making my jaanu work? I can't give you the money or what?'

'It's not about the money. It's about me doing something special for you.'

He rolled his eyes.

I elicited a fresh batch of tears and held his hand. 'Please, jaanu. I want to take care of you too. I want to be a good jaanu, your *shona* wife.'

His face scrunched up in pity. Like I had hoped against hope, he found this cute. 'All you girls are just silly. Fine, jaanu, you can work,' he said, and then added after a pause, 'But I want to see him first. And as soon as possible.'

7 February 2003

Raghu and I were waiting for him at Countdown.

'Should we order something?' asked Raghu. 'A boss meeting his employee's fiancé won't wait for the fiancé to order.'

'You're not my boss.'

'For today I am,' he said and ordered two Cokes.

Meghnad came just as the order did, and he made a big show of his entrance. He shook the cashier's hand, shook the owner's hand, then made sure people saw him and acknowledged him before he took a seat with us.

'So you're him,' he said. 'Raghu Ganguly.'

Raghu changed in an instant. The nonchalant, lost look in his eyes was swiftly replaced by a cold stare and boredom. His face screamed that this was a waste of time.

'And you're getting married to her. I forgot your name,' he said in a newsreader's tone, impassionate and matter of fact.

'You would have known if you were from this city, but you are not. I'm Meghnad. You're from Delhi from what I hear.'

Raghu stared at him, and stayed silent for a long time. He wanted the conversation firmly in his hands and making Meghnad wait for his answers was how he was doing it.

'Correct.'

'Why did you come here? From a big city like that? You were in some *locha* (trouble), I'm sure,' said Meghnad and asked what I knew he wouldn't get an answer for. 'What did you do? Accident? Beat up someone? What are you running away from?'

Raghu stayed silent again, and said, leaning forward, 'Death.'

Meghnad's eyes grew wide, and then he slammed the table in delight. 'I knew it! It's in your eyes. What? What happened? Drove over a pedestrian? Or a motorcyclist?'

'Forget I said that.'

'OK, fine,' said Meghnad. 'We won't get into it. Let's get to the point.' He leaned forward, and looked menacingly at an unaffected Raghu.

'We should.'

'So, she's working for you, but as you know, she's mine. She doesn't want the money. What you are paying, I can give her twice that. I can buy out your entire thing. I'm carrying more in my pocket. What she's doing is passing time, OK. OK?'

'Hmmm . . .'

'So it will be better if you don't make her work too much. Is that clear? *Warna ladke bahut hai mere paas.* (Otherwise, there are a lot of men at my beck and call.)'

Raghu didn't answer. Instead, he sipped on his Coke.

Meghnad continued with a smile, 'And anyway, I will have an eye on you.'

Raghu answered, his voice as cold as steel, 'If you'll be spending that much time on me, do send a few students my way. They won't be disappointed. We are the best in town.' He slurped through to the end of his Coke noisily. 'I better be going. My students are waiting for me,' he said and got up. 'Can you take care of the bill?'

Meghnad looked surprised, but he accepted. Perhaps he liked it that Raghu had accepted his superiority.

'He seems fine,' said Meghnad. 'But if he so much as looks at you differently, let me know. I will gouge his eyeballs.'

Raghu was still at the tuition centre when I got there. His class had stretched over to two hours from one, and the parents of the students were waiting outside. They had been watching silently as their sons nodded and asked questions. I told the parents to recommend our coaching institute to other parents around them. It's a lost cause, though. IIT preparation is a zero-sum game and no parent is going to help anyone else's kids.

After the classes, we sat down and started making notes afresh.

11 February 2003

It was too early for Karan Bhaiya and Anshuman Bhaiya to be up and about. So I was surprised when I saw them turn sneakily around the corner on the scooter, talking in hushed tones, and their shirts in tatters. I hid like I have been doing for the past few days. The truce at the Vaids, negotiated on the basis of Manish Chachu's sexuality, seemed fragile and I wanted to not exist for Buaji, Dadaji or anyone for that matter.

Everyone has been walking on eggshells, trying not to step over each other's toes, and remind each other of the uneasy compromise. Of all the people, Karan Bhaiya, the paragon of masculinity, is hurt the most. Almost as if being homosexual is worse than being from a lower caste. He has been treating Manish Chachu worse than even my mother. He has been walking out of everywhere Chachu is, refusing to touch anything that Chachu touches as if he's some leper, and even addressing him by his first name. Yesterday he had even gone as far as to say to Sumitra, 'Chachi, you should have waited a few more years. I would have taken care of you.' Buaji had slapped Karan Bhaiya, but he hadn't backed down. It's as if Manish Chachu's homosexuality was chipping away at his own manliness.

I climbed over the gate and hid behind the electric board and watched them trudge in with the scooter.

'That madarchod! You said Bengalis can't fight for shit,' said Karan Bhaiya.

'We will see him the next time,' Anshuman Bhaiya said, limping.

As they came closer, their bloodied noses and split lips came into focus.

'I told you we should have taken a rod. One swing and—'

Anshuman Bhaiya scoffed, 'And what? Kill that madarchod? Are you out of your mind?'

'We could have scared him, made him leave town,' said Karan Bhaiya.

'Don't tell anyone about it,' said Anshuman Bhaiya.

Then they disappeared inside the house, wiping their faces on their torn, dirty shirts. I turned on my heel and ran.

My heart only stopped thumping when I saw Raghu at the coaching institute, showing no signs of having been in a no-holds-barred fight with my brothers. He looked up nonchalantly when he saw me at the door and said, 'I'm fine.'

He looked fine, a far cry from the battered faces and ego that Karan Bhaiya and Anshuman Bhaiya had returned with.

'I had a cricket bat. One of the students had left it back,' he said, smiling.

'Show me your face,' I said.

There were bruises and cuts, but he had already neatly bandaged them.

'I'm sorry,' I said.

'It wasn't in your hands, was it? You brother are class acts.'

'God knows what they were trying to achieve.'

'Don't confront your brothers regarding this. We have a good thing going. You don't want to jinx that. We need to just concentrate on the work ahead. Just a few more good months ahead of us and we will achieve what we want.'

I felt ashamed at what had happened and wanted to set things right. Raghu only made it harder by not being offended at all.

He continued, 'We don't have the time or the energy for this. There's a lot of work to be done. I'm thinking of adding

Hindi too. Would you able to teach that? Eighth to tenth standard?'

'Without a sweat.'

We got back to work.

17 February 2003

The morning seemed like it was a new beginning to my life. There was sunshine and good tea and warm hugs and cosy things and love and everything I had ever dreamed of. When I got to the coaching institute in the morning, there were five sets of parents waiting patiently for me. FIVE. They did annoy me when they demanded to talk to the teacher or the owner of the coaching institute and not some girl. I had half a mind to send them packing, but they had seemed eager to part with their money, and money wins all.

'I own and run this place,' I told them and saw their faces immediately fall. They did a double-take, and maybe wondered if they had misheard about the teacher, the institute, and if this was all a scam. A couple of them even stepped back, unsure of whether they had come to the right coaching institute. I kept watching them, seeing them squirm in doubt, and said, 'You're here for admissions, aren't you? I can take you through the fee structure and the class schedule if you want to see it.'

'Beta, you're—'

'Never had the resources to prepare to go to a good college, but you do. Let me tell you how we can go about it.'

The parents, now feeling much better, stepped forward and sat on the chairs. The rest came naturally to me. Out of habit, some wanted to negotiate, but it was their fault that they had put me in a nasty mood earlier. As they filled up the forms, I wanted to raise my hand, snap my fingers, and ask Chhotu to give the parents celebratory tea. I was still toying with the idea when Raghu walked in, carrying a tray brimming with plastic cups of steaming tea.

'We will take good care of the children,' he said to the parents.

'He's going to teach your children,' I said and took out the notes that we had prepared, now cyclostyled and bound beautifully. 'These are personalized notes for just our students. You can't get them outside in the market or buy them separately. It gives a distinct edge to our students.'

The parents nodded dutifully.

'We also want the parents to play a more active role in this. We don't want you to pressure the kids, but to share their burden. Preparing for IIT needs a calm mind, so we would need you to sit with your child, discuss his studies with him and encourage him,' I said.

Raghu rolled his eyes.

The parents were taking mental notes. The anxiousness they'd exhibited had slowly given way to a certain understanding of the process and respect for this one-room– one-teacher institution.

That's when an overtly smart parent asked Raghu, 'Have you taught anyone who has cleared IIT?'

Raghu lied skilfully, surprising even me. 'I have taught in Delhi. But that market is all money, no soul. I didn't want to get stuck in the rut, so I came here so that I can genuinely help people. You can see why our fee structure is so generous.'

The parent nodded.

'I have all the details and I will call you once I make their time table,' I told them. 'You have to tell your kids that from this moment on, they have to put all their energy into what we teach here and not what happens in school. Can you do that?'

They nodded.

When they left, I exulted and jumped across the tables and did a little happy dance, while Raghu sat silently, watching and smiling.

'I'm sorry,' I said. 'I thought I was dancing in my head.'

He said, 'It was beautiful.'

I ran straight to the PCO after the classes ended and called Divya Di. I must have waited an hour, and when the phone finally rang and I was called, my knees were shaking and my fingers trembled with excitement.

'YOU WOULDN'T KNOW WHAT JUST HAPPENED!' I screamed over the phone.

'Same! You go first!'

And I told her breathlessly about the five new students, about the new fee structure I sold them, and how much money that meant for us.

'What is it that you wanted to tell me?' I asked her, still dizzy with excitement.

Divya Di's voice faltered a little.

'You need to hear me out completely and think with an open mind,' she said.

'Spit it out, Di.'

'Advaita, you know Meghnad is not going to let you be,' she said. 'I mean what you're doing . . . it's great. But I know how he is. He's not going to let you live your own life.'

'What do you mean?'

'Do you think Buaji will keep quiet about you being just a receptionist when you walk out of the house and marriage? How difficult is it for him to get a few guys and wreck the institute? Scare the kids and the parents away? Have you thought about that? It's not safe for you there.'

'Please, Di, you're overreacting.'

'Advaita, if you reject him, you can't stay in Dehradun any longer. You can't even stay in Delhi!' said Di.

'Please, Di. Of course I can!' I protested, my voice breaking.

'Don't be a fool, Advaita. Calm down and listen to me!'

'What's the worse he will do?'

'He's not going to let you breathe. I don't know why Mumma and Papa are encouraging you in this,' said Divya Di.

'I am disconnecting the call. I don't have time for this nonsense.'

'Advaita, listen to me—'

'WHAT!' I shouted.

'Listen carefully,' she said. 'I have got through the first round of the Emirates—'

'I DON'T CARE!'

'Will you please listen!?' she snapped. 'It's an airline based out of Dubai. I will have to clear two more rounds and a medical test, and they will give me a job as an air hostess. It's good money, and will also give me a place to live. So here's what you, Mumma and Papa are going to do.'

'WE WON'T DO ANYTHING!'

'Send Mumma's and Papa's passports to me. Come to Delhi and gets yours made on *tatkal*. I will get your visas done, and all of you are coming with me as soon as I clear the rounds.'

'I AM NOT!'

'You will do exactly what I ask you to do!'

'Why would I leave everything and come there! For the first time I've got something going in my life! You do whatever, but I'm not leaving and neither are Mumma and Papa!'

'You're really *that* stupid, are you?'

Tears streamed down my face. 'What if you don't make it? Aren't there two more rounds?'

'I will make it, Advaita, you know that.'

'YOU NEVER KNOW! YOU ARE NOT THAT GOOD ALSO!'

When I got hack home, Mumma asked if I had had a word with Di today and I told her that I hadn't. I won't take the escape route she had found. I had found my own, and Mumma and Papa were going to stay with me.

20 February 2003

They didn't react at all. They just stared at me looking for words that wouldn't hurt me.

'Mumma,' I said. 'I don't want to leave this. For the first time I am getting somewhere and . . . I don't want to run away from this.'

Mumma and Papa looked at each other and sighed.

Mumma said, 'Advaita beta, we know. I understand, but you have to think clearly about this. Whatever you two decide, we will go along with it.'

Papa added, his voice shaking, 'Mumma is right. And the decision doesn't have to be made right now. There are still two rounds left, aren't there?'

'My passport needs to be made right now. If she gets though, the visas need to be stamped,' I murmured.

Mumma and Papa exchanged a look that lasted for the blink of an eye and then Mumma spoke, 'Look there's nothing wrong in getting that made. We will not use it if we don't need it.'

If only they had slapped me and told me that they had taken the decision for me, I could have been rightly furious at them, and stomped out of here.

'Mumma. You're on Di's side.'

'Advaita, it's not like that.'

'There's nothing to be scared of!' I said. 'What is the most that will happen? Dadaji will throw us out, Meghnad and his family will throw a few tantrums, but sooner or later, they will let us be! I will take care of everything.'

'Is that what you really think?' asked Mumma.

'Yes,' I lied.

'If that's what you think, then that's what you should do,' said Mumma. 'I will tell Divya that we won't come.' She ran her fingers over my face and hugged me.

Now as I write this, it's slowly starting to sink in. Di is going to stay in Dubai. Not for a day, for a week or for a month, but for as long as she holds her job. She's going to be an NRI. An NRI?! And we would be too if we leave with her. We would be staying there. It would be a different life, away from our past and this city which hasn't given us anything but unbridled pain and humiliation.

Am I being selfish? Would I have expected Di to fall in line if I were in her place? Yes, I would have, but Di wouldn't have agreed. Or maybe she would have. She's ready to give up her modelling dream for this. She was so close. She could have been Miss India if she tried.

But it's so hard to even think of abandoning BCC. It's finally started feeling like . . . home. Is that why Mumma and Papa never attempted to run away? Was it fear or was it a sick form of nostalgia? Given a choice, would I choose to come back to my home town, to the house I grew up, no matter how horrible the situation was?

And what about Raghu? What do I do with him? Just leave him in Dehradun at the mercy of Meghnad and my brothers? For the first time since I met him, he doesn't seem lost or broken. He looks happy. After drawing him out of the hole he was living in, how could I abandon him, my best friend?

21 February 2003

Di didn't take the news lightly. She screamed and shouted and bawled over the phone and threatened to smash my head against a wall, and drag me with her to Dubai if I didn't come along willingly.

'Would you have done the same?' I asked her.

'Of course, you idiot! I would have done the same,' she shouted. 'I would have packed up and left that very second. Listen to me, you dimwit, I am going to take Mumma and Papa away. If you try to stop me, you're going to get it. If you want to stay in that wretched town, with those wretched people, it's your call. You're welcome to destroy your life, but I am taking Mumma and Papa with me. You're now going to go back home like a good girl and tell Mumma and Papa to send their passports to me, OK? And you will get yours made. Am I clear?'

'I am doing no such thing!' I said.

'I'm going to slap you hard!' she said. 'Look, Advaita, I don't have time for this, OK—'

'Neither do I,' I snapped. 'And unlike you, I run a business here!'

'What has gotten into you? Are you absolutely out of your mind? Wait. Wait! I know what it is. You're in love with that boy, aren't you?' she said.

'No!'

'Of course you are! You are in love with him,' she said.

'I am not, Di, and you need to—'

'I have nothing to say to you, Advaita,' she said. 'I don't have time for this. You're the last person I want to fight with. If you can't see that this is the best opportunity we will ever get to run away from our previous lives, I won't waste time convincing you because clearly you have more trust in a fucking boy than your own sister.'

'I don't!'

'Well, you do. Didn't you say you would know that you're in love when you ditch your family for a boy? Well, that time has come and you have picked a side!'

'NONSENSE. What if you lose your job—'

She banged the phone down.

When I got back home, I sat Mumma and Papa down and told them of my decision. They didn't have to suffer because of me.

'There's no reason you should stay here,' I told them. 'I will find a place to live once you leave with Divya Di. You deserve a better life.'

Mumma looked at me strangely. 'Ah!' she mocked me. 'Deserve a better life and what-not? Look at how your daughter is talking.'

Papa started to laugh too and slapped his thighs hysterically.

'Where did you learn to speak like this?' she sniggered. 'We are not going anywhere. If you stay here then, so will we.'

'Kids these days,' said Mumma to Papa, 'they think they are so smart.'

Papa laughed and mimicked my words, calling me cute.

'What's so wrong in what I said?' I asked Mumma, indignant.

'You will know when you have kids of your own,' said Papa.

'I have been hearing this nonsense for years now. I will know when I have kids! If your brain turns to mush when one has kids, I don't want any!' I said and stormed out of the house.

Raghu had just finished the last class when I entered. He looked up and said, 'Look who's here. I thought you had left me.'

I flinched for a moment. It was as if he knew everything that was going on.

'I would never do that,' I said. 'There's something I need to talk to you about.'

'Tell me. We have time, and I have just put the pot on.' He smiled. God. That smile. I couldn't possibly take that away from him.

I tried to be as dispassionate as I could about the entire Divya Di drama so as to not influence him. But even as I was speaking, I saw the light drain out of his eyes, as if he was already imagining the institute shutting down, or us no longer being friends, and separated by miles of land, water and desert. He tried not to show all this on his face, but it did. He was disappointed, sad, but most of all, he felt abandoned.

'I think you should go too,' he said after hearing me out. Despite the obvious disappointment, he sounded like he meant it.

'It will be everything you ever wanted,' he said. 'You can do something there. I have heard there's plenty of work in Dubai.' He smiled a disingenuous smile and it was the first time I had seen him do that. It was pathetic.

'I am not going to just leave you in the lurch.'

He cut me off.

'Listen, Advaita. I'm going to stay here and run this. Maybe not as well without you for support, but I am not going to leave the students midway. And you know, you can come back when things cool down, can't you?'

'I wanted you to make me stay. I don't want to go.'

'But you know you have to, right?'

'You can't possibly think that?' I asked.

'It's your best option. It's a safe option, and you should take it,' he said.

'I can't leave my best friend,' I said.

'What kind of a best friend would I be if I didn't see that it's the best decision for you? It's the least I can do for you.'

'It feels wrong.'

'You came to be my friend at my most cynical moment in life, when I only saw the worst in everyone, when I firmly believed that all I will ever get from people is hurt. At a time when I believed I would just grind down minute after minute, day after day, till the end of time, just exist, live. I was broken.'

'And I fixed you?' I asked with a sad smile.

'Let's say you put a Band-Aid over the thing. Don't give yourself that much credit too.'

We both chuckled pitifully.

23 February 2003

Raghu has been trying his hardest to pretend like nothing has changed between us. The more normal he acts the antsier I get.

He has assumed that the decision has been made. The conversations have become hollow. They exist only to fill time. It's as if we are already at the railway station, the train's about to leave, and there's nothing left to say that hasn't been said before. I see bits of the Raghu I had seen when I first met him coming back. There are times I see him stare vacantly at the books, and when I point it out, he brushes it away. I don't blame him, I would have been much worse had I been in his place.

Every time I have tried to start a conversation, he has shut me up, telling me that I shouldn't waiver from what I had decided.

But what have I decided?

Mumma and Papa are on the opposite side of the spectrum. They believe that I have decided to stay. We talk about BCC, but not about Di's new job, her life-changing move to another country.

I haven't called Di, and from what I can make out, Mumma and Papa haven't talked to her either.

The last person I wanted to see tonight was Meghnad but there he was, and why not, he had paid in full for me. I had just mopped the floor and wanted to doze for a while when he rang the bell and came ambling in before anyone could open the door. It was eleven in the night.

His feet were unsteady and he stumbled twice, knocking over a vase.

Buaji and Fufaji smiled immediately, lighting up like thousand-watt bulbs.

'Beta, careful,' Buaji said.

But the closer he got to us, the surer we were that he was drunk. His eyes were bloodshot, and saliva dribbled down his lips. He struggled to keep his eyes open. A small bottle peeked out from his pocket. He reeked of sweat and alcohol. Three buttons of his shirt were open, and he had dragged in mud with his boots.

'We will watch a movie. Me and my fiancée! Right now!' he announced, trying his best to mask how drunk he was. He kept swaying around the room trying to make the world stop spinning.

Mumma and Papa came running out and saw Meghnad stumbling around and uselessly trying to stand straight and act sober.

'Hello! Hello! My in-laws! I love my in-laws, pranam, pranam,' he said and touched Mumma and Papa's feet, almost falling over.

'Hi,' he said and looked at me and winked. 'Shall we go? I have big plans.' He chuckled. 'It will be a lot of fun!'

Just as he turned, Papa clutched his hand firmly. 'You should sit with us and eat,' said Papa.

Meghnad slapped his stomach and said, 'Papa! I knew you will say that, but I am full. I am here to take my to-be wife. Can I do that? I need to tell her I love her! I need to love her! Is that not what I am paying for!' He laughed playfully again. It was all a joke to him. I wondered how much of this he would remember the next day.

'You should sit with us,' said Papa, his voice harsh and stern.

Meghnad now realized that Papa was serious, and his grip harder than any man would have dared to hold him. He pried his arm free and said, 'I thought I was getting married into a good family. But what use is marrying into a family who can't maintain good graces. She's my fiancée!' He glared at Papa.

'She can't go,' said Papa.

'Papa, *par vo to parayi ho gayi hai* (she's not yours any more),' said Meghnad playfully.

He then turned towards me and smiled. Even Buaji and Fufaji were at a loss as to what to make of all this. Karan Bhaiya and Anshuman Bhaiya stood there, feet bolted to the ground, conflicted. Karan Bhaiya even took a step forward to stop Meghnad, but Anshuman Bhaiya held his hand, not out of malice, but knowing that their words wouldn't stop Meghnad. Even to them, Meghnad's actions were reprehensible.

Meghnad took a few steps towards me when the words escaped my mouth. 'I am having my period. The first day.'

'What do you mean?'

I saw his face fall, his lips curve in a grimace, his eyebrows burrow, and a sense of disgust cloud his face. He stood there looking at me, and said, 'Ah, again!' he said, and turned away from me. 'Such a waste of good alcohol!'

Without a single word, he turned to leave. All of us watched him, flabbergasted, as he stumbled a few times before he found the door. We waited for his car to start. But he was too drunk. He slept off at the wheel. Mumma cried herself to sleep holding me. Papa hobbled around the courtyard, just in case Meghnad woke up from his slumber and tried taking me away again.

It's early morning now as I write this. My hands are still trembling, and it feels like I am getting a slight fever. He woke up ten minutes ago and drove off without a second look towards our house. I don't want to write this, but the only thought that kept running in my mind all night was . . . I could have been raped by my fiancé last night. And it would have been just the start. I can't get it out of my mind.

24 February 2003

Mid-afternoon, a hung-over Meghnad and I were at Countdown.

Unashamed, he had come to pick me up at the house. I made tea for him as he sat brazenly in the living room and apologized half-heartedly to Buaji about his drunken behaviour, and Buaji gleefully accepted. He brought flowers for Mumma and Papa and touched their feet. Mumma and Papa wished for his long life.

'If young boys don't do this, then who will?' Buaji had said.

He pestered me to talk to him, and my silence made him angry, as if it was my fault and not his.

'I am not hungry,' I said.

'Oho, don't be like this. It wasn't a big deal.'

'If you say so.'

'How can you be still angry about it? Even your Mumma and Papa were fine with it. You can't still be angry,' he declared and rolled his eyes in frustration.

'Can you drop me home before evening? Mumma and Papa are going to be extremely upset if I am not home by then,' I said.

'Oh c'mon! I was drunk. Couldn't you see that, jaanu?'

'Yes, I know. Everyone knows that.'

'I won't do that again. What else do you want me to do? I said sorry, I don't see what's the big deal! Should I now fall at your feet now, huh?'

'I didn't ask you to do that,' I said.

'We should leave if you're not eating,' he said.

He asked for the bill before I could answer and then led me to his car.

'So you're not going to talk to me?' he asked irritably.

'I need to go to Delhi.' The words just bubbled out of me, unhindered.

'Where did that come from? You're not going anywhere.'

'I have work there,' I said dryly.

'*Dimaag fir gaya hai kya*? (Have you gone mad?) You're not putting a step out of Dehradun.'

We drove around silently. Every few seconds he would look at me, his irritation with me rising every passing second. I couldn't even bring myself to cry today. I just felt pure, distilled hatred for him. No matter how hard he tried to elicit a response, I remained frigid. I didn't say a word, didn't yield an inch. With every passing second, his anger and irritation with me rose. He could have slapped me, but I was ready for it. Ready to get hurt even. It was a little victory to see him try to impatiently break my silence.

'*KYA BAKWAS HAI*! Fine, you can to go to Delhi. But for that, you will have to forgive me for yesterday and smile. OKAY? OKAY? Smile and forgive me!' he said.

'I forgive you.'

'Say it like you mean it,' he growled.

I mustered up a smile and said, 'I forgive you!'

He grinned, easing up. 'You're such a tease, jaanu. I don't see the love. You're just saying the words, shona, you're not feeling them. Feel them and then say them to me.'

'I really forgive you.'

'No, it's still not there, feels like I'm making you do it.'

'I forgive you, jaanu,' I said, as coyly as possible.

'Ah, now that's something. Say that again. You're getting better,' he said and put his hand over mine.

'I forgive you, jaanu,' I said even as the word grated on my tongue.

'It's okay but it's still not there,' he said and clutched my hand even tighter.

He was grinning now, and despite my questions, didn't tell me where we were going. My heart thumped as he drove in circles around Rajpur Road and then parked the car in a relatively deserted spot.

'Why did we stop here?'

'For you to show that you've really forgiven me.' He looked at me and ran his fingers on his face. He said with a smile, 'You know what? I can't wait to get married to you. Then I don't have to come to your house drunk and out of my senses. Then I can love you when I want to,' he said, his eyes glinting.

'Jaanu.' I smiled and he held my hand even tighter. It was about to come. I knew it, it was in his eyes. Spit and bile rose up in my throat even as I tried to smile. His body leaned into mine, his foul breath hung in the air. I fought against my body, trying to not give in to the disgust and the anger welling inside me. And then his lips touched, at first softly, but before I could say or do anything, he thrust his tongue deep inside my mouth. I wondered if he could taste my revulsion; I could taste his naked lust. My eyes were open and so were his. After the first few moments, I closed my eyes and tuned out, thinking of Di, thinking of Delhi, of passports, of watching Dehradun grow tiny from the vantage point of a soaring aircraft, of a house in Dubai. When he was done, he leaned back and wiped his lips, a nasty grin on his face.

'I love you, jaanu,' he said.

He took my hand, looked at me and smirked, and slowly took it to his crotch and kept it there. He kept looking at me, willing me to enjoy it, and I tried to look away, but he held my face and looked on lustfully, enjoying his power over me. My hands clenched into a fist, but he kept rubbing it against his jeans. My body slowly shut down. Tears flowed. At first a trickle. He looked at me first with surprise and then with anger and confusion. Yet, he didn't stop, as if my revulsion and tears were turning him on. I looked away and he kept rubbing my clenched fist over his crotch. A few minutes passed and his body trembled like a dying animal, his eyes rolled, and his legs stretched out. Then he let my hand go.

I stopped crying.

'What happened?'

'Nothing,' I said.

He put his arm around me and said, 'We are getting married. We are allowed these things! Especially now that I am letting you go to Delhi, *itna to banta hai* (this much you owe me). And don't be such a prude. You know you liked it.'

A little while later, I asked him to drop me home, and he did.

He called me thrice in the evening and twice in the night, sometimes repentant but mostly angry, even as I kept telling him in a low, soft, lying tone that I was fine and he didn't need to bother himself with what he did to me.

'You're such a villager! This is 2003!' he screamed on the phone.

The last call was at five in the morning.

25 February 2003

He stared at me in horror. I couldn't bring myself to tell Raghu about what Meghnad did to me in the car yesterday. I just told him that Meghnad had spent a night outside our place two nights ago, sleeping in his car.

'What?' he said, aghast.

I didn't tell him I had stayed up the last two nights thinking what would happen if Meghnad was to come home again, piss drunk. Where would he stop? What would Meghnad do to me?

'It wouldn't have been sex, Advaita. It would have been rape,' he said.

'I was trying not to tell myself that,' I said.

'You know what this means, right?'

'I don't,' I lied.

'There's no time to waste,' said Raghu. 'You have to pick your battles. If your sister doesn't clear the rounds—god forbid—we will have to fight this man, but if she does, you should leave the city. That's what's best for you and your family.'

'I'm tired of hearing that. Of Mumma and Papa hoping I would realize that. Why didn't they tell me that they feared Meghnad would make my life hell even if BCC worked!? I wouldn't even have tried!'

'Hope is a strong emotion, Advaita.'

Like always, my wretched luck was a step ahead of me, beating me, mocking me. I felt stupid sitting there in that room, the smell of fresh paint still there . . . the tables, the chairs, the notes . . . all for nothing.

'You did your best,' said Raghu. 'If anything I wouldn't know where I would be if it were not for you.'

'You're just saying that,' I said.

'I know it seems futile for you that everything you did was worth nothing, but for me it was everything. I look forward to you coming here.'

'But—'

'It won't be the same when you leave.'

'Raghu.'

'I couldn't save you from your fate, but you saved me and that's worth something.'

'Of course it is,' I said. 'But—'

He held my hand and said, 'I let you help me. It's time you let your sister help you. Knowing you, it wouldn't be for long.'

'You think so?'

'Absolutely. You should call your sister,' he said.

'Wouldn't she be waiting for that,' I said. 'She will rub my nose in it for years now.'

Why do men always win? Why do they get away with everything?

27 February 2003

Di didn't rub my nose in it. Instead, she cried her heart out and told me how much she missed me and how it'll be a new beginning for all of us.

'Now make sure you don't screw up,' I said.

'Ha! I won't,' she said with her trademark cockiness.

Mumma and Papa are aware of it too. But they are too nervous about Di making it.

'I will believe it when we are sitting on the plane,' Mumma says that twice every day.

Mumma's and Papa's passports are ready to be sent to Di to get visas stamped on them. We are all supposed to get tourist visas to get into the country and later we will all get permanent visas. It's only I who doesn't have a passport. We all know it's too risky to get one in Dehradun. And there's no way I can go to Delhi to get one made unless Meghnad gives me explicit permission to do so and talks to Buaji about it.

'If we have to run away, let's all leave right now!' I had said yesterday.

'And what if your sister doesn't get through—'

Mumma stopped Papa mid-sentence lest it turn true.

2 March 2003

That bastard was waiting downstairs when I left BCC. I pretended to not see his car and walked straight on. He drove behind me, honking like a madman. I kept walking. He got down and slammed the door and ran towards me.

'Hey? Can't you hear? I have been honking! Am I fucking mad or what?' he grumbled.

I turned to him, my eyes pools of tears, then expressed the requisite surprise and said, 'Mumma has told me not to look at a car that honks at me.'

'You're crying?'

'I am not.'

I wiped my tears. He held me and pulled me close.

'WHO MADE YOU CRY?' he thundered.

'It's nothing,' I said.

'It's not for nothing that my baby is crying. JUST TELL ME! NO ONE MAKES MY JAANU CRY.'

'I was asked to leave my job,' I said softly.

'What? That bastard. How the hell could he do that to you, jaanu?'

'I don't want to get into it. Let's just go, please. He will shout at me again,' I said coyly.

'That madarchod shouted at you?' he said, rolling up his sleeves.

'I told him that you would talk to Buaji about letting me go to Delhi. I know you're busy, jaanu, and you couldn't tell her about you allowing me to go. So I begged Raghu to wait for a day or two for the permission to come, but he shouted at me and asked me to leave the room. He said he has seen dozens of eye-candies like me who have goonda boyfriends.'

It took a few seconds to hit him. 'What did he call me?'

'Nothing—'

He was already charging towards the building.

'MEGHNAD! Stop!'

He stopped and turned towards me, 'I will show him what being a goonda means. *CHAL MERE SAATH* (Come with me).'

He held my hand and let it go only when he entered the room. Raghu looked up and within a flash, Meghnad was at his neck, wringing it with all his might.

Raghu coughed and spluttered.

'*KYA BOL RAHA THA BHE, BETICHOD*! (What were you saying, you daughter fucker!) Repeat it. BOL. Say it again,' he said and loosened his grip.

'But . . . I need . . .'

'LISTEN, YOU PIECE OF SHIT. I CAN SHUT THIS SHOP OF YOURS IN A DAY. *SAMJHA*?'

'What . . . what do you want?'

'She will go to Delhi,' said Meghnad and released his neck. He turned to me. 'You will stay at a guest house of my choosing. I will send a driver from here with the two of you.'

'Listen—'

He swung at Raghu and got him square on the face. Raghu stumbled back, his lips split, mouth bloody.

'ROD *PADEGI AGLI BAAR SAALE* (You will be hit by a rod the next time).'

And that was the end of the discussion. Meghnad stormed off with me in tow.

In the car, he held my hand with both of his, and said, 'If he ever bothers you again, tell me. No one will know who shot him.' He chuckled, his eyes gleaming.

'I am sure he won't cross any lines now.'

'Are you happy now, jaanu?'

I nodded.

He held my face and rubbed his thumb against my lips. 'I am not a bad person, it's people who make me do bad things. Look how angry that boy made me. But you're not like that, you make me happy, jaanu. I will miss you when you are in Delhi.'

'I . . . I will miss you too.'

His thumb was inside my mouth now. I could taste metal and dirt.

He said, 'What we did in the car that day? Once you come back, I will teach you how to do it with your mouth.'

4 March 2003

After Meghnad's expected but surprisingly aggressive outburst against Raghu, things fell into place easily. He came to our house and told us that they needed to send me to Delhi, that he had given his word and his word meant the world to him, as if he was a Rajput prince, and not a petty criminal who had made a fortune out of looting people. Buaji agreed, giggling, telling him that the minute the alliance had been set, I was his to govern. But, hours after he left, Buaji walked around the house like a zombie. Who knows what was going on inside her wicked head?

At some point I heard her complain to Anshuman Bhaiya, 'Did you see how she has ensnared Meghnad with her guile?'

'As long as our deal stands, Mumma, she can go around selling herself the way she wants to that man,' said Anshuman Bhaiya.

When I left the house, Buaji, Karan Bhaiya and Anshuman Bhaiya waved from the gate, looking like ghouls, the light of their eyes lost somewhere. I was in Meghnad's car, and I picked up Raghu on the way. The driver Monty had been asked to keep a strict eye on Raghu.

It wasn't supposed to be a very long drive but the driver, Monty, stopped after every one hour and updated Meghnad wherever he could find a PCO. He wasn't discreet about it.

'Haan, sir. Everything OK, sir. No, sir. They are only talking about the coaching institute.'

The driver, who was by far the largest man I had ever seen, was listening to everything that Raghu and I talked about, as instructed. Needless to say, all we were saying was horseshit, made-up stuff about the education conference, the state of coaching institutes in India and what-not, and to be honest, it was a lot of fun. Soon I dozed off.

When I woke up, I saw Raghu staring out of the window, tears in his eyes. That's when I realized I hadn't asked Raghu even once if he would be OK to go to Delhi, the city that had broken his heart, the city he had run away from. I felt sorry to have dragged him out here. I wanted to talk to him, but Monty kept staring at me through the rear-view mirror.

'It's a hard city, Delhi, isn't it?' I asked.

'Huh?' he broke out of his reverie and turned to me. He nodded softly.

'Will everything be OK? With the conference?'

He sighed and said, 'It will be OK. As long as we complete what we are here for.'

For the rest of the journey, while I slipped in and out of sleep, Raghu gazed outside, the pain slowly engulfing him, visible, tangible, coursing through him like ink on blotting paper. He woke me up when we reached the guest house. I should have been overjoyed at the prospect of seeing my sister and plotting my escape, but I found no happiness in seeing Raghu go through the motions as if someone was wringing every last bit of joy out of him.

The driver and I had adjacent rooms.

'I will see you in the morning,' said Raghu and shook my hand like a boss would.

He then went away. Meghnad had made sure we were in different guest houses.

Three hours later, there was a soft knock on my door. I opened it and there she was. The saviour of the Vaids—Divya

Vaid. She rushed in and quickly closed the door behind her. She hugged me for what seemed like a longer time than she had been away from us, and for as long as her tears dried out.

'I'm staying in the room next to you,' said Divya Di.

She looked fresher, happier. Or was she always this beautiful? We held hands, looking at each other like long-lost lovers.

'You have Mumma and Papa's passports and all your documents?'

I nodded.

Divya Di said, 'I know someone here who can get your passport made in three days.'

'How do you know people in Delhi?'

She smirked. 'The hope of sex makes men do anything. But how did that bastard let you come?'

'Long story,' I said, not wanting to go into the details, or what Meghnad had promised he would *teach* me once this trip ended.

'How are Mumma and Papa?'

'Hopeful,' I said. 'And scared, of course. They don't say it aloud. You know how they are.'

'It will be all right,' said Di. 'We will finally be free, leave everything behind, have a new home.'

She smiled and I hugged her, hope tingling inside both of us. It wasn't safe for her to stay any longer, so she got up to leave.

'How do I see you tomorrow?' she asked.

'Raghu and I will go to Pragati Maidan. I will see you outside Gate No. 5.'

'Done. We have lots of things to do in one day. Make sure you get some sleep.'

She left the room. For the rest of the night we knocked on the headboard in our rooms to remind each other that we were still there, and that it was not a dream. We were indeed going to run away.

I was happy, but I couldn't stop thinking about Raghu . . .

5 March 2003

Monty picked me up sharp at nine. Raghu was already in the back seat, looking even worse than yesterday. It didn't seem like he had bathed, or even slept.

'Are you ready?' I asked him.

He nodded.

'Bhaiya, take us to Pragati Maidan,' I said to Monty.

Monty dropped us at Gate No. 1. He didn't suspect a thing when we entered the grounds where a bunch of conferences and business-y things were happening. Anyone would have believed our lie. We trotted from one hall to another, taking sharp turns, hiding behind pillars and disappearing into stalls to find out if we were being tailed. Once we were sure that no one was tailing us, I told him I needed to go. 'What will you do?'

Raghu looked around and said, 'I will be around.'

'Are you sure?'

'Go do what you have to do.'

'You can come with me if you have nothing to do,' I said.

'Advaita, stop worrying about me,' he said. 'I will go to the canteen and eat something. You have a good day. I will see you at Gate 5?'

I nodded and he walked away from me. But I couldn't turn and leave. I tailed him to see if he was OK.

He didn't go to the canteen. He walked around aimlessly for a bit, bumping into people and apologizing, and he got out of the grounds. Once outside, he haggled with a few auto drivers, settled with one, and left.

'What took you so long? I thought you had been caught,' scolded Di.

'I just . . . nothing. Can we go now?' I asked.

For the rest of the day, we hopped from one dingy office to another, getting affidavits made and stamped, filling up forms and standing in lines. Every now and then, a frown, a shake of the head of the tout would worry me, I would see it all fall apart, and then there would be a loophole waiting to be exploited, people's palms to be greased, and our derailed escape plan would be back on track. It was tense, and I had to remind myself to keep breathing. It was nerve-racking.

Di seemed to know a lot of people on a first-name basis which was strange because it hadn't been long since she had been in the city, and she smiled a lot, the kind of smile I hadn't noticed on her face before.

The last man we met had touched Di's arm, and said, 'It will get done in two days. Don't worry.'

She had smiled exaggeratedly and said, 'Then I will treat you to dinner.'

I have known her long enough, heard enough lies from her to know that this was one too. The man bought into it, his eyes lit up, and he even blushed a little.

We went to her PG where she cooked what I believe were a hundred packets of Maggi. I won't lie. It tasted extraordinary. She regaled me with stories about Dubai and what all we should do together.

'Just let them send the tickets and then we are never coming back,' she said.

For the next hour or so, we revelled in these concocted futures and ate some more and drank some more tea. It was all a bit surreal. Raghu has always told me that the Vaids seemed to live on hope, and that sets us apart, but I never truly believed there would come a day where all our imagined futures will come true. Not in Dehradun, but in a faraway land in Dubai! It was like a fantasy and except for Divya Di who has been to Dubai, it seems a little too much to digest. It felt like the earth would shift and everything would fall apart. This happiness seemed too good, and hence too fragile.

When I got back to the Pragati Maidan grounds, Raghu was waiting for me at the canteen. He looked significantly more tired, which was the exact opposite of what I felt.

I had experienced freedom, and frankly, this freedom tasted like Raghu's tea. Later, Di came to my room, and emboldened by the successes of the last two days, she decided to sleep next to me.

'I want to spend some time with Raghu tomorrow,' I told her.

'Of course. That boy seems to be in love with you. That's the least you can do for him.'

I didn't reply to that.

6 March 2003

We went through the same charade again. If anything, Raghu looked lifeless, even worse than before, as if he was rotting inside. Every time I looked at him, he seemed to have withered a little more.

The driver dropped us off at the gate and we went inside. Raghu told me he would wait for me at the canteen, and then like yesterday, I left the ground. Only this time, I followed him in another rickshaw. It was a long drive from Pragati Maidan, and every time my rickshaw passed his, I saw his dead, sorrowful eyes. He got down outside a posh housing society. He sat on the pavement and lit a cigarette. Twice I wanted to go and ask him what he was doing there, but better sense prevailed and I waited. An hour passed and then two, he finished two packs of cigarettes, just sitting there, looking at a first-floor apartment. Was this where he lived? Or Brahmi?

Then a beautiful dusky girl walked towards where he was sitting, and without a word sat next to him. They didn't look at each other, didn't greet each other, didn't even acknowledge each other's presence. They just sat there like two passengers at a bus stop.

She looked about the same age as Raghu and for the longest time they had nothing to say to each other. They sat there staring at the apartment. I would have believed they were strangers had she not taken a cigarette from him and lit it. A while later, the girl got up and left. And after about half an hour, Raghu got up and turned. I barely ducked in time but not before I caught a glimpse of his miserable, tear-smeared face. He wiped his face with a handkerchief, hailed an auto and left.

My amateurish sleuthing had yielded nothing apart from the image of the apartment I could frame in the fractured timeline of Raghu's life. I was waiting for an auto when someone tapped my shoulder. I turned.

'Who are you?' asked the girl.

It didn't take me long to realize that it was the same girl who had bummed a cigarette off Raghu. She was taller than me, with skin the colour of dark chocolate, and the most melancholic eyes I had ever seen.

'I'm . . . I'm . . . don't tell him,' I blurted out.

'Are you in love with him? Are you the reason he's in Dehradun? He's never in a city for this long,' said the girl.

'Me? No. You're getting it all wrong.'

The girl eyed me distrustfully as if I had encroached into a place I shouldn't have. She looked vicious.

'You're friends with Raghu?' she asked, her voice almost mocking.

'Yes, why?'

'You look nothing like her, not even close.'

'Brahmi?'

She didn't answer and hammered me with questions instead. 'How did he meet you? Does he talk to you? Where are you from? What did you do to him?'

'I should go now,' I said, turning.

She grabbed my hand.

'You need to tell me everything,' said the girl, her eyes smouldering. And then suddenly, she became soft. 'Hi. I'm Richa.'

'There's nothing to say!' I said, wanting to get away from this slightly deranged girl.

'You didn't answer any of the questions I asked you,' she said.

'I don't need to talk to you.'

I started walking away from her, but she followed me. 'Did he tell you anything about himself?' she demanded. I kept walking. She said, 'I have his diary. I know everything! Everything you want to know about him!'

I stopped in my tracks.

'So you do want to know about him, don't you?' she said, smiling deviously. 'Wait at the park. I will get the diary. You tell me everything about him and you, and I will tell you about him.'

I steeled my voice and said, 'Fine.'

I waited for her at the park, knees shaking, sweating, despite the slight nip in the air. I felt light-headed as she walked towards me with a leather-bound diary with the year '1999' embellished on it in gold.

'Tell me all that I need to know,' said Richa.

'How do I know you're not carrying anyone else's diary?'

'You're not as dumb as you look,' she said. 'Can you identify his handwriting?'

'I can,' I said, having gone through hundreds of pages of Raghu's notes for typos and other errors.

'Here.' She touched the diary. 'This is the first thing he wrote in this. Read it from here. Don't touch the diary.'

I saw the writing, it was unmistakably his. I started to read.

. . . *Hey Raghu Ganguly (that's me), I am finally putting pen to paper. The scrunch of the sheets against the fanged nib, the slow absorption of the ink, seeing these unusually curved letters, is definitely satisfying; I'm not sure if writing journal entries to myself like a schizophrenic is the answer I'm looking for. But I have got to try. My head's dizzy from riding on the sinusoidal wave that has been my life for the last two years. On most days I look for ways to die—the* highest building around my house, the sharpest knife in the kitchen, the nearest railway station, a chemist shop that would unquestioningly sell twenty or more sleeping pills to a sixteen-year-old, a packet of rat poison—and on some days I just want to be scolded by Maa and Baba for not acing the mathematics exam, tell Dada how I will beat his IIT score by a mile, or be laughed at for forgetting to take the change from the bania's shop. I'm Raghu and I have been lying to myself and everyone around me for precisely two years now. Two years since my best friend of four years died, the one whose friendship I thought would outlive the two of us, engraved forever in the space–time continuum. But, as I have realized, nothing lasts forever. Now, lying to others is fine, everyone does that and it's healthy and advisable—how else are you going to survive in this cruel, cruel world? But lying to yourself? That shit's hard, that will change you, and that's why I made the resolution to start writing a journal on the first of this month, what with the start of a new year and all, the last of this millennium. I must admit I have been dilly-dallying for a while now and not without reason. It's hard to hide things in this house with Maa's sensitive nose never failing to sniff out anything Dada, Baba or I have tried to keep from her. If I were one of those kids who lived in palatial houses with staircases and driveways, I would have plenty of places to hide this journal, but since I am not, it will have to rest in the loft behind the broken toaster, the defunct Singer sewing machine and the empty suitcases. So Raghu, let's not lie to ourselves any longer, shall we? Let's tell the truth, the cold, hard truth and nothing else, and see if that helps us survive the darkness. If this doesn't work and I lose, checking out of this life is not hard. It's just a seven-storey drop from the rooftop, a quick slice of the wrist, a slip on the railway track, a playful ingestion of pills or an accidental consumption of rat poison. But let's try and focus on the good. Durga. Durga . . .

My hands felt cold. I felt my throat go dry. I wanted to skip pages and run through them in a tearing hurry, but she slammed it shut.

'You never thought he wanted to kill himself, did you?' she asked, relishing my ignorance.

I shook my head. And in another moment of softness, she touched my hand and said, 'Neither did I. Or I wouldn't have let anything happen.'

'Why . . .' I murmured, words still not coming to me.

. . . my friend had been mysteriously found dead, his body floating in the still waters of the school swimming pool. He was last seen with me. At least that's what my classmates believe and say. Only I know the truth . . .

Things were slowly falling into place. For an infinitesimal second, I closed my eyes and imagined if Raghu were to be dead, and it was unimaginable, the pain too sharp, too deep. To have it happen in real can break anyone. But where does Brahmi fit into all this? 'Who are you?'

'Do you want me to tell you? Or do you want to read what he wanted to say about me? For that you will have to tell me how you first met,' she said.'

I promptly told her about how I had caught him stealing a book that I intended to from the library.

'Here,' she said. 'Read . . .'

. . . Last year, Richa had accepted me as the love of her life when I inadvertently walked into the bathroom while she was bathing. She was the first woman I had ever seen naked, and I was the first man who had seen her like that. Ever since that day she shies away from me whenever I'm in the room, blushes excessively when I ask for extra tomatoes or a cup of dahi, steals glances at me till I smile and accept the existence of that secret between us. She's beautiful with her thick, black hair melting into her skin and she has the body of a woman, no doubt about that, but I feel nothing for her. That's unfair . . .

She snapped the diary shut before I could read further.

'I was his neighbour for sixteen years. He should have fallen in love with me but . . . no . . . he fell in love with her. A suicidal, stupid, stupid girl. Brahmi.'

'What—'

'Enough,' she said. 'Tell me how you kept meeting. What did you do? How did you trap him?'

I was offended at the insinuation, but I wanted to know more about Raghu, so I told her about the first few times we met, about Raghu's incredible tea, amongst other things. She sat there listening, unblinkingly, but with a sort of scepticism, as if I was lying.

I stopped after a bit when I thought I had told her enough. 'Where did he meet Brahmi?'

'What do you know about her?' she asked.

'Only that she broke his heart. And probably committed suicide. I didn't ask him, I didn't want to pry,' I said.

She spat on the ground angrily. 'She did much more than that. And what kind of a friend are you? Didn't want to pry? What does that mean? What kind of friends don't know everything about each other?' And with disdain, she opened up a page in the diary. 'Read,' she almost commanded.

. . . I was prepared to forget every name as soon as possible but one name stuck in my head, entangled in my thoughts like a chewing gum stuck so badly in my long hair that it needed to be burnt off. That name is Brahmi Sharma, the class monitor . . .

She skipped a few pages and pointed to another paragraph. Richa didn't even have to stop and look at the pages. She had committed every page of the diary to memory, just like I was doing right now.

. . . I have been searching for something to hate in her. Her hair is long and shiny. It is usually tied into a scruffy, untidy pony, and is absolutely un-hateable. Her face is amiable, with an odd pimple here and there. She has a lissom and athletic body, with perfect round mounds, bursting with puberty; she's at the cusp of turning into a young woman. Her uniform is not as orderly as the good kids in class and hence not irritating at all. But then, today, something hit my eyes like a flashlight during load-shedding—her bony wrists. Like a

child's drawing, there are cut marks zigzagging the entire length of her *wrist. Then every time I saw her during the day, my eyes rested on* *her wrists. The little ridges are telltale signs of someone having used a* *knife or a paper cutter on those hands . . .*

'So Brahmi was suicidal—'

'Why can't you just read?' snapped Richa and flipped to another page.

She slammed her hand on the diary just when I started to read.

'Wait! Tell me what happened after you saw him for the first time. Did you seek him out? Did he seek you out?'

'It was by accident that I saw him, on top of a bus,' I said. I told her about the accident site and the time I saw him in the hospital when a friend was admitted.

'These are too many coincidences for me to believe you.'

'I have no reason to lie to you,' I said. 'Can I read please?'

. . . This past week I have been praying to all seven of *Baba's gods—Ganesh, Saraswati, Durga, Kali, Kartikeya, Ram,* *Lakshmi—for a fresh batch of pimples on Brahmi's face so I can be the* *hero with my handkerchief dabbed in Baba's perfume . . .*

. . . While Brahmi Sharma struggled with the crossword, I counted *the little ridges on her wrists. Some were deep, straight and longish,* *others lighter and half-hearted jabs. They looked like hieroglyphics,* *like tattoos of the brave . . .*

She snapped the diary shut again. I now knew why she had asked me to read the diary from her hands. I had half a mind to snatch it from her and make a run for it.

'But . . . what happened?'

'It all started with his Dada falling in love with a Mussulman girl,' said Richa. 'Read . . . and hurry up, please. Aren't you too dumb for him? You're a painfully slow reader.'

. . . How stupid is Dada to think he can spend a night with a *girl he loves in a hotel room and not get married to her? Of course,*

he's getting married to her. I'm not an idiot to think that staying a night together could mean a pregnancy, but there are certain moral obligations that come when you say you're in love. Maa and Baba didn't throw the word 'love' around so frivolously and neither did they teach us that. Maa and Baba never said we-were-figuring-out-what-we-wanted-to-do after they professed their love. Quite unlike Dada who tells her he loves her, stays in her room, and then behaves as if he's not going to get married . . .

. . . Is nothing sacred anymore?

Richa looked at me and said, 'His brother was playing with fire. Daring to fall in love with a Muslim girl despite Raghu's parents being strict, orthodox Hindus. But our Raghu? He was too foolishly in love with Brahmi to intervene, to make his brother see sense. Brahmi was the light of his life. Nonsense!' She flipped to another page. 'So you just kept meeting him? Why?' she questioned.

'Yes.'

'Why? Why would he want to meet you?'

'Because we became friends. That's what friends do. They meet and they talk,' I said, impatiently.

'How many other *friends* has he in Dehradun?'

'Just me.'

'Oh! So Brahmi gets to be the love of his life, and you the best friend? Fucking brilliant! And I—'

'We had a deal, can I read, Richa?'

She rolled her eyes angrily. 'Read . . . *fucking best friend.*'

. . . After a long time I wanted to live on, not because I didn't want to disappoint anyone but because I wanted to stay alive for myself! In those few seconds—that seemed to last a lifetime—I didn't see Maa, Baba or Dada, I saw her. I saw my future as clearly as day. In the future that flipped in front of my eyes like a graphic novel, I saw myself clearing IIT, scoring much higher in the entrance test than Dada, and then I saw myself graduating

from IIT, then calling Brahmi's mom, and informing them of my existence. I saw them liking me, and then in two more years, I saw myself slipping in the possibility, quite randomly in a conversation with Brahmi, of us getting married, and then I saw her take it to her family and them agreeing to the union on the grounds of my loyalty and success . . .

'Then what happened?' I asked.

'Things started to fall apart,' she said. 'His parents were livid at their son's affair with a Muslim girl. They threw Dada out of the house. They stopped talking to Raghu because he had hidden the relationship from them.'

'Then?'

'Did you stop at being best friends? Or did you fall in love?' she asked.

'We run a business together now.'

'Wah!' mocked Richa. 'A business! No wonder he doesn't come to Delhi any more. Why did you suddenly need to run a business?'

'I needed the money,' I said.

'And you guys aren't in love? Just friends, huh? Sounds like horseshit,' she grumbled angrily.

'What happened next?' I asked impatiently.

. . . Maa and Baba, who had stopped talking to me for keeping Dada's secret, thought it was best I started going to school again to divert my attention. I know they sent me so they could mourn in peace. The thin walls of our house can barely contain Maa's wails . . .

'But as much as Raghu was wrecked, he was in love, and that made everything all right for him,' said Richa. 'Even when Dada and the girl Zubeida, whom he called Boudi, got married. It wouldn't be long before she was pregnant. He was obsessed with Brahmi, he would do anything for her, that stupid boy.'

Flip.

. . . I sat on the pavement facing her window. I saw a silhouette in the window which I'm not sure was her. It was stupid what I did and I knew it sitting there, but I couldn't make myself get up and leave. I felt myself heal, the auricles and ventricles found their place again, the tendons snapped back, the blood flowed in my veins once more. Then I got up and came back home . . .

'He obsessed over her. That stupid girl was everything to him!' scoffed Richa. Flip. She added, 'At least she saved him.'

I thanked god she hadn't asked me any further questions and went on to another page in the diary.

. . . Despite everything that has happened in the last few weeks, I am the farthest I have ever been to doing anything stupid. I feel I'm tethered to Brahmi like a stupid lovelorn goat. I can go round and round her, close or far, but I can't disentangle myself from her. I want to see her again, talk to her, know her stories if she would tell me, and just be around her. So in true goat fashion, I left Ashiana Apartments for Brahmi's place. Had it been a movie, I would have barged in, given a credible explanation for how I found her address, and then got on my knee and told her that she meant quite a bit to me. But since it's not, I hovered around awkwardly, came back home and got an earful from Maa, who gave me the staple 'Is-this-house-a-guest-house-for-you!' line . . .

Richa kept getting angrier with the flipping of every page, and it got the better of her. She forgot to ask me anything. Flip.

. . . Later we decided to say the words 'I', 'love' and 'you' in different combinations and wondered how if only spoken in the correct order these innocuous words turn powerful and all-consuming. We backed it up with physiological evidence when she placed her hand on my chest and felt it thump. We decided we would give each other three short missed calls in the evening just in case we missed hearing it from each other . . .

Richa heaved angrily. Flip.

. . . I have chosen not to tell Maa and Baba of Boudi's pregnancy right now. Today I'm going to revel in the imagined future of a little kid calling me Kaku and seeing me as his or her hero. And since we are going that way, he/she's going to call Brahmi Kaki, and he/she's going to love spending time with us rather than his/her stupid, stuck-up parents. In my imagined future, Dada and Boudi are scraping past their expenses, while Brahmi and I are the power couple but with a lot of time on our hands to live a fulfilling life . . .

Richa composed herself.

'I saw him lose himself in her. Every night he would sneak out unnoticed. But I would be right there,' she said, pointing at the balcony on the second floor. 'I watched him every day as he slowly slipped away from me and walked into her gangly arms.'

. . . I stole from Baba's wallet, sneaked out, took an auto to Brahmi's house, and stood under the streetlight beneath her window. A while later, the lights of her room went out. A candle flickered behind the frosted-glass window. The window opened with a groan and a creak. She poured wax from the lit candle on to the ledge and fixed two more candles and lit them. The flames burnt yellow and blue, and she smiled at me in their pale glow. She mouthed, her eyes lowered in shame and shyness and things I have never associated with her, 'Now what?' On the pavement, I drew in bold letters with the chalk I had taken from school. 'I see you.' She let her fingers linger around the flame and smiled. She scribbled in the air—I see you. We spent the next hour writing messages to each other on the pavement and in thin air. Then she rested her chin on the ledge and I sat on the pavement and we stared at each other. The candles were about to be extinguished when she said—tomorrow. The flames died and it was dark again. The window closed. I came back home looking forward to tomorrow . . .

'That girl was always strange,' said Richa. 'Absolutely wrong for him. God knows what he saw in her. Tell me?

Would you fall in love with a girl like that? There's nothing in her, nothing!'

'Maybe—'

'Look! Look at this! How she's gushing over the fact that she could fly kites better than most!' she ridiculed.

'What was he thinking!'

' . . . she flew kites?'

'Yes! Why are you looking at me like this? Read this,' said Richa.

. . . Brahmi had insisted we celebrate Independence Day the way it was meant to be celebrated—by flying kites. Before long we realized why. Brahmi was a kite warrior if there's ever been such a thing. She decimated Sahil, Rishab, Arundhati and me with consummate ease, her manja cutting through our combined ranks like a hot knife through butter. Sahil and Rishab had dressed in their finest combinations of orange, white and green to impress Arundhati whom they were meeting for the first time and, from what I could gather, found attractive. The first few losses were put down as a fluke, the next few were attributed to Brahmi having a good day, and the last few were spent grunting angrily. It took us two hours and sixteen kites to accept Brahmi's superiority . . .

I was still reading when she snapped it shut.

'I was reading!' I said.

'What's so interesting in her flying kites! Anyone can do that! I too have learnt it now,' she said. 'You know what really grates on me?'

' . . . '

'That he would risk his life for that girl. Didn't he think of anyone else before doing what he did?'

'What did he do?'

'He risked getting impaled on construction rods. For what? Just to talk to her?'

. . . I said a prayer and climbed up the scaffolding, taking Lord Hanuman's name at each step—like him, I would leap for love. It

was harder than it looked and I was out of breath by the time it came for me to jump. She asked me to not do the five-foot jump, but it was too late. She knew it too. Catching my breath, I leapt, I missed, and I hung shoulder down from the parapet, my legs dangling precariously. Brahmi gasped and outstretched her hand quite uselessly. It took me all my might and more to pull myself up to the ledge. I climbed into her room, my T-shirt in tatters. The blood from the minor bruises had already started to clot. After she had whispered words of concern and we discussed in gestures how dangerous it was to sneak in like this, we became acutely aware of the silence and the darkness of the room. She lit a candle and asked me to be absolutely quiet. I could hear the clock ticking in the living room, I could see the fear on her face. There wasn't much in her threadbare room, just a bed and a small cupboard, but what wouldn't I give to be here with her, for this to be our little world. If one could be envious of inanimate objects, I was, of this room, which held stories even she wouldn't remember now. The room knew what made her laugh, what made her cry, the boys she loved, the boys she hated, the boys for whom she felt both; it knew how short the days were and how long the nights, knew her desires and her fears, her peeves and her likes. We knew how dangerous it was, so we maintained a funereal silence. A little later, she kept her head on my shoulder and held my hand. We breathed softly. Our chests rose and fell at the same time. She wept softly and I found myself weeping in response . . .

'It kept getting worse,' said Richa, frantically flipping pages, her fingers trembling.

. . . We came to a stop at Nizamuddin railway station, where we ate fried rice from a stall. Every night seemed endless till it was time to leave. And the next night, aeons away. Time's plasticine, malleable; when love's in the equation, it's as relative as Einstein theorized it to be . . .

Richa snapped the diary shut. 'Don't think I forgot about asking you questions about Raghu and you. I didn't want to break the flow. This part really gets me. As much as I hated him being with that girl, he was really happy with her. It was disgusting.'

'Hmmm . . .' I was impatient to read more.

'Tell me why wouldn't he come here in a month to meet his nephew? Clear that up for me, please? You say you're not in love, you're best friends, whatever that means, and nothing more. Than why doesn't he come?'

'Boudi had a son?' I asked.

'Let's not skip paces. What exactly do you get out of each other? Give me that answer and I will tell you,' she said.

'I don't know, Richa!'

'Hey, hey! Don't take that tone with me. I will leave,' she said, snapping the diary shut.

'Richa, I don't know what to tell you,' I said, exasperated.

'Tell me about yourself. Tell me all that there's to know about you. Since you're too stupid, too daft to know for yourself what he saw in you, let me do that for you,' said Richa condescendingly.

I tried not to get pissed off.

I succinctly gave her a dispassionate account of the story of my family, and how Raghu was helping me run away. While I was finishing it, for the first time I saw Richa smile. She stopped me midway.

'I have heard enough.'

'What—'

'Read this,' she said. 'This is when Raghu's parents accepted his brother's wife and took good care of her. It was all a ruse. They had their grandson in a Mussulman girl's belly, so they accept even the girl.'

  . . . *In the evening, we went to Boudi's house. Her bump is considerably larger now. Only yesterday, Maa helped Zubeida Boudi redo the stitching of her burqa. Maa's guessing it is going to be a boy from the size of her bump. It's surprising to see how irrational she can get despite her education. For the most part of the evening, Maa sat right next to Boudi, one hand firmly on her stomach as if she didn't trust her with the life growing inside her . . .*

There was something Richa wasn't telling me. She had smiled when I had told her my story, but it wasn't like a happy or even a knowing smile. It reeked of sadness.

She didn't ask me anything further. 'Read this. This was when he got to know that the girl's parents were long dead.'

'What?'

'She kept telling him they were out of town. That she lived with her father's brother.'

'Why would she do that?'

'She was nuts. What else! What do you expect from her?'

. . . She reached out for my hand and hugged me. We cried for a bit, which was liberating. Then she left without a promise of when she would be back to see me again. I couldn't bring myself to ask the one thing that was gnawing at my insides—why does she lie to people about her parents?

She skipped a few pages.

'After all that he did for her, what did she do? She betrayed him!' said Richa, indignant, throbbing with anger.

'How?'

'She wanted to leave the school, move in with her cousin and join a call centre. Can you imagine?'

'She must have her reasons! How do you know she was being treated well there? She didn't even have her parents—'

'I would have died for a boy like him,' said Richa.

. . . I waited for her till 11.59 and then at 12, I made a resolution to stop moping over Brahmi's prolonged absence, to scruff her out of my heart, to not think endlessly about her, but at 12.01 all I could think of was to pick up the phone and call her, hear her voice. I wanted to cry and bawl and run all the way to Brahmi, to be her knight in shining

armour, get a job in a call centre, have a house and TV, and whatever Vedant has. Why couldn't I be the hero just fucking once?

She turned over a few more pages.

'Then she just upped and left,' said Richa. 'Leaving him alone. Can you believe that? And she went missing for days on end. No calls, nothing. Who does that? You should have seen how Raghu was during the time, an absolute wreck. Read, read all of this! That girl made him feel like their relationship was over!'

'Why would she do that?'

Richa looked away and didn't answer.

'Everything came crumbling down,' she said.

'In whose life?'

'Both.'

'What happened to Brahmi? Why did she not keep in touch?'

She said after a long pause. 'She was being suicidal again, didn't want to drag him into the mess. The cousin . . . was a pervert.'

. . . I saw Brahmi today. It sounds innocuous if I put it like that. I waited for three mornings outside her office. It wasn't a decision based on reason. It was what my body, my heart and my mind yearned for. I struggle for words to describe what it was like. Maybe a little like burning, like everything was on fire, and only she could quell it. It sounds silly I know but that's the closest to how I felt . . .

. . . I don't miss her voice, I don't miss her touch, I don't miss her presence—yes, I don't miss her at all. And why will I miss her? It's not as if I think she was a part of me. It's not as if the last few days of my life have been spent in abject despair, or as if I spent every waking minute reliving everything that we shared, everything that seemed real and true and everlasting, or as if I have mourned the loss of every possible future I have seen with her, or as if sometimes the pain is so hard to bear that I fiddle with the paper cutter . . .

I gasped. 'But . . . but . . . Did he . . . did he try to kill himself?'

'Not until his brother . . . Anirban died in that awful fire.'

'What!'

'Months before his son was born.'

I choked on my words as she turned to the page. In places, it had been smudged by tears. I couldn't bear to read it.

. . . Between Dada's realization of the blue spark, and his heart coming to a stop, Dada would have felt everything. The second Dada would have switched the light on in that living room filled with the LPG, and seen that spark billow into something more, he would have been filled with horror. Dada would have wondered how it would be, the fire, the din of the blast, and then the force crushing his body. In the first few microseconds, Dada would have taken it lightly, thought the flame would be little and brief, but in the very next moment he would have thought otherwise, his body floating, golden flames licking every part of him. He would have felt the searing heat, he would have felt the skin melt off him, his organs would have singed, every tissue Maa gave Dada from her womb for nine months shrivelling, charring. Dada would have felt the unbearable, physical pain of his body disintegrating. Fists clenched, jaws locked, vocal chords strained, he would have screamed. And then the pain would have become too much . . .

Both Richa and I hid our tears. I wondered how many times had she cried reading this, and if the tears on the page were hers too. 'Raghu's parents blamed it on Zubeida. Took away her child and asked her to convert.'

'Did she?' I asked, shocked.

She nodded. 'That was the last straw. Raghu's parents stripped Zubeida off her burqa, her name, her holy books, dragged her to the temple and made her convert. It was horrible. They even made her wear wedding bangles and then broke them. The entire colony watched the monstrosity.

Imagine looking up to your parents all your life only to realize they are beasts! It was terrible, too much for Raghu to take. He left the house vowing not to come back again. They made . . . they made that nonsensical pact, to end their lives together. It seemed to them that that was the only way out. They moved into the house where his brother lived . . . and died.'

. . . The kitchen and the living room are wrecked, blackened with soot, the walls half broken, the blood washed off, but the bedroom is surprisingly untouched. The flat has no running water or electricity, but it's a house. Brahmi said she would have her bag ready tomorrow . . .

The words scraped my mouth and I bled. I asked, 'What happened that night?'

'Brahmi saved Raghu,' said Richa. 'At least that's what she thought she was doing. She wrote on the last page of the diary for him to read before . . . they would jump off together . . .'

I snatched the diary and turned over to the last few pages.

. . . Hey Raghu,

I am at the ledge and you think what you're writing is the last of what you will ever write. You're thinking I will read it and smile and I am sure if I do I will smile, but there's no time left for me. You are a lovely person, Raghu, you have the power to be happy and to make others happy, and you should be that person more often. You have the power to love, and the power to change, and you're a survivor unlike me. You're brave, but I'm not. Didn't we always talk about how brave it is to die? No, it's not. It's brave to survive, to live the years god has given us, to hold close our happiness in times of sorrow and to live on. You can do that, I can't. You have the capacity to live for others. Like this morning, didn't you agree in a second when I asked you if you wanted to see your nephew? You did, because you have an unending capacity to love, to give, to live for others. And what kind of person would I be if I snatch someone like you away from the world?

Ask yourself what your answer would have been if I had given you the option of staying in your dada's flat, just you and I, scraping by, existing. You would have picked me and life. You would have done anything to keep me happy. It's because you're a nice person, Raghu. You believe love overcomes all, the deepest of pains, the hardest of times. You gave me the best few months of my life and I'm thankful for that. You were the only part of my life that was worth living for. Don't beat yourself up when I'm gone because it won't be your fault. I was always a goner. A bit crazy, mental, as my relatives always thought of me. I died the day my parents died. After that it was just a matter of time. Now I think all I was waiting for was you, to fall in love with you, to have someone love me as selflessly as you do; you were god's consolation prize for my defeat in life. You saw me differently, and I can't thank you enough for it. But I can't be with you, Raghu. I can't drag you into my sadness. So let me go. Look up and smile at me. Before I jump off this ledge, I want to look at you one last time. Don't try to run or talk. It's too late. Just look at me, smile at me, and don't be shocked. This is our last moment. I want us to smile. You're probably crying right now. That's OK. You will cry for a few days, mourn my absence, but you will get over it, Raghu. You deserve all the happiness in the world. You have a lot of time. You have a long, fulfilling life to live. You have to live. For my sake. And someday, you will find someone who will love you more than I ever did, and that day you will thank me. Now it's time for me to go. When I jump, don't follow me, don't try to save me. Save yourself instead. If you have ever loved me, don't come after me. Now look up at me and smile. Don't cry, smile. Yes, that smile. That sunshine. That light, my love. It's my time to go. Bye, Raghu. I love you. I will always love you.

She jumped.

When it slowly sunk in—and it took a lot of time—I started to bawl uncontrollably and Richa had to drag me away from the park which had started to fill up with children and old people. Before I knew it, we were on the stairs of the building where Raghu once lived. I could feel everything come alive around me. Raghu and his love who died, leading him towards a downward spiral of guilt; his dead brother who dared to love and left their world in a shambles; and his burqa-clad wife who gave up her identity to keep her child; his devious parents who loved their sons a lot, but loved their religion a little more, and the love of his life, the stupid, lying Brahmi. I felt a sadness I had not felt before. It was as if someone had crushed my heart. It was suffocating.

Richa took me home, and straight to her room.

'The house is a little dirty,' she said.

I was still crying.

'You need to stop, or my mother, when she comes, will think there's something seriously wrong,' she said and wiped my face with her towel. Then she held my hand. 'You're a little baby, aren't you? How old are you?'

'Eighteen,' I said, not knowing how that mattered.

'After that stupid girl jumped off the roof, I thought he would know better,' said Richa. 'But no. That boy kept running after her.'

'How—'

'She didn't die that night. It wouldn't be until a month later that she . . .' Her voice trailed off. She continued after a long pause, 'No one knew that Raghu was on the roof too, that he too . . . It wasn't until I found the diary on him in the hospital that I knew what Raghu and Brahmi had planned to do. I know what it took for me not to burst into Brahmi's ICU and strangle her with my bare hands. Brahmi had nearly killed my Raghu. You know what was the worst of the month that Raghu spent there? He had this foolish hope—both of them—despite the doctors not giving a sliver of hope of survival. Any fool could see that she wouldn't survive, no one could after a fall that ghastly. It was disgusting to watch him spend every waking minute by her bedside, looking at Brahmi, as if she was a marvel. In spite of her lies, her subterfuge, he was there, loving her and praying for her. He didn't let a single tear fall lest Brahmi see it. While Brahmi flitted in and out of consciousness, barely being able to say more than a word, Raghu would talk to her endlessly of things they would do after she was discharged. He didn't question her decision to end her life even once! He would just spend day after day staring at her like a madman. I missed school to sit and watch him love the girl who least deserved it. Why couldn't Brahmi have died that night? Sometimes I felt it was just god's way of making me miserable. I didn't want the front-row seat to the love of my life destroying himself for someone else. But it was also for the first time, he talked to me . . . like a friend. At that point, I took heart that I was the only one he talked to.

I was hoping she would die soon, leaving Raghu and me to navigate the dark sadness, hand in hand. He would eventually fall in love with me, I thought. Sooner or later, he would forget Brahmi. She would be like a blimp on his mind's radar, before he found the girl he was truly in love with.

'Twice, I saw him telling off his parents, even his brother's wife. A few days later, Brahmi's Tauji, the man who Raghu held responsible for Brahmi's actions, was beaten within an inch of his death in the parking lot. No one knew who the attacker was, but Raghu's knuckles were bruised the next day.

'He wouldn't even talk to his friends, or his Bhabhi, despite them paying for Brahmi's treatment. He saw Brahmi's pain only, and didn't see the rest of us. It was infuriating. I thought more than once to tell the police that he had tried to fling himself off the roof as well. I quite liked the idea of people dragging Raghu off Brahmi and separating them. That's what kept me going those days. It was sinister, but that's what love does to you, I guess. I kept hoping Raghu would lose hope, go home, but he didn't. Not even when Brahmi was put on a ventilator and everyone from the doctors down to the nurses knew that she wouldn't survive.

'Even when her vitals dropped, her hands got cold and she lay dying, he would find a ray of light. "Look, the saturation level is up! Look, her heart rate is fine. Look, I saw a finger move," he would say and give a forced smile. It was pathetic. But that's the kind of love I yearned for. Moronic as it might be, I wanted to be on that bed, to be the one Raghu talked endlessly with. It made no sense. But watching through that little round disc of the glass on the ICU door I would have given up everything to be on that bed, half-dead. At least I would have valued it. They say we shouldn't speak ill of the dead, but why shouldn't we? She destroyed him.

'At some moments, even I rooted for Brahmi. Not because I saw the sense in their love, but because I feared what would happen to Raghu when Brahmi died. It wasn't a question of if, but when, and I was scared to the bone. I kept telling myself that everything would be fine, that he would cry for a day, a week, a month at the maximum, dry his tears and hide his grief, and then move on with his life. I couldn't have been more wrong. I can still hear his screams, everyone in the hospital can too, I'm sure, when Brahmi flatlined once. He had to be physically removed from the hospital, for he smashed a doctor's head against a wall. My misery still didn't end. Brahmi, the one who had so desperately wanted to die, was revived.

'He sat in the parking lot for two weeks. He would just sit there and stare, like a dead man had been placed upright. Not once did he move for food, for water, for anything. The hospital authorities reached out to Tauji but they refused to come. Sahil, Rishab and Arundhati, Raghu's friends had come

and settled the bills without which Brahmi couldn't have
been kept on the ventilator. And a few days later, it was his
friends who had broken the news to him. Brahmi had died in
her sleep. Raghu had thrown himself at the door, wanting to
see Brahmi one last time. He was denied that by the hospital
authorities.

He got beaten up by the guards when he tried to enter
the electric crematorium without authorization. He stood
there, bleeding, as they turned his lover to bones and ashes and
dust. Everything gone. I was right there seeing him crumble,
my heart in my mouth, terrified. When his friends emerged
with her ashes, he fell to their feet for it. Once he had them,
he disappeared. I didn't see him for a month. I thought . . .
I thought the worst. I had read his diaries, he wasn't short
of ways to end his life. He had a death wish right from the
beginning.

'His parents filed a missing report which was squashed
because he had reported to the police station. He still didn't
come home. I spent hours at the balcony waiting for him. It
wasn't until his nephew's first birthday that he came to me.
He wanted to give his nephew a gift. We sat together on the
pavement and celebrated his birthday. He had smiled that day.
I thought he would go back home to his parents. Because not
only was it his nephew's birthday, his Maa and Baba had burnt
his Boudi's burqas, her plaques, her books. The loss of two
sons had cut deep.'

'He didn't go home?' I asked.

'No,' she said. 'He would come every couple of months
and watch them. He would answer none of the questions I had
for him. And then you came along. His first friend?'

I didn't know how to respond to that.

'But I know why he's happy again. You remind me of
her.'

'I seem nothing like her.'

'No, you're not. You're much prettier, which makes me angrier. But in a lot of ways, he's doing what he couldn't do for her. He's helping you leave, isn't he? Trying to make your life better?'

'But—'

'It may seem like you reached out for him, but could it be that he knew of you from before? He must have heard about you from someone?' she asked me like it was a question, but she seemed sure of it. I had Altaf's name in my mind, but I didn't say anything. I thought of how he had said 'Dr Vaid's granddaughters', of how he knew everything about me even before he had met me. Had he bumped into me? Or was it all planned? Did he always mean to insert himself into my life? Was none of it an accident?

Richa continued, 'He's in love with you.'

'No, we are . . . are just friends.'

'Sure, you think that. But he doesn't. You think he would go to the trouble of making a friend when I am sitting right here? I know him better than that. He's always wanted to be a hero. He must have found you, and thought of you as his redemption. Do what he couldn't do for Brahmi. Save you. Just because you call yourself his best friend doesn't mean you know what I do,' she said. 'I know him. He's in love with you. It's only thing that explains—'

'You can't say for sure.'

'Can't I?' she sniggered, malice and anger clouding her face. 'Then why the hell is he writing a stupid diary again? I saw it in his hands, a few pages filled up.'

'There's no way you can say for sure,' I said, trying to make sense of everything.

'You should leave now, Mumma will be home soon,' said Richa, and led me to the door. Then she said in a low voice,

'After you are gone, he will be with me. Maybe this time, he will choose the right person.'

I walked down the stairs, my vision blurred and world spinning. All the time that I had spent with Raghu muddled with his past now, with Brahmi. On the way out, I saw a woman dressed in a burqa with a toddler clinging to her, giggling, calling out, 'Maa, Maa, Maa.' They were smiling, big wide smiles. The boy looked back and called out to his grandparents, Raghu's parents, who trudged along slowly. They looked older than what I had read in the diary, the father's hair almost white and the mother's eyes sunken. They called out the kid's name, Anirban, and smiled weakly. They looked tired and sad.

9 March 2003

Our passports have come.

On a random page on each of the three passports is a stamp of our freedom. Mumma and Papa have kept them carefully hidden. Neither of us is getting enough sleep. Like me, I am sure they too daydream of the time she will call us and tell us about the ticket and the offer letter, of how we will have to sneakily leave in the middle of the night. How she will tell us, in all excitement, that we need to directly reach the airport. At the airport I would try not to be embarrassed by doing things wrong—presenting the ticket to a guard and not to an airline employee, or trying to open a window that doesn't open. But in all these dreams, I turn and see Raghu standing there, waving his hand, smiling his stupid smile, and mouthing the fact that he loves me.

I could be imagining it, but we are not the same any more. Is it because now when I see Raghu I see what he has been through, the darkness, and the pain? Or is it because I now know of his love for me? Or does it have to do with me abandoning him? In the past two days I have caught him stealing glances at me and then freeze up and act as if there was nothing to it. And now that I'm going, he's not going to burden me with the truth. He's used to carrying his truths himself, isn't he?

I have been through the timeline of our friendship in a bid to understand where it could have happened. Failing, I wondered if there was a window of time I had missed and when I should have fallen in love with him. It would have been easier then. Two people in love with each other, separated by forces beyond their control, but vowing to come back together later. That's something I could have lived with. But this . . . this just makes me angry. This is an inauspicious and a heartbreaking start to a new chapter and neither of us deserves it. It just keeps reminding me of what he had written in his diary.

If we were intended to live most of our lives in pairs, why didn't we come with the names of our soul mates imprinted on our hearts? Why do we stumble from one name to another till we make a choice, right or wrong? Why would she fall in love with me when I would never love her back? The checks and balances of love in the world will never settle. It will always be a CA's nightmare.

Richa was right about the diary Raghu had started to write. It's in my hands. I stole it this morning. There's all but one entry in it. It's not dated. I have not read it, I'm scared to. What if it's Raghu's declaration of love? It would be disconcerting to know that he *loves* me when I don't love him that much. But I shouldn't be feeling guilty, should I? Of course, I love him deeply as a friend. After my family, he's the only person I care about and would do anything for. Why do I feel bad even though there's no way of saying if my love is any less than his? Just because his is romantic love and mine's not? Isn't true friendship the most powerful relationship in the world? From the little I have seen, you can fall equally hard in love innumerable times in a lifetime, and one love story often overwrites the other, and once past the expiry date, you don't want the same love back. But none of the friendships you have are the same. You always miss the friends you make in school, and you miss them differently from the ones you make at work. And no matter how ugly the fallout, years later you would still want them back. Wouldn't you?

I should read his diary without feeling any guilt (apart from, of course, the guilt of stealing it). Now I'm doing it.

I feel out of practice.

It feels strange to hold this pen again, a bit like a betrayal, and I'm no stranger to betrayals.

It all started from my betrayal of Sami, my now-deceased best friend from school, didn't it? He died on my watch. I could have saved him, but I couldn't. I watched him drown in that pool; I was too scared to jump in and save him. I saw him take his last breath, watching me with accusing eyes. What was that flapping for life that set everything in motion? How could I forget Dada's betrayal of Maa and Baba's love? Or Maa's and Baba's betrayal of their grandchild? Not to forget Dada's rude egress like he was in a hurry to move away from the sadness. And then there was Brahmi, the biggest betrayal of all. The liar. The illusionist. The girl who left my heart broken in a million little pieces.

Every night after she was gone, I would tell myself I was dried out, that the tears won't come, but they always did. She took that feeling of hope away from me. We don't realize how important hope is in our lives till it's snatched away cruelly. I hope there's chicken for lunch. I hope I score well. I hope that girl likes me. I hope I get a job. What do you do when you don't have hope? How do you keep living your life? You can't.

I lived on. Not because Brahmi's dying words meant anything to me, but because it was my little revenge against her. When I meet her again, after dying in ripe old age, I will tell her that it isn't that hard to live without hope; that I did it and she was foolish to do what she did. Or maybe I would have told her the exact opposite. I would have told her to regret what she did, leaving me to live a miserable life, which I did nothing to improve just to spite her. A revenge lived in the form of my life.

But none of the plans included this girl I have come to love.

Should I read it further? Should I? I should.

None of the plans included this girl I have come to love.

I don't feel bad about writing this. I don't feel shackled. I don't feel judged. I have thought about this.

I saw her first a year ago, I remember it clear as day.

The board exam results for the twelfth standard had been declared. I was there to see how one of my students had done. She was there, away from the students who crowded in front of the board, and she muttered silent prayers, tightly clutching her mother's hand. And when she knew she had made it, she had danced in full view of everyone till her mother stopped her.

For a moment, I felt disgusted at how happy she was while others around her were anxious about their future.

At that time she had what most didn't: hope.

Over the next few days, I dreamt of that cute girl dancing without a care in the world, embarrassing herself and her mother. The more I saw her, the more things around her got blurrier and she came into focus; the untainted joy on her face, those dancing, twinkling eyes. She was what people often describe as cute. The only definition of which in my mind is when people retain their childlike innocence even when they grow up. Advaita certainly had that, her eyes disproportionately big for her little round face, her nose too bunched up, and her lips glistening as if she had just drunk milk. She waddled around like a little duck, eyes wide with curiosity. She had slowly become the little flicker of happiness in my day. I treasured playing that moment over and over again in my head.

A few days later, I saw her talk to Iqbal and Altaf at the market. Iqbal was addicted to my tea and me to the stories of the girl he had seen growing up. Every evening he would sit there and tell me anecdotes of the little girl he considered a sister. I would drink it all in, putting together her lifetime of joy, misery and love. I hadn't known it at the time but I was falling in love with her. I was too consumed with the guilt of feeling something—even though unnamed—towards a girl other than Brahmi. It seemed like a blatant betrayal. Hadn't I loved her enough that all it needed were a few years and then death to move on? What about all those promises to love each other till the end of time reduced us to dust? The burden of guilt seemed heavy at first and then tapered as I felt angry at how weighed down I felt with her memories.

The more I thought about Brahmi, the more I veered towards Advaita. I started seeing Advaita around more frequently. It was uncanny. I liked to believe it was the universe putting us within a few yards of each other repeatedly. But it wasn't until the day I went to the library, for work, I like to think at the time, that she noticed me, and luckily was interested in me because I had stolen a book that she had wanted.

I struggled to come to terms with what I had started feeling for this girl. Looking at her sipping my tea, hungrily eating the namkeen I gave her and talking endlessly and excitedly, gave me what I had lost before. Hope. She was everything I was not. She knew it as a fact that a day would come and she would find happiness for not only herself, but her family. Unlike me, she was a fighter.

I had felt my heart stop when she called me her best friend, her only friend. At the same time, a deep fear of the power to disappoint, and the vulnerability to get disappointed struck me, but I was helpless. I was happy. I was truly, truly happy in that moment. And every time I think of it, I find myself smiling. She saved me, she kept me from living a life without joy; she told me it was possible to be happy if one just fought on, and that's rare. From that moment on, I wanted to be her best friend and give her everything she would require of me and more. Not that she ever needed it, but I wanted to protect her, fight her battles for her, take her sadness away.

I felt alive again. I felt happy again.

For the first time I wasn't thinking of days in terms of hours. I was thinking about what I would do next week, or the week after that. That a month after this one exists, a month that can be filled up with things to do, people to meet, places to go. She made that possible.

Time was no longer my enemy. It became a friend. It was moving, and the faster it moved, the sooner I could see her.

I know better than to expect my feelings to be reciprocated. She's already done the impossible for me. I don't expect anything else. It will be hard when she leaves, but she has to do what's best for her and the family. It's what she has always wanted and I am happy for her.

I love her.

I shouldn't feel bad. I shouldn't feel bad.

10 March 2003

He was sitting on the pavement, his shoulders drooping, cheeks caved in like an old man, and staring straight ahead, his eyes vacant.

'Raghu?' I called out.

He got up and walked towards BCC. I ran after him

'Will you tell me what happened?'

He stopped at the gate, and said, pointing towards the room, 'I think he knows. You have to run.'

The tables had been burnt, the chairs broken and wrecked systematically, the whiteboard hammered to little pieces, and the papers stripped apart, stamped on. I felt sick to the stomach. Someone had taken a hammer to my dreams.

'Go home.'

I fell to my knees, scooping up the papers, trying to put the chairs together, crying, the reality slowly sinking in, my hands freezing. I picked up the notebooks and diaries and course material, and stuffed them inside my bag. Raghu, the boy who loved me, the boy whose heart I was going to break, held me till I stopped bawling, and told me that I should go home.

He shook me angrily. 'Stop,' he exhorted. 'Go home right now. Do you hear me? Look at me. Listen to me! It's done! You have to leave.'

He dragged me away from the room. As he walked me towards the bus stop, we crossed a few bewildered parents and kids who were walking towards BCC.

We got into the bus. He held my hand and kept telling me, 'It's going to be fine . . . it's going to be fine . . .'. But every time I looked at him, I could see the fear in his eyes. I looked at how he clutched my hand, like he would never let go, that he would put himself between me and anyone who would try to hurt me.

Raghu kept his eyes on me till I turned the corner towards my house. There was an eerie silence that crept up on me even before I opened the main gate. From the window I saw shadows of people, moving around in circles, throwing up their arms in anger and despair. I opened the door and what seemed like a million pairs of accusatory eyes turned towards me, boring into me, burning into me. For the next few minutes, accusations and insults and abuses ran freely. I was called randi, *najayaz*, and they cursed me for having lived beyond my mother's womb. I was grabbed and slapped and shouted at, and so were Mumma and Papa by Buaji. Karan Bhaiya and Anshuman Bhaiya stood nearby, legs apart, hockey sticks in hand, ready for instructions. Dadaji sat on the sofa watching it all unfold, the architect of all of that was happening, legs crossed, hands folded. In front of him on the table lay our passports with our visas signed and stamped, the tickets to our freedom.

Manish Chachu and Sumitra stood mute in a corner, watching silently, not protesting this time. At some point, Dadaji nodded ever so slightly at Karan Bhaiya and Anshuman Bhaiya, and they moved in quickly. They grabbed at my hair and slapped me. All my pleas fell on deaf ears.

'Not the face,' said Dadaji.

Anshuman Bhaiya, always the wimp, the boy who has never won a fight against anybody, rained punches on my stomach.

'Enough,' said Dadaji and got up.

He picked up the passports, which were now dripping with oil.

'The others,' he said and Karan Bhaiya gave him a bunch of old, yellowed papers.

Dadaji, meticulously, as if hardened and perfected by practice, stacked them all up in the middle of the room. Birth certificates, identification proofs, school and college certificates, bank account numbers, medical records, driving licence, college ID cards. Every proof of our existence.

'You walk out of this house and you don't exist,' he said as he set all the documents on fire.

The first flames shot up ferociously, surprising everyone with their angry, yellow licks that laid waste to our future. Mumma and Papa stood dumbstruck.

'Meghnad is not stupid,' said Buaji. 'Going around with that boy in Delhi! Meeting your sister! Do you think he had sent just one man after you?!'

Karan Bhaiya tightened his grip around my arm.

'You will get married to Meghnad. There's no running away from here. This is where you will live and this is where you will die,' said Buaji, and looked at Mumma and Papa. 'You had once chance and you threw it away. Such bastards you are! Loyalty means nothing to you! Give you a finger and you want an entire hand! Filthy cockroaches! Bhaiya, you should have crawled into the gutter your wife came from rather than get this whore here!'

'Advaita won't get married to him!' screamed out Mumma. 'She's won't!'

Buaji looked at me and said, 'It's either that or we take care of your friend Raghu.'

Dadaji voice boomed from the background, 'He will meet the same fate as Altaf.'

'What do you mean?' stammered Manish Chachu.

In that second that stretched out for what seemed aeons, the shock turned into realization—things suddenly fell into place, like gears, one fitting into another, the machinery of intolerance and hatred—that Dadaji, Buaji and Fufaji were murderers, yes, that's the word, that's what they had done, they had orchestrated it, they had organized the mob and got him lynched. Altaf's death had nothing to do with the garden-variety misunderstanding of a Muslim being mistaken for a terrorist; it had everything to do with the fact that he had dared to fall in love with Manish Chachu. They had gotten Altaf killed.

Buaji turned to me and said ominously, 'We had no choice, did we? Your chachu was getting reckless and these things don't get hidden for long.'

The realization soon gave way to fear, and all I could visualize was a crowd converging on Raghu with a tyre and kerosene, of them bashing him up with hockey sticks, tying him, and then hanging the burning tire on him.

'That bastard dared to . . .' said Dadaji, anger eating the rest of his words. 'He deserved what he got.' He looked at Manish Chachu who was still dumbstruck, as we were. 'You did this to him.'

Buaji held Sumitra by her hair. Sumitra screamed. Buaji shouted, 'Now? Go now and tell what my brother is! Go!'

She let Sumitra go. Sumitra held Manish Chachu's hand; his eyes suddenly seemed to have lost their light.

'You take a step out of the house and we will tell everyone that the child inside of you is from an *ashiq* of yours. We will see who believes who! It will be your word against ours!'

Instinctively, Sumitra's hand crept up her stomach as if shielding the unborn child's ears from Buaji's words. We all looked at Sumitra who seemed shocked that Buaji knew about the pregnancy. There's no way she would have told her.

'I will get married to him,' I said.

My words weren't taken at face value.

'Did we ask you for permission?' Buaji thundered.

'LOCK THEM UP,' said Dadaji.

Mumma, Papa and me were boarded inside, bolted and locked, and we were told we wouldn't be allowed to even visit the washroom without Karan Bhaiya's or Anshuman Bhaiya's permission. The harder we shouted, the worse treatment Raghu would have to endure, we were told.

'You're getting married next month,' declared Buaji.

12 March 2003

It's been two days and I have barely stepped out of the room.

Mumma and Papa were also confined to the room for an entire day, but then Mumma was needed around the house to cook and clean and serve, and Papa had to be let out to keep up appearances in the neighbourhood. I have been let out only to visit the bathroom and for baths. Other than that, I have stayed in and festered in my own unhappiness. At nights, Karan Bhaiya and Anshuman Bhaiya have taken to banging our doors and shouting expletives at us, trying their best to strip away all our dignity.

'We made a mistake,' I told Mumma and Papa yesterday. 'We shouldn't have thought that—'

Mumma had cut in and told me to never talk like that again. She keeps asking me to keep hope even though she knows it's of no use.

Yesterday, Karan Bhaiya threw a bedpan into our room and told me that it's what I was going to use for the next month. No more bathroom breaks for me. It was only when I, in a fit of rage, started to break that he ran and wrested it away from me.

'I shall make you pay for this, you crazy girl!' he said and left the room.

Every few hours, either Buaji or Fufaji come to the door and repeat their threat against Raghu.

'Only we know how we have stopped Meghnad from doing something stupid. We can't let this wedding fall apart,'

Buaji said in the morning. 'But after you get married, what do we care what he does with you? In that household, women are seldom seen outside once they get married.'

Divya Di has been calling the house number and every time she calls, Buaji tells her that we have changed our mind. 'They don't want to have anything to do with you,' Buaji tells her. I can assume Di did not believe her; and during her last call, Buaji had shouted abuses at her.

I was scared for Di. What if she came to Dehradun to check what was happening to us? So today morning, when she called and Karan Bhaiya picked up, I screamed in the background, 'DON'T COME HERE! THEY WON'T LET YOU GO! JUST STAY AWAY!'

Karan Bhaiya banged the phone down and stormed inside my room. He grabbed me by my hair and asked me to stand in a corner of the room, facing the wall. He then unzipped and peed on the bed.

'That's what you deserve, whore,' he said and left the room.

I cried but not for long. There are only so many times you can cross a line and expect a reaction. I turned my thoughts back to Di. I prayed that she would understand that this was not her battle to fight right now. And the more I thought of Di, the more I found myself thinking of what she would have done had she been in my shoes. She wouldn't have gone silently into the night. What could I do to not lose everything entirely, to have a modicum of dignity?

Mumma held me last night and whispered in my ears, 'When the time comes, don't fight. He will only hurt you more.'

There's no way I am listening to Mumma. If Meghnad wants to break my spirit, he has to do it himself, earn every bloody badge of honour, and make me give up. What happened in the car won't happen again. Every time he takes me out, he will have to fight me for it. Maybe one day I will win. Of course, I didn't tell Mumma that. I am preparing not to tell her a lot of things because what hasn't she done to carry her miseries and mine. After Meghnad takes me away, I will lie to my mother that I am happy and she would see straight through my lies and not question further.

I have not dared to ask them about Raghu. I'm thinking if I don't ask about him, they would think he doesn't matter and then forget about their threat. What must he be doing? Knowing him, he wouldn't have left town no matter how menacing Meghnad's threats were. He would have stood his ground like the fool that he is, taken it on the chin, but for what? Stupid, stupid love. Stupid, stupid best friends?

What's scarier is the thought of Meghnad not letting him leave town. Did they lock him up too? Is he OK? Is he . . . alive? When will I see him again?

13 March 2003

A bulb flickered to death.

I could see him crouched in the corner of his ransacked room, bleeding from his head, swaying, too tired, too fucking tired to do anything.

Meghnad was staring at me, smiling, his hand firmly on my knee, slowly rubbing it. My voice is stuck in my throat, choking me, killing me, my ideas of resistance and rebellion dying a slow, writhing death. Why did I even try? Why?

'Do you see him?' asked Meghnad, thrusting the video camera in my face, playing the video for the third time. He laughed out loud. 'Look at him duck! Look! OPEN YOUR EYES AND LOOK, KUTTIYA!'

All the four men in the video had handkerchiefs tied snugly across their faces, but it wasn't hard to recognize Meghnad, his driver Monty, Karan Bhaiya and Anshuman Bhaiya. They grunted and shouted and wielded rods like swords and swung them indiscriminately at Raghu. Raghu had tried to get up a few times, swung and got a couple of them on their faces with big, powerful jabs, but the harder he managed to hit, the swifter and crueller was their assault. Rods and kicks rained down on him mercilessly. The crunch of the rod against his legs, ribs, the sound of Meghnad's knuckles against his face sounded inhuman. Every time I saw the video, I felt he wouldn't survive this. In between the beatings, I heard Meghnad say, 'LEAVE THE MADARCHOD ALIVE.'

I heard Monty shout repeatedly, '*TANG TOD SAALE KI!* (Break the bastard's leg!)'

He finally switched off the camera, kept it aside, held my hand, and caught Mumma and Papa's eyes and said, 'Your son-in-law will always protect her. Whoever looks at her will have to pay. You are the luckiest parents in the world!'

He ran his fingers over my face, starting from my eyebrows and then slowly came down to my cheeks, and lingered them on my lips, moved them to my cheekbone and lightly tapped my face like you would do with a dog. Once, twice, till they were more like little slaps.

'I thought you were a nice girl,' he said. 'Not like your sister, that whore.'

'Meghnad—'

'*Abbe chup!* Shut up!' he shouted. 'Not a word,' he said and held my face. 'Not a word. See what you make me do? I don't want to be harsh with you. I love you, more than I loved your sister.'

'Then let my parents go,' I said.

'Let them go? Go where? To your whore sister?' said Meghnad. 'You really think I will send them to her? Let her just come here. Oh, what fun that would be!' His eyes glinted madly.

'Leave her out of this! She has done nothing!'

'Nothing? Really? I don't think so. Can you imagine what her face would look like if someone just accidentally . . . you know . . . drops acid on it? It would happen in an instant. No one would know where the guy came from, where he went,' said Meghnad, his eyes dripping with malice and intent. 'Ah, that beautiful face. I wonder what her employers might think of it.'

Mumma and Papa started to cry, and he smiled, explaining to me in detail about how many different ways he could carry out this act.

'What's the most that will happen, huh?' he said. 'Let's say you do find something to convict me? How long do you think I will be jailed? It won't be for life I'm sure, but on the other hand . . . your sister . . . she will be ruined, won't she? Tch . . . tch. All that beauty gone in an instant. So sad.'

'Please please please leave her alone.'

'Are you going to tell me what I can or cannot do?' he said and held my hands in his grubby, sweaty, criminal hands. 'So the next time you talk to her, tell her what I told you. Tell her that I forgive her for breaking my heart. She can stay out of Dehradun and I will let her keep her beautiful face. That sounds fair to me. What do you say, Mummy?'

Mumma was too terrified to react. He laughed, touched their feet and left, locking our door from the outside. Papa held my hand and cried. He tried all he could do to make me not think of what they did to Raghu. How limp his left leg looked, his eyes bleeding, lips all tattered.

Now we waited with our ears pinned to the doors, for Divya Di's call, and when the phone rang Mumma and Papa shouted and screamed and cried and begged for them to open the door. It wasn't until Mumma screamed like an animal and threatened to slash her wrists and mine that Buaji opened the door. Our deaths would be mighty inconvenient to the rest of the Vaids.

Mumma, her voice broken from all the screaming, made Di swear that she wouldn't come to Dehradun, not even think about it, and when Di fought with her about this, Mumma and Papa repeated their threat of killing themselves if she even tried.

'We will be fine. You take care of yourself. Eat well and don't forget to drink a lot of water,' Mumma told her.

Buaji took the phone and slammed it down. Karan Bhaiya and Anshuman Bhaiya herded us back inside and bolted the door.

14 March 2003

I kept telling myself that I would get used to the oppression that Meghnad would subject me to, that I was made of sterner stuff, I'm my mother's daughter. After all, aren't there people worse off than I am? At least I would not starve to death, or be sold off as a sex slave.

Last night, there was a big bonfire in the courtyard. My attention was drawn towards it when I heard Buaji scolding Karan Bhaiya and Anshuman Bhaiya for it. They put it out hurriedly before Dadaji noticed, collected the debris, stuffed it into a gunny bag and dropped it at my door. Buaji was still shouting in the background.

'He's gone,' said Karan Bhaiya. 'We checked and this was all he left behind. Books, books and more books!'

Both brothers chuckled.

'He ran away like a little rat,' said Anshuman Bhaiya. 'Like a little rat! He was too tiny for Monty to catch.'

Karan Bhaiya sniggered wickedly. 'Don't worry, though. If he ever comes back—' He cracked his knuckles.

They trotted away, mighty pleased with what they had achieved, and troubled Sumitra to make pakoras for them, because chasing well-meaning boys away from a town must be tiring. I wondered where Raghu would have run to. Delhi? Who would he be sitting on a pavement with? Richa? I wished I could meet him once, apologize, and tell him how much he meant to me. I wanted to tell him how special he is, how loving he is, and how unlucky Brahmi was to not spend a lifetime with him, and how stupid I felt for not being in romantic love with him! I wanted to tap his head and scold him for falling for me! I would chide him for making me feel that the love I feel for him is in any way inferior. I wanted to hug him and let him thank me for saving him and thank him for saving me. I wanted to have another cup of tea with him.

I picked up the gunny back and brought it inside, too weak to check what was left, and asked Mumma to dispose it of which she promptly did.

'You will meet him again,' said Mumma.

'He didn't need to be dragged into this,' I told Mumma.

She had been working tirelessly to prepare me for what was ahead, tempering my anger. And of all the things she kept saying to me, the one thing she said with the most emphasis was to keep my eyes open and my brain sharp.

'Sooner or later,' she said, 'you will find an opportunity to leave everything behind. It may come in a week, or a month, or a year, but you have to take it. Don't come back here, don't worry about us, just run. I don't know where you will go, what you will do, but find a way to go to your sister. Do anything, but don't come back to this house. Don't make the mistake we did.'

Whenever she said this, she didn't say it as desperate bid, she meant it, and she wanted me to devote every minute of every day looking for that window of escape. It was what she demanded of me, so that I would eventually find happiness, because that was not going to be my victory alone but hers as well.

15 March 2003

Like every night, today too she had hugged me tightly, as if wanting me to slowly go back to her womb, change my gender and be born as her son. Wouldn't life be so much easier? Unlike Karan Bhaiya and Anshuman Bhaiya, I would have carried the Vaid surname with me, and with that I would have had certain privileges and none of this would have happened.

'Sleep,' said Mumma and sang me a lullaby I hadn't heard in years. She patted my head till I drifted off in her arms.

It could have been twelve or one or four—locked in that room, I had lost track of time—when there was a light knock on the door. We all sat up.

'You keep sleeping,' said Mumma, scared if it was Meghnad again, drunk.

'I will get it,' whispered Papa.

The door was knocked again and this time we heard a voice.

'It's me,' said Sumitra.

We looked at each other, befuddled.

Mumma got up and opened the door. Without a word, Manish Chachu and Sumitra walked inside, held our hands and led us outside. The door of the house was ajar. It was dark outside, the neighbours all fast asleep.

Their grips on our hands were strong, tight, their steps determined. We left the house and soon we were walking towards the end of the lane, barefoot and still in the clothes we had worn to bed. We didn't have a single rupee on us, and yet none of us wanted to say a single word, or even turn and look at the house, or let the thought even cross our minds. A white Omni van with blacked-out windows waited outside, and Manish and Sumitra bundled us inside with a sureness that would be hard to muster in a day. They must have been planning this for days. They didn't talk to each other either, just little nods of the head, a slight touch on the arm. Manish Chachu drove like a madman, his eyes boring into the road, and Sumitra looking at us in the rear-view mirror as if to check if were still there. It was natural, we didn't believe it was happening either. The roads were deserted. If Meghnad's men were out there, it would be easy for them to pick us out.

Mumma clutched my hand tighter. The roads were clear and we must have reached there in ten minutes, but it seemed much longer. Every stray light, every person on the road seemed to be trailing us. No one talked about what was happening, but everyone knew. The walk from the parking lot to the platform was the longest, the hardest, and we walked with our heads hung low, hiding from whoever might recognize us. I felt claustrophobic; my body seemed to shut down on me. Then the announcement came about our train—it was before time. How often does that happen? We all clambered up without waiting for people to get down. We were cursed, shouted at, shoved, but we powered through. We would have run all the way to Dehradun if that's what it took. All of us sat with our knees shaking, faces towards the window, hands clutching the railway seats just in case someone tried dragging us out of the train. No one said anything to each other. I had expected Manish Chachu and Sumitra to get up and deboard, but they didn't. Sumitra sat next to me holding my hand, and Manish Chachu stood vigil at the train door. Thrice I thought Meghnad's men were staring at us from the other platform. I felt cold, and my breath stuck till they walked away without so much as a second glance. The train started to pick up speed. I wondered if Manish Chachu and Sumitra were running away too. Had they too had enough? Where would they go?

But the faster the train went, the easier I breathed. I had left behind the town I had grown up in and I felt nothing but joy. My heart thumped with happiness as we sped past the last few settlements of the town. I closed my eyes and vowed to never come back to Dehradun. We looked at each other, and now we could afford to smile.

'We are waiting for two more people to join us,' said Manish Chachu.

And as if on cue, he appeared out of nowhere. There he was in our berth, bloodied and bandaged, but smiling.

'What!' I half screamed.

And right behind him was Divya Di.

Mumma, Papa and I looked at them, not sure if we were imagining the entire thing, if we were losing our minds. Then Di came and hugged and kissed me, even slapping and scolding me for scaring her. Raghu touched Mumma's and Papa's feet and they asked him if his injuries hurt.

'He contacted me,' said Divya Di.

'And us,' said Sumitra.

'There was no other way,' said Raghu, playing it down.

I thought about Richa's words. Of his need to be a hero, of redeeming himself, getting over the hurt.

'I'm carrying a girl,' Sumitra said. 'We got it determined from a clinic. That's the last place I would want her to grow up.'

'I sold the shop,' said Manish Chachu. 'That would get us through a few months. She will start working, we will both find jobs, we will get by.'

The technicalities of our escape from Delhi were discussed, but all of this was white noise to me. I had tuned out. I hugged my sister and looked at Raghu, who, after all that I had put him through, had dared to come back for me. The boy who loved me, the boy with a broken heart.

Later outside the train toilet, Di seemed to know what I had been thinking and said, 'What will you do now?'

I shook my head. 'I don't know.'

'You will never quite find anyone like him, you know,' said Di.

'That I know.'

For the rest of the train ride, Raghu and I stood at the door, the cool wind hitting our faces with a ferocity we weren't used to, and we looked out.

There was nothing to say. He knew I had read his diary. I could see that in his eyes, and I felt a bit stupid to have made it a big deal in my head. Raghu was at complete ease with me not being in love with him. Was it even better for him? Because if we couldn't be together, there was nothing for him to lose in the relationship, or was I just consoling myself by thinking like that? It was nearing morning when we sat down and he held my hand. I have never felt better.

'You will always be my best friend,' he said.

'I—'

'You don't have to apologize for not being in love with me,' he interrupted.

'Will you be OK?' I asked.

'Of course, the hard part is over. I don't think we would have been much better had you been in love with me,' he said. 'Thank you for all that you have done for me.'

'I did absolutely nothing.'

'Let's agree to disagree about that.'

'But don't you feel deceived or let down that I don't—'

'Why would I? You gave me what no one else could—hope. You have already done enough.'

'I don't want to be another Brahmi, leaving you when you need me. It's not acceptable to me.'

'You have shown me you can choose to be brave, you can choose your future over your past, you can choose to love other people, you can choose to be not sad any more.'

'That doesn't sound right,' I said, frowning. 'Will you choose to be in love with someone else in a few years' time? That doesn't feel particularly nice to me.'

He laughed. 'If anything, you have taught me to be open to all possibilities, haven't you?'

'If the girl's not nice, I will kill her.'

'I don't expect anything less.'

And I hoped in those moments that it was love, but . . . it wasn't.

16 March 2003

Our hotel is in Paharganj, and it's all neon lights and noise and car honks here. I saw more white-skinned people in the first hour here than I have seen in a lifetime. It's the first time I have lived in a hotel room (and it's quite nice, there's room service, and there's an electric kettle and they give free newspapers, imagine that!), and I didn't think it would be under these circumstances. To be honest, I thought the first time would be on either Di's or my wedding day, and we would have a room all to ourselves for our clothes and our make-up. But I would pick this a thousand times over. Raghu, Divya Di and I slept on blankets spread on the floor, and Mumma, Papa, Manish Chachu and Sumitra adjusted on the two single beds.

In this little hotel room for the first time ever, I felt Chachu and Papa had some kind of a relationship; that they were now not strangers who had spent years living in the same house. The words didn't come easy at first. Manish Chachu hadn't called Papa 'Bhaiya' in years, but once he did the trickle of words turned into a gush.

Growing up, I had always felt that Manish Chachu was embarrassed about Papa. He maintained a distance from him, not only in the house but even outside. They would walk past without a single nod of the head. Manish Chachu was a handsome man, the torchbearer of the Vaid name, and Papa a bent, hobbling cripple, a regret of the family, someone who had outlived his life.

From the time they got to Delhi, they talked only to each other, raking up memories from the lost years, laughing and wistfully remembering a relationship that had never existed. Every time Papa tried to thank Manish Chachu for saving us, Chachu would get weepy and apologize to Papa for his neglectful behaviour over the years. 'You have what no one else did in the family,' I heard Manish Chachu say. 'You had the courage to love and be with the person you loved. We are all cowards but not you.'

'When you have nothing else, you cling to the love you have,' Papa had said, rather heroically.

While Papa and Manish Chachu built a relationship they never had brick by brick, Sumitra and Divya Di easily slipped into the role of friends.

Divya Di's hatred for Sumitra now seemed a faraway joke.

Once Di told Sumitra about how she had sought out Vibhor Gupta in the farthest corner of Rohini, a Delhi suburb, and hit him with an iron rod, the ice between them thawed. It was like they had always been best friends. They even stepped away from me a couple of times to talk about things which weren't supposed to be for my ears. Divya Di kept teasing Sumitra by calling her Chachi. Now for the first time ever, in this hotel room, apart from the four of us, I felt we had a family—a loving family, the members of which knew each other's pain, and did everything to alleviate it. This was everything I had ever wanted.

All this while Raghu looked on, pretended to read the newspaper, made tea multiple times a day for all of us, watched the TV news on mute, made himself scarce, but I know him enough to discern what he felt when he saw us—a sense of longing. I caught him smiling sadly more than once as we all sat around and ate and talked loudly.

This morning, Manish Chachu and Sumitra took the train from Delhi to Mumbai where they will stay till the whole thing blows over. Sumitra's childhood friend stays there and she has agreed to take Sumitra and Manish Chachu in. They were sure of not returning to the house again.

As much as we wanted to, we couldn't go to drop Manish Chachu and Sumitra at the railway station. It was too risky. It was Richa who did so. I felt guilty for having thought of her as a bit of a crackpot. It was she who had booked the tickets, and it was under her name that we were staying in the hotel.

There have been times I wanted to thank Richa but I don't know what difference it would make. She's doing it for Raghu, not for me. I have seen her look longingly at Raghu, and it breaks my heart. No matter how warmly Raghu treats Richa, it never seems enough, and no matter what Raghu tells me about being OK with what we have, I never stop feeling guilty.

'Will they come looking for us?' I asked Di.

'What do you think?' she asked, a sense of dread clouding her face. 'But he won't find anything. We will be gone within a week.'

Her words weren't reassuring. Raghu and Divya Di have told us that this hotel is untraceable amongst the hundreds of similar hotels that dot the area, but even then Raghu stays up at night, staring out of the window, squinting at every car that slows down in the lane. Mumma and Papa haven't called any of their acquaintances in Dehradun lest they snitch on us. And on our behest, Richa has repeatedly tried getting in touch with Dadaji over the phone, from different PCOs. But all the calls have gone unanswered. That also means Karan Bhaiya and Anshuman Bhaiya are looking for us.

I don't want to think about what they would do if they find us. We all wake up every time headlights flash against the window of our room.

19 March 2003

Richa told us that Manish Chachu and Sumitra reached
Mumbai on time and that there was nothing to worry about.
But worry is what every hour of ours is made of.

Yesterday, the men Divya Di had eked out favours from
to get the passports made refused to help her more if she did
not fulfil her promise. 'The bastard wants to sleep with me,'
Di had said loudly, not really realizing that Mumma that Papa
were right there. 'I will find a way out, just give me a day.'

Richa, who had been listening to the entire conversation
intently, nudged a distracted Raghu who hadn't been saying
much.

Then Raghu, breaking out of his reverie, said, 'I . . . I
think I can help.'

Raghu hesitantly made some calls to three people—Sahil,
Arundhati and Rishab. The three names I had heard before.
Richa had told me about them. They were the ones who had
been around Brahmi in her last few days, after Raghu had
been kicked out of the hospital. They had been the ones who
had managed Brahmi's last rites.

In the evening, Sahil Ahuja, a strapping young boy, and
two more of Raghu's friends, Arundhati Bhattacharya and
Rishab Batra, were sitting in the room with us, their eyes on
Raghu. They looked questioningly at Raghu who didn't meet
their eye, out of shame or discomfort, I don't know. Two
years had passed since they had last seen him and they were
at a loss for words. Neither of them brought up the topic of

Brahmi or where he had gone missing. It was highly possible that Richa had already filled them in and told them not to ask a lot of questions. They knew of our predicament.

Sahil was the first to speak. 'I know a few people who can get this done. Had done some tweaking for the software they use, can definitely get it done.'

Richa later told me that Sahil was some sort of a computer prodigy and had learnt everything on a laptop that Raghu had given him. He owed Raghu everything.

'You should stay at my house. Mom will be angry if she gets to know you are staying in a hotel,' said Karan to Raghu. 'There's plenty of space for everyone. You can't be staying here.'

'You don't have to take the trouble, beta, we are good here,' said Mumma, equally surprised as I was. If a friend had abandoned me and gone missing without a trace, I wouldn't have come rushing to that friend, opened the doors of my house, and embraced him with open arms.

'It's your favourite, it's for all of you,' said Arundhati, the rather beautiful Bengali girl who held Rishab's hand all through. She was Raghu's neighbour and it was through Raghu that she had met Rishab; the two of them looked in love, greeting-card, teddy-bear love. She stretched out a steel tiffin box. Then she added after a pause, 'Your Maa sent this, Raghu.'

Something seemed to shift deep in his heart, buried under all the hate and dislike; he felt something, a sharp pang, a sense of nostalgia came over Raghu's face, and he smiled a little.

'Are you leaving for Dubai too?' asked Sahil.

Raghu shook his head. 'No.'

'We are always there for you,' said Rishab. 'Mom keeps telling me to get you home. You should come someday.'

Raghu looked over at Rishab, and then at Arundhati and Sahil, and said after a long pause, 'I will.'

Noticing the awkwardness, Divya Di took over the conversation. She handed over the forms, the photocopies of all our documents that she had thankfully kept with herself.

'Three days is enough,' said Sahil. 'I might have to—'

Rishab interrupted and said, 'Don't worry about the money. I will talk to Dad about it, he should be able to help us out. Sahil, just let me know.'

Sahil, noticing Raghu's discomfort, said, 'We should be going now, lots of work to do. I will—'

Mumma, who had been sitting quietly, butted in, 'You're meeting us for the first time and you will go *aise hi*? No way, you're Raghu's friends and he's family to us. Eat and go. I'm not going to hear another word about it.'

Arundhati and Rishab protested feebly, but Mumma can be quite persuasive if she wants to.

'I will order room service,' I said.

'There's no need, didn't Arundhati beta say there's food for everyone?' said Mumma and quickly picked up the tiffin box. 'Come, Advaita, help me.'

I followed her. I whispered. 'Mumma? What are you doing? Didn't you see how strangely—'

'It's his mother's food, he's bound to love it. How can he not?' said Mumma.

'It's not a movie, Mumma. You have no idea—'

'Don't teach me things,' grumbled Mumma. 'Hand me those plates quickly now, don't waste time.'

There was dal, rice, *muri ghonto*, fish of two kinds, brinjals, and what-not; it seemed like a feast, and if this is what Raghu missed all these years, I feel even worse for him. The room instantly filled up with the heady aroma. Plates were passed around, and everyone dug in hungrily. Only Raghu hesitated. He gazed at the food for some time, and slowly started to eat, taking small morsels, as if eating quickly would mean forgiving his family. I played a little mental game in my head. If he cleared his plate before us, then it wouldn't be hunger but a sense of nostalgia, lost love, longing, wistfulness and hope. And he was the first to finish and take a second helping which was as big as the first one. He looked over his shoulder to check if anyone was looking. He caught me staring; I was proved right.

Arundhati followed me as I took another helping and whispered in my ear, 'Thank you for bringing him back, but never do something to him like that girl before.'

Before leaving, Sahil reassured Divya Di that the work would be done. Karan added, 'I will tell Dad if it gets stuck anywhere.'

And just like that, Arundhati Bhattacharya broke into tears and hugged Raghu. Raghu held her back, and whispered in her ears, 'It's OK, it's OK, I'm fine now. I'm not going anywhere now.'

She let him go, little rivulets of tears still flowing on her face, and then slapped him square on his face. 'We were right there! I was right there on the other side of the wall! You could have told me than write it in that stupid diary! Wanted to die, my foot!'

'Arundhati—'

'SHUT UP! Do you have any idea how foolish we looked? We were kids, Raghu, and you DID THAT TO US! YOU DID TO US WHAT BRAHMI DID TO YOU! WHY?' snapped Arundhati, her eyes glowing.

'I—'

'Don't insult us by apologizing, Raghu. She's right,' said Sahil. 'Richa showed us the diary. I had never felt so . . . inadequate.'

'We don't have to talk about this,' said Rishab.

'Shut up, you don't have a brain only,' said Arundhati. 'Next time you even think of doing something like this . . .' She raised her hand as if she would slap him again.

'Enough,' said Sahil.

Raghu stepped forward and hugged Arundhati and quietened her down. 'I'm OK.'

'I have your books to return. Come home, OK?' she said.

'I will try to.'

After they left, Raghu didn't seem like himself. He sat on the window and burned up two packs of cigarettes.

'I never felt answerable to them,' he said when I sat next to him. 'There was no reason for me to feel guilty about not keeping them in the loop back then. I didn't think they could help, I felt telling them would be a waste of time.'

'So, what has changed now? You seemed to be affected. Were you?'

'School's ended, it's been two years. Did I break something in them? That was something I didn't want to accept. Now I know I mattered to them, and what I did affected them deeply. Arundhati is right, I betrayed them like Brahmi and my parents betrayed me.'

'So—'

'Now I can't help but think that if you just vanish someday, how would I feel? If I get to know there's a bundle of secrets you have been hiding, I would probably never make a friend again.'

'I will never vanish,' I said and held his hand. To lighten the mood, I added, 'How did you do it?'

He chuckled sadly, 'I'm not telling you my trade secrets. What if you use them?'

'But you should never disappear like that ever again.'

20 March 2003

Our worst fears were confirmed this morning. Sahil and Richa were sure they saw Meghnad and his friends at the passport office. They had been walking up and down the lines, peeking into people's papers, cracking knuckles, and angrily talking amongst themselves. In the three hours that it took Sahil and Richa at the office, they hadn't moved.

'How far will she run? She will go to Dubai, na? I will catch her there,' Richa had heard them say.

Sahil and Richa had submitted the documents without a hitch, and Sahil's point of contact in the office told him that the passport would be done in three days, and no police verification was required.

This wasn't the only place Meghnad and his cronies had been to. A little later, a shaking, terrified Divya Di came running back to the hotel and breathlessly told us she hadn't been able to submit the documents to the airlines office because she had spotted Meghnad's friend loitering about near the main gate.

'He won't find us here,' Raghu assured Mumma and Papa who had been wringing their hands ever since Sahil had confirmed their presence. 'We just need to stay low. It's a big city, they won't find us if we avoid the places they will expect us.'

In the evening, Arundhati and Rishab came bearing food again. Raghu taunted them playfully, 'Don't you have anything else to do?' It was the first time I had seen Raghu say something in jest, small talk, and it made me smile.

'Unlike you, we go to colleges, attend lectures and what-not; and you also have a girlfriend whom you have to help escape,' Arundhati gave it right back.

'Friend, she's a friend,' said Raghu awkwardly.

'Haan, haan, only she's a friend,' said Rishab. 'The rest of us are *chutiya*s.'

While the food was being unpacked and served, Sahil took Divya Di to the side. When I asked what it was about, he said it was regarding the documents, nothing to worry. Raghu watched on pensively, as Arundhati passed on a bunch of papers with recipes written down by Raghu's mother to Mumma. Mumma thanked Arundhati and asked her to thank Raghu's mother in turn. The handwriting reminded me of his, the curved letters, the exaggerated italics, it was as if Raghu himself had written it. When I asked Mumma if she really needed the recipes, she didn't give me a convincing answer. 'A child always needs his mother,' was the only thing she said to me.

When they left, a hassled Divya Di said to me, 'I had asked Sahil to check on Vibhor.'

'What do you mean?'

'I had a hunch. Meghnad found him, and beat him enough to put him in a hospital. Multiple fractures and partial loss of vision in one eye,' said Di. 'But Raghu's right, this city's too big, they would never find us.'

It wasn't until very late that we went to sleep, double-locking our doors with the locks Sahil had got us. We even shifted our room to the one closest to the exit of the hotel, just in case.

Like every night, Raghu and I talked ourselves to sleep.

'Do you miss them?'

'I feel angry at them.'

'But do you miss them?'

'I don't revel in their misery like I used to.'

'You will talk to them?'

'I don't think they will have the words to apologize.'

'Did you apologize to your friends?'

Raghu said sternly, the hurt bubbling to the surface, 'They were my parents.'

'And that's why you should forgive them.'

' . . .'

'Promise me you will try?'

'I miss that house.'

'Is that a promise?'

He didn't answer. After a while we both dozed off.

It had been just an hour when Raghu woke us up with a jolt. 'WE NEED TO GO!'

No one asked any questions. We were ready for this eventuality. Mumma, Papa, Divya Di and I all got up and packed our clothes in a couple of minutes. The room had been paid for, so we ran out, and caught the first auto. Raghu sat in the front with the auto guy and screamed into his ear to drive fast.

'Where to?' asked Divya Did.

'Rishab's house,' said Raghu.

No further questions were asked. It was three in the night, I checked, when we were ushered into Rishab's living room. His mother, a gregarious woman with a loud voice, didn't ask us a single question and welcomed us warmly. I assumed Rishab had filled them in on everything. Two servants brought us tea and biscuits. Rishab's father ambled into the room, rubbing his eyes, and reprimanded Rishab for not driving to get us. It was only to Raghu they didn't talk warmly enough. I am not sure whether they were scared or angry with what Raghu and Brahmi had made their son go through.

'No one will come to this house,' said Rishab's father menacingly, a kinder version of Meghnad. 'They won't be able to touch you. *Hamare bhi bahut contact hai* (We too have a lot of contacts).'

'Tell us if you need anything,' said Rishab's mother. She instructed the servants to show us where to sleep, and to give us clothes to wear for the night.

When Mumma and Papa, who had never been at the receiving end of such benevolence, tried to thank them, it was dismissed. Raghu was supposed to shack up with Rishab and they gave a large room with the biggest bed I had ever seen for Divya Di, Mumma, Papa and me.

'You should have come here earlier only,' said Rishab. 'Why did you decide—'

Raghu said, 'If Meghnad was following Advaita to Delhi, he would know that Advaita met Richa. They could find out where Richa lived and get to us. I could be wrong—'

'What you did was for the best. You can stay here for as long as you want,' said Rishab.

Mumma asked him hesitantly, 'Your mother . . . they know—'

'Richa told us. They are happy to help you. Anyway, I think all of you should rest now. If you need anything, just ask,' said Rishab.

Rishab and Raghu left the room. I couldn't help but join them. Neither of them seemed to have any problem. We went up to the terrace where the boys lit up cigarettes for themselves.

'Don't mind my mom. She's still a little angry with you. She meets your mom quite a lot, you know how women are. They think you overstepped,' said Rishab.

'You can't blame her.'

'Arundhati used to cry every evening and my mom had grown rather fond of her, so . . .'

'I understand,' said Raghu.

They smoked hungrily.

A while later, Rishab said, 'I scored eighty-three in English, board exams. Sahil got ninety-three. Imagine us dumbos, scoring that much. Uncle taught us, he insisted on it, he wouldn't take no for an answer.'

Raghu didn't say a word.

'Did you meet his mother too?' I asked.

'Your mom taught us mathematics, even Richa. She teaches my younger brother too when he comes back from the hostel—'

'I don't want to—'

'They did horrible things to you and your Bhabhi, I know. They own up to that now, believe me they do. And I sincerely believe that if your Bhabhi can forgive them, so can you, can't you?'

'I don't want to have this conversation.'

'*Abbe gadhe*, don't look elsewhere, look at me.'

'We are not talking about this,' snapped Raghu.

Rishab shook his head, 'Actually, we do need to talk. Because god knows what you keep thinking in that shitty brain of yours.'

'Rishab—'

'Don't Rishab me,' he said and raised his hand in mock anger. He then grabbed Raghu's collar and pushed him against the wall. '*Maarunga*, I'll hit you. See, I know . . . what happened.'

Raghu pushed Rishab away and said, 'YOU DON'T KNOW ANYTHING!'

'FUCK YOU! Three days in a week I saw your parents cry in this house, in Arundhati's house! They would tell everyone who would listen what happened! THEY EMBARRASSED THEMSELVES OVER AND OVER AGAIN JUST SO SOMEONE WOULD FIND YOU AND GET YOU BACK. You need to give them a break.'

Durjoy Datta

'YOU NEED TO FUCK OFF, RISHAB—'

'You fuck off! They have been calling us, talking to Richa through the day to ask you if they can meet. You can at least talk to them—'

Raghu said, steeling up, 'We will talk about this later.' He stubbed his cigarette and stormed off.

'What's his problem? Why don't you tell him something?' said Rishab to me. 'Cigarette?'

It was early morning. A little while ago, Richa called and told us that three boys had accosted her outside the house, and demanded to know if she knew a certain Raghu. It was only when Raghu's and Richa's parents raised a hue and cry that the boys drove away.

21 March 2003

Mumma is now like a child in Disneyland.

Despite the fervent protests of Rishab's mother, she has taken over the kitchen, insisting that only she will cook. Rishab's mother pleas were rejected, and they soon withered when Mumma cooked an elaborate breakfast for all of us in half the time Rishab's servants would. Mumma wasn't being helpful or paying back for what they were doing to us, it was just that the kitchen, with its sparkling marble slabs, fancy knobs and chimneys, and the shiny china was too much to resist. Much to the chagrin of Rishab's family who prided themselves on being great hosts, she spent most of the time in the kitchen.

Rishab's elder sisters and their husbands were home too, and they were spared the details of our presence there. But all of them couldn't stop gushing about the food Mumma cooked.

Raghu, Sahil, Arundhati and Rishab had spent almost the entire day on the roof, smoking. There was no point eavesdropping on them. Most of the time, they sat silently, sucking on the cigarettes, listening to a tape that Arundhati had brought. Sometimes they would switch it off and Arundhati would sing. Rarely did I hear someone talk. And when they did, they kept it short, and the other three would nod, and they would retreat into silence. Raghu seemed to be at home with that, a sense of calm pervading his face. He smoked less urgently, less desperately, smiled more often. I chose to not go outside and interrupt their company. After I leave, they were the ones who would be around him, helping him build his life all over again if he chooses to. He needed them to be around, to fill in the blanks of his life. I watched him as he slipped into a role he seemed to be at home with—a friend, a boy capable of being happy. I felt possessive about him, like I was losing him a little. It was what I had heard people talk of, the pain that's bittersweet.

Richa, who had been asked not to come to Rishab's house lest Meghnad tail her, called at Rishab's house to talk to me.

'Hi?'

'How good are you at remembering dates?' she asked me.

'Why?'

'Twenty-fourth March, that's the date.'

'Yes, that's the date we are leaving for Dubai, I know,' I said.

'That's also the date Brahmi died.'

It took me a second to pull from my memory Raghu's diary, and the entry on 24 March.

'It's the same day you're going to break his heart, aren't you? Have you thought about that? Or are you too busy celebrating your freedom?'

'It's not the same, we are still going to be friends, we are always going to be friends.'

'If there's one thing he's good at, it's hiding pain. If he did it to us all these years, there's no reason why he can't do it to you. You wouldn't know what's happening behind that face, I didn't when it was gawky, and you wouldn't now when he's . . .'

'What do you want me to do?'

'If you can't love him the way he loves you, at least be with him, hold his hand, tell him that it will be fine. He needs to be told that. Everyone he once held dear has disappointed him, and no matter how we come together for him now, it will take a lot of time. You can't take an eraser to your past. Do what I would have done if he loved me like he loves you.'

The call disconnected before I could say anything. For the rest of the evening, I stood outside the door of the roof watching Raghu with his friends, praying that his healing process had started. Richa had set the cat amongst the pigeons. Now I wondered if Raghu was putting on a brave front to make my move to Dubai guilt-free. It slowly started to eat me from inside. I waited for Raghu's friends to leave and confronted him.

Raghu laughed it off when I put it to him. 'What's your use if you can't make me forget that day?'

'But—'

'Will the day be sad? Is the coincidence just cruel? Of course. I have gotten used to a cruel god. I have resigned to the fact that there's no way around it. But I'm happy, Advaita, as happy as I can be.'

'But you loved—'

'My love for her didn't save me, but your friendship saved me. What do you reckon is more powerful, huh?' he said.

'I have nothing to worry? There's nothing you're hiding? Because I have been told you're good at that. If there is, you need to tell me right now or I will slap you so hard you wouldn't know whether it's day or not.'

'I'm so scared.'

'You need to take this seriously,' I said.

'I will take it seriously when you do,' said Raghu.

'What does that mean?'

'You seem to be very happy about this, going to Dubai, aren't you?' he asked.

'Yes, I am,' I said and added after a pause. 'I mean, I would have liked to run our coaching institute, but then we can't really get everything, can we? Didn't you also say that's the best we can do right now?'

'It's not about the coaching institute. You don't have to hide it from me that you can't bear to look at your parents right now.'

'I—'

'Don't even try to lie,' he said.

'. . .'

'You need to put it in words.'

And just like that, I started to cry like a child. He put his arm around me and called me stupid. It hit me right where it was meant to. I had been hiding from this, and so had Divya Di.

'They won, didn't they? Those bastards won. They chased us out of the house, out of the town. They turned us into little rats,' I sobbed into his arms. 'Mumma and Papa, they haven't known anything else other than Dehradun, and we are dragging them across an ocean to a country they have never seen. They can tell me all day that they will be the happiest being with their girls, but I know that's not true. It makes me angry that even a win sounds like a defeat. I feel scared for them.'

'Advaita—'

'What will they do there? Sit in the house and do what? Stare at the walls?'

'That's never going to happen. You don't know your mom, within the first week, she will have a bunch of friends who would want her to stitch for her! And your father? He will be the life of old-uncle gatherings, smiling and laughing the hardest at silly jokes—'

'Meghnad? He will find someone else to torture, won't he? Divya Di and I will escape, but he will find someone else to torture, won't he?' I asked.

'Life isn't fair, Advaita. I learnt that long back. People aren't by nature kind and humane with a streak of evil in them. It's the other way around.'

'We should just forget about Meghnad and feel powerless instead?'

'Yes.'

I wiped my tears and melted into his embrace. It seemed to be my only choice. To choose happiness, not all-encompassing, victorious happiness, but happiness all the same. That's what women do I guess.

Oh. I forgot to mention. The passports came today.

Three days from now, Raghu and I will be miles apart, dipping biscuits into our tea alone. Doesn't matter what Raghu says, that's not what victory sounds like.

23 March 2003

I have new clothes, and so do Divya Di and Mumma and Papa. Rishab's parents bought more clothes for us than we had ever owned as a family, and wouldn't take no for an answer. All this love is making me sick in the stomach. It doesn't seem real. Does such love for strangers exist? What are they hiding? Even Raghu's parents have sent us clothes and jewellery and they haven't even met us. All this love is revolting. To know that there are families and friends as loving as these, it's reprehensible that my family is the way it is, who didn't make it easy for us even after driving us out of our own town. It makes me furious.

But to think of it, Raghu's family is capable of much evil too; at least my family didn't pretend to play nice, their wickedness had always been bare. So maybe I shouldn't feel too bad about it.

But I can't bear to leave India.

It's also wrecking my heart to leave Raghu. All I want right now is for Divya Di to take Mumma and Papa to Dubai and leave me behind. For the last two nights, I have been toying with the idea of falling in love with Raghu. I'm sure if there was a switch I would have flicked it, and had it not worked, I would have pulled the wires, smashed the circuit box to make it work somehow. I would do anything to be in love with that boy.

Divya Di and I have always discussed that if I were ready to leave my family for any boy or man, I would have to be in love. Right now, I am all for them leaving me behind with this man. Is this love though? Is this what I have read about or seen on television? I don't know. Maybe I'm just scared that I will never feel the same kind of love for anyone else, ever. What if this is the most I will ever feel? But would it be right to tell him that I might not be in love with him, however, who knows with time? Or would I be repeating what Brahmi did to him?

Maybe I'm scared that he will be lost without me here, although I might be giving myself a little too much credit there. There are others now who can take care of him much better than I can. Maybe this is where our journey ends.

This morning, without a warning or explanation, despite everyone's reservations, Raghu sneaked me out of the house. He was caught by Rishab at the gate but he let us go, and gave us the key of his car with the tinted glasses.

'Where are we going?' I asked Raghu.

'You will know.'

The drive took an hour long; the sun was yet to come out. Raghu remarked how much the roads had changed, and that the traffic had trebled, small talk that he was quite bad at. Was he taking me to his home? Was he meeting his parents? My hands went clammy and my knees shook like a tong. Unlike me, he was surprisingly calm.

He stopped outside an apartment building and everything snapped right into place. Snatches of what I had read in his diary came rushing to my head, and my hands went cold. Why would he get me here? Richa's words came flooding to my head. Could you really know what's going on in Raghu's mind? Had he been planning something? But why would he?

He parked the car and let me outside.

'This is where it happened,' he said, his voice serious, his eyes glazed over. For a moment, he stared at the concrete unblinkingly and then looked up. He let out a deep sigh and closed his eyes. I felt I shouldn't be there. He composed himself and turned away from the site.

'Why—'

Without answering my question, he walked towards the building. I followed without a word. We climbed the stairs, and stopped at a crumbling flat. Where a door should have been, there was only a big hole in the wall. It was dark inside, and an eerie silence surrounded me with every step I took.

'Are you sure—'

Raghu paused for a bit, stared at what lay in front of him, held my hand and led me. It took me a little time to adjust to the darkness and the dank smell.

'This is where we spent the last few days,' he said softly. He looked wistfully around. The house, blackened with soot, and littered with garbage, didn't look habitable at all. But maybe two years ago, they had found a way to live here.

'We made that pact here, decided to end out lives here,' said Raghu, trying his best to stop his voice from quivering. 'How stupid were we.'

'. . .'

'Seems like a long, long time ago.'

'Is this the first time you have been here since that day?'

'I have been here a few times in the past few days,' he said. He looked at me and said, 'I am not scared any more of coming here.'

He held my hand and walked me to the roof of the building. I was terrified. There was something very . . . dead, about the place. A pang of sadness pierced through me and coursed through my veins. I had no idea what Brahmi looked like and yet I could see her there, at the edge of the wall, staring down, her hair blowing in the wind, Raghu in the corner, reading the diary at first with foolish romance in his eyes and then with confused anger, feeling betrayed by the love of his life.

I could see him sitting reading that diary and then running to stop Brahmi, realizing it's too late, and then peeking from the edge of the roof, terrified, shaking, knowing what he would see and yet wishing, praying that it wasn't true. The thoughts clouded my mind and before I could come to tears, he held my hand and walked me towards the edge. I wanted to run, I wanted to wrest my hand free and go back home. Every second I stayed there I felt my heart shrink, the grief of a past time wrapping around it, drawing the life out it. We sat with our legs dangling and he said, 'I feel nothing, Advaita. I feel nothing. This . . . this steep drop seemed like an escape, a hatch door away from the pain, a quick, painless exit, but no longer do I see it that way. I look at what lies ahead.'

'. . .'

'You made that possible.'

'I don't want to take the credit.'

'It is true,' said Raghu.

'I—'

'You want to have one last tea before you leave tomorrow?'

'Why are you even asking?'

He poured us two cups from the thermos he had carried that I hadn't noticed before.

'I'm going to miss you,' I said, my heart easing a little.

'Come back to see me when you get the time.'

'You should come to Dubai.'

'I am not sure when I would get the time.'

'Are you seriously acting pricey—'

'I am thinking of going home,' said Raghu.

It hit me like a hammer.

He continued, 'Before Anirban Junior makes memories without me, I want to be there. I don't want to regret that.'

'And your parents—'

'I will see when I get there,' he said, smiling. 'I got to try, right? All these friends of mine rallying for me, for you and your family, the least I can do is give it another shot.'

I hugged him. 'I don't want to cry,' I said.

'You should. God knows when we will get the chance again.'

And with that, we both cried.

24 March 2003

I am scared. I am on the flight right now, but none of this means anything. I want to crack open the window and leave. I am crying. The flight attendant has been hovering around, asking me if I needed something, if everything was OK. I want to scream at her that nothing was OK, that they need to stop this flight right now and save my best friend! Di, Mumma and Papa have been telling her, and the other passengers who have been turning and looking at us, that I was fine, that I was missing my best friend. I'm not missing him! I'm guilty of destroying my best friend. Should I not cry!

Mumma and Papa have been holding my hand and telling me that it will all be fine, it will all be fine, but I know nothing will be fine. They are all lying. It's because of them that this has happened. It's all on them. Had they not stopped me, had they not been selfish, had they not been terrified like I was, Raghu would have been . . . It's on them. Raghu had to pay for us.

I am telling them that I'm OK but I am not OK. I don't want to be on this plane, I don't want to be with them any more. I want to be in Delhi with him. I would rather die than be on this plane. Please stop. Please. Stop. I can't write this.

Two cars . . . we were in two cars . . . why . . . why wasn't I in the car that he was in? I could have been, I should have been, why was I so stupid? I had a lifetime with my family, why wasn't I in his car? Why was I with Mumma, Papa, Divya Di and the driver? When I saw Raghu laugh with his friends, when I saw Rishab stand up and poke his head out of the sunroof, when I saw Arundhati slap Sahil playfully, I wanted to be in that car, with them, with him. We lost track of them in a maze of half-constructed flyovers, and my heart had sunk, but then they were back at our tail. I could have been next to him. Only twenty minutes to the airport. I thought, I thought, they are the friends Raghu will live with, he needed to be around them, establish that friendship again, and I made the foolish decision to not travel with him. I should have been there. I should have been in that car! I could have saved him. I could have done what he had credited me with, instead . . .

We lost them again at a turn. And then I found them again in the rear-view mirror. I saw Raghu. I saw him smile at me. So happy, so relieved, just like we had decided. We wouldn't cry because then it would feel like we would never meet again. He waved at me and smiled that charming smile. Two minutes, just two minutes later, a Tata Safari cut in out of nowhere. Their car swayed and swerved to a stop. We had barely made it through the red light. Theirs had stopped on the other side. The doors of the Tata Safari opened. Rishab tried moving the car out of the way, but the Safari had blocked it. Four men, handkerchief around their mouths jumped out of it. The driver stopped our car, and climbed out of our car to see what was happening. Morning rush hour, the traffic flew unabated towards us, unmindful, frenetic. Mumma held my hand as I tried to run into the traffic and towards them. Time slowed down.

The four men came into focus, rods and hockey sticks in hand, with one of them carrying a canister with yellow liquid splashing around in it. Karan Bhaiya. Anshuman Bhaiya. Monty. Meghnad. They charged towards Rishab's car and banged at the tinted windows. We could hear them shout. Meghnad brought a rod straight down at the windshield, cracking it. I heard Meghnad shout at Monty, '*KAHA HAI SAALI! DAAL ACID SAALI PAR! DEKHTA HU KAHA JAATI HAI SAALI!* (Where is that bitch! Throw acid on her! I'll see where she goes!)'

Karan Bhaiya and Anshuman Bhaiya who had been hammering at the car's door with their hockey sticks now swung them at the windows, breaking them instantly. They thrust their hands inside through the broken windows and jimmied opened the two doors. I tried to run towards them, but Divya Di gripped my hand. Mumma put her hand around my mouth. My screams died down.

'*JALA DE SAALI KO!* (Burn that bitch!)' said Anshuman Bhaiya, not knowing that behind the tinted windows were only Raghu, Sahil and Arundhati. They all walked out, hands raised in the air, trying to talk. I tried to scream, but Mumma's grip on my mouth was too tight. I heard Karan shout for the police. Rishab ran headlong into the traffic and was knocked over to the side by a speeding scooter. People converged near Rishab who lay writhing on the ground, holding his leg. His driver looked on, too scared to move. I now saw Karan Bhaiya and Monty opening the boot, scouring the car for us, furious that we weren't there. They dragged out a screaming Arundhati and asked her where we were. Raghu strode towards Arundhati. Meghnad stopped him, but Raghu pushed him away gruffly and he stumbled a few steps backwards. Arundhati was screaming till her voice slowly gave way, and the words 'STAY AWAY, STAY AWAY' became just lip movements.

Raghu charged at Monty and pushed him away from Arundhati. And he had just held Arundhati when Monty slammed an open hand on Raghu's neck. Raghu stumbled back and Meghnad held him by his neck. Raghu struggled free and landed three quick punches on him, drawing blood. Sahil was jostling with Karan Bhaiya and Anshuman Bhaiya who were raining the hockey sticks down at Sahil. 'WE NEED TO STOP THEM,' I said, but the words didn't come out. Divya Di and Mumma were dragging me towards our car lest they spot us. One of the hockey sticks broke when they brought it down on Sahil's leg. Sahil bellowed in pain, but managed to knock them both off their feet. However, Monty who had grabbed Arundhati by her hair now, swung his rod at the back of Sahil's head and he collapsed on the road. Bystanders watched. I screamed and screamed in the little hollow of Mumma's palm. Divya Di said, 'THERE'S NOTHING WE CAN DO! THERE'S NOTHING WE CAN DO! THEY WILL LEAVE THEM, BUT NOT US!' The horror in front of our eyes continued. Meghnad and Raghu exchanged brutal blows, cracking knuckles against jaws and ribs. Both spat blood from their mouths, their lips torn, and their eyes swollen shut from the blood. Raghu slammed his head into Meghnad's nose and blood spouted out. Meghnad grabbed his rod, flung it at Raghu, but missed. Meghnad, dripping blood from his mouth, stumbled. Raghu charged at him, kicked him twice in the face. He held him up, gripped his throat, but Monty's rod swung at the back of Raghu's neck.

More people surrounded them, standing mute, watching the bloody scene. No one did anything. My shouts still silenced by Mumma's fear, by Divya Di who had slapped me to keep me quiet. Karan Bhaiya and Anshuman Bhaiya looked around, now terrified of being caught. Meghnad shouted at a fallen Raghu, 'WHERE IS SHE!' Barely conscious, Raghu stumbled to his feet and charged at Monty, and brought him down to the ground along with himself. The canister tumbled. Meghnad said, 'TELL ME! WHERE'S SHE!' Karan Bhaiya and Anshuman Bhaiya exhorted Meghnad to leave. 'THE POLICE WILL BE HERE,' they shouted. Meghnad refused

to budge. Monty swung hard. Something broke. Raghu's
scream pierced through the air. The rod was now red with
Raghu's blood and gore. He rolled over, half dead. Terrified,
Divya Di started to drag me towards the car. Mumma and
Papa held me. 'Listen, listen, that's the police, you can
hear the siren, they are coming, it will be OK, we need to
leave,' shouted Divya Di. 'Just come.' Papa and Divya Di
commanded the driver to drive us to the airport. The driver
protested feebly, but he too was paralysed. I felt the life drain
out my body. Mumma dragged me to the car and slammed
the door. They were right there. Rishab and Sahil in a heap,
disoriented. Karan Bhaiya and Anshuman Bhaiya panicking
hearing the sirens. Monty and Meghnad both clambering,
getting on to their feet, standing over Raghu who had been
bleeding as if a tap had been left open. The driver put the
car into gear. Raghu's hands, chest, the road, all stained
with blood. Meghnad bent over, asking questions. '*BATA
BHENCHOD!* WHERE IS SHE! *CHODUNGA TERE
SAAMNE MAA, BETI DONO KO!* (Where's she? Will
rape the daughter and the mother in front of you!) Till when
will they run!' Karan Bhaiya and Anshuman Bhaiya were
already stepping backward towards the car. Monty kicked
Raghu in the stomach. Once, twice. Raghu spluttered more
blood on to the road. The driver hesitated. Divya Di shouted
at him to step on the pedal. Meghnad's shouts got fainter. But
his face got angrier. He spat on Raghu. He opened his zip,
I think, to piss on him. Raghu stumbled to his feet. Monty
was about to step forward when Rishab and Sahil pounced
on him, bringing him down with a thud. Meghnad swung a
kick and failed, he slipped and fell. Raghu rolled over, and
climbed on him. The driver drove further away, honking.
Meghnad shouted, 'MADAR—' His words were cut by a
tired punch from Raghu. Meghnad shouted, '*SAALE, AAJ*

TO BACH JAEGA, but tomorrow? (You will be saved today, but tomorrow?)'

Raghu punched Meghnad like a madman. I saw Meghnad's face flopping from one side to another like a lifeless doll. I didn't see it at first . . . Meghnad reached out to take a gun from his back . . . He looked to the side, and at that moment, his eyes locked with mine, and I saw an evil I hadn't seen before, I flinched and caught Raghu's eyes. That's when Raghu did it.

I saw it.

It happened painfully slowly.

I saw it all; even as Raghu reached out towards the canister, I clenched my jaw, terrified at what would come next; he brandished it before Meghnad, and my eyes flitted towards Rishab and Sahil who looked on, frozen in terrified anticipation; they too knew what would happen, the devastation Raghu was about to cause. Then he opened the cap of the canister. I saw Karan Bhaiya's and Anshuman Bhaiya's mouths open as they screamed, regret writ large on their faces, and relief that it wouldn't be them who would be splashed with the stream of acid that would burn through everything without mercy. When he tilted the canister, the splashing, corrosive liquid spilt out; all I could then think was of Anirban Junior, of Raghu's sister-in-law, and of the life Raghu had been about to mend being obliterated, burnt, laid waste by the acid. As the first drop fell on Meghnad's face, I thought about Arundhati and Rishab and Sahil who would lose their friend again, all that wait coming to nothing, in those thirty seconds they would lose him again. Meghnad screamed an inhuman scream, a bloodcurdling scream, and in that infinitesimal second between the first and second drops, I had imagined rushing to Raghu and stopping him from destroying his life, but nothing was fast enough, and with the second drop, I could see the skin burning, the eyes disintegrating, melting, and I felt guilt course through my body like lava. It was us it was meant for, not him, and with every second that he held the canister up, the acid flowing through it determinedly, it was eroding everything, not only Meghnad's face, but also Raghu's much-deserved chance at normalcy. Seeing Meghnad's distorted face and hearing his pathetic scream, even Raghu screamed. My eyes started to blur, and it wasn't until the canister was empty, when Meghnad was no longer Meghnad, but a lump of molten flesh, that Raghu realized what he had done and he threw the canister aside, and crumpled to the side.

Rishab and Sahil pulled him up. On the side lay a writhing, screaming Meghnad, his arms and legs shivering, melting, dying. A last gasp, and then nothing. A few jeeps carrying policemen converged towards the scene. Raghu got to his feet. Our car sped on.

I am shaking now thinking of the last time Meghnad had looked at me. With unfinished business, with revenge in his eyes, that vileness, that threat all too apparent. Raghu had noticed that. He had looked at me and then at Meghnad and something had changed in him. It wasn't a crime Raghu committed in a passionate moment, in self-defence. He knew what he was doing when he opened that canister. He had weighed his options. He had knowingly destroyed his second chance at a future. He had chosen my freedom, my safety and my life over redeeming his own.

Raghu Ganguly, my best friend for life . . . had killed a man?

25 April 2003

We were at a television shop. The NDTV news ticker rolled past.

The road-rage accused, Raghu Ganguly, who claimed the life of one, is still on the run.

Mumma, Papa and Di saw it too and ushered me out.

30 April 2003

Mumma, Papa and I were eating dinner when the phone rang.

It couldn't have been Di. She was on a flight to the US and wouldn't land for the next three hours. We all looked at each other. The phone doesn't ring in this house unless it's Di calling from a faraway country. After we shifted back, Sahil and Arundhati would call us to talk about Raghu's disappearance, but even that trickled to a stop. Nothing changed in those conversations. He had vanished without a trace.

It was Mumma who picked up the phone.

'It's for you,' she said.

'For me?'

'Who's it?' I asked, my worst fears bubbling to the surface. *Had the police found him? What will happen now?*

'Some girl named Brahmi Sharma,' said Mumma and handed the receiver to me.

My fingers trembled as I spoke. 'But . . . you . . .'

'I was made to go away,' the girl said from the other side, her voice reminiscent of Raghu's, authoritative and sure. '. . . by his friends. I wasn't good for him, I was told. It was true.'

Her words hit me like a jackhammer. Flashes of what Richa had told me came rushing to my head. I frantically searched for a meaning.

. . . Tauji but they refused to come . . . Sahil, Rishab and Arundhati, Raghu's friends had come and settled the bills . . . And a few days later, it was his friends who had broken the news to him . . .

Brahmi had died in her sleep . . . Raghu had thrown himself at the door, wanting to see Brahmi for one last time. He was denied by the hospital authorities . . .

He got beaten up by the guards when he tried to enter the electric crematorium without authorization . . . He stood there, bleeding, as they turned his lover to bones and ashes and dust . . . when his friends emerged with her ashes, he fell to their feet for it. Once he had them, he disappeared.

'You were . . . you died.'

'Rishab and Sahil told him I died. I wasn't meant to survive anyway,' said the girl. 'These are details for another time. I need to meet you. We need to find Raghu.'

I knew what I had to do . . .

YOU MAY ALSO LIKE

The Boy Who Loved
Durjoy Datta

**The only thing you cannot plan in life is when and
who to fall in love with . . .**

Raghu likes to show that there is nothing remarkable about
his life—loving middle-class parents, an elder brother he
looks up to, and plans to study in an IIT. And that's how he
wants things to seem—normal.

Deep down, however, the guilt of letting his closest friend
drown in the school's swimming pool gnaws at him. And
even as he punishes himself by hiding from the world and
shying away from love and friendship, he feels drawn to the
fascinating Brahmi—a girl quite like him, yet so different.
No matter how hard Raghu tries, he begins to care . . .

Then life throws him into the deep end and he has to face
his worst fears.

Will love be strong enough to pull him out?

The Boy Who Loved, first of a two-part romance, is warm
and dark, edgy and quirky, wonderfully realistic and
dangerously unreal.

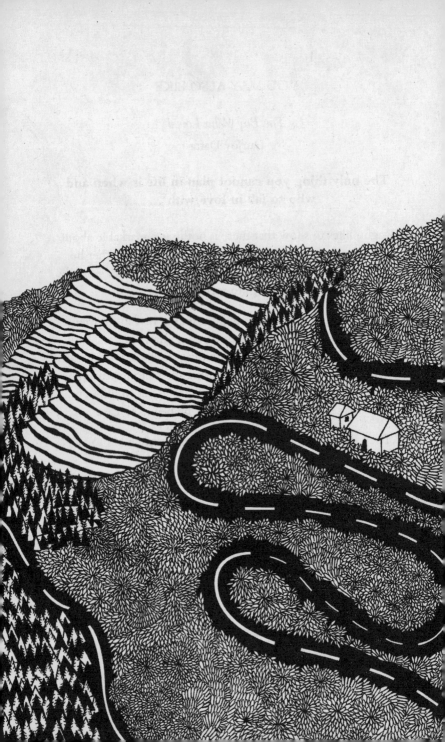